THE DARK
CORNERS

A Luke Tremayne Adventure

THE DARK CORNERS

Malice and Fanaticism: Wales 1656

GEOFF QUAIFE

Order this book online at www.trafford.com
or email orders@trafford.com

Most Trafford titles are also available at major online book retailers.

Printed in the United States of America.

ISBN: 978-1-4907-2684-7 (sc)
ISBN: 978-1-4907-2685-4 (hc)
ISBN: 978-1-4907-2686-1 (e)

Library of Congress Control Number: 2014902030

Trafford rev. 01/30/2014

 www.trafford.com

North America & international
toll-free: 1 888 232 4444 (USA & Canada)
fax: 812 355 4082

THE LUKE TREMAYNE ADVENTURES

(In chronological order of the events portrayed)

LEADING CHARACTERS

Cromwell's Men

Luke Tremayne (Colonel)	Cromwell's special agent
Sir Evan Williams (Captain)	Luke's deputy
John Martin (Lieutenant)	Luke's third-in-command

The Local Community

Inhabitants and Friends of *Llanandras*

Sir Daffyd Morgan	Magistrate and landlord
Sir Cranog Morgan	Daffyd's son and successor
Lady Alis Morgan	Daffyd's second wife and widow
Lady Glynnis Morgan	Cranog's wife
Simon, Lord Kimball	Alis's cousin
Lady Rhoslyn Morgan	Daffyd's niece
Merlyn Gwent	Steward, lawyer
Tudor Gwent	His nephew and assistant

Inhabitants and Friends of the *Priory*

Sir Conway Jenkins	Landowner
Captain Ned Jenkins	Eldest son and soldier
Lawrence Jenkins	Son, lawyer and steward
James Jenkins	Son, chaplain
William Price	Drover and businessman
Emlyn Vaughan	Farmer and horse breeder

The Wider Rhyd Community

Dilys Bithel	Witch
Huw Cadwallader	Freeholder, parish constable
Edwyn Cadwallader	Huw's son, lawyer and steward
Morgan Derfel	Independent rector of St. Brioche
Bronwyn Hedd	Dairy maid, cunning woman
Kynon Hedd	Her son
Tecwyn Hedd	Laborer, Kynon's uncle
Gwyn Jones	Leader of Fifth Monarchy Men
Darryn Lewis	Shepherd
Kendric Lloyd	Baptist preacher
Garyth Morris	Blacksmith
Rhun Talbot	Renegade trooper and fanatic

Others

Lady Penelope Abbott	Disgraced noblewoman
Black Barris	Smuggler
Olwyn Price	Rhayader businessman
	Brother of William Price

Real Historical Personages

Oliver Cromwell	Lord Protector
John Thurloe	Cromwell's head of intelligence
James Berry	Major general for Wales
Vavasor Powell	Anti-Cromwell preacher
Walter Cradoc	Pro-Cromwell cleric

Historical Prologue

Throughout much of 1655 and 1656, Oliver Cromwell, the Lord Protector, faced uprisings and conspiracies from Royalists, parliamentary Republicans, Levellers, a variety of religious fanatics, and most seriously disaffected senior officers of the army. Confronted by these security risks and rising costs, he created local militias to be paid for by the defeated Royalists and divided England and Wales into ten regions, each to be controlled by a major general. The strength in Wales of Royalists, Catholics, and sectarian extremists—Baptists, Fifth Monarchy Men, and Quakers—made the Principality a potential problem. The apparent political apathy of the Welsh made Cromwell even more nervous. As a matter of urgency, he needed to shed light on this dark corner of the land.

1

Mid-Wales, autumn 1655

KYNON HEDD WAS TERRIFIED.

His uncle Tecwyn was making another unwelcome visit.

Kynon was still grieving the tragic death of his father, Mabon.

Mabon, a laborer; his wife, Bronwyn, a dairymaid; and Kynon had lived in a small cottage on the land of their employer, Rowland Parry.

Parry now permitted the new widow to keep the cottage, provided her twelve-year-old son replaced his father and worked on the Parry estate.

Bronwyn detested her brother-in-law who worked only intermittently. Since his brother's death, Tecwyn had tried to assume a protective role over Bronwyn and her son. She repelled his bullying and lecherous advances at every turn. He was a violent adulterer, liar, and thief who had only escaped serious punishment over the years because of Mabon's constant intercession on his behalf.

Bronwyn held Tecwyn responsible for her husband's death. Mabon had died during the annual drove of local cattle to the English markets when he was trampled to death by a couple of rampaging kine. Tecwyn's behavior provoked the cattle to stampede, and witnesses claimed that he failed to warn his brother as the frenzied beasts headed in Mabon's direction.

Tecwyn's repulsive appearance mirrored his character. He was a square-built individual with very short legs and long powerful arms. He had a sloping forehead and a ruddy pockmarked face with a large bulbous nose and bulging eyes. His reddish brown hair was cut short. He was supposedly clean-shaven, but stubble dominated his unkempt appearance.

He removed his dripping sheepskin cape and sodden leather hat, revealing crumpled gray trousers and a filthy creamy brown shepherd's smock. His muddied high boots had seen better days.

Bronwyn was anxious to be rid of him. "What do you want?" she asked crossly.

"Dear sister, I need Kynon to join me on a late-season drove."

"What do you mean *a late-season drove?* The local cattle have either been driven into our barns or to England months ago."

"They are not local. I met a man in the Red Kite who wanted someone to guide coastal cattle through this area to the English border. I agreed to meet them at the Pass at midnight."

"Why are coastal cattle coming through the Pass? At this time of the year, it's easier and safer to take a route much further to the south. And why do you have to meet them at midnight? Nobody moves cattle at night, especially in our dangerous terrain."

Tecwyn did not answer.

Bronwyn continued her tirade, "And why do you need Kynon? He has no experience, and the death of his father on the last drove makes him a very reluctant participant. Who is the master drover? Kynon will not work for that rogue Price. It must be Davies."

Aneurin Davies was a local lad who made such a fortune as the drover-dealer for the local farmers that he had also become a wealthy farmer. In recent years, the English-born William Price had challenged Davies's droving monopoly, successfully dividing the local community.

Davies relied on the traditional Welsh method of buying the cattle for the drove with promissory notes, which were converted into cash on the successful sale of the cattle in England.

Price had ready cash and bought the cattle for his drove on the spot. Most cattle owners faced the dilemma of ready money in their pocket or loyalty to one of their own.

Bronwyn's loyalty was to her Welsh friend. She despised Price's undermining of Davies by his conspicuous display of money.

Tecwyn finally responded to the torrent of criticism. "Don't create unnecessary problems! It is neither Davies nor Price. It is a dealer from the coast."

"Kynon is too young, and Goodman Parry needs him to complete his chores. There must be dozens of experienced men available."

"No, sister, most of the locals who work on the droves will not work for anyone but Davies or Price, and many of them have stayed in England for the winter. I have tried unsuccessfully to recruit three or four drinkers from the Red Kite."

"Kynon is not available. Now leave!"

"Then, sister, could you do me a lesser favor? In coming through the sleet and slush, I realized that my boots are holed. My hose is sopping wet. As I must be at the Pass by midnight, there will be no time to repair them. Could I borrow my brother Mabon's special boots?"

Mabon and Tecwyn's father had been a shoemaker and cobbler. As a wedding gift, he had made Mabon a very special pair of boots. They were made from the best leather and took four times longer to craft than normal boots.

Bronwyn was furious. "Tecwyn, have you no feelings? Mabon died in those boots, and he made clear from the moment he received them that they would go to his eldest son."

Tecwyn had had enough of his scornful sister-in-law.

"You ungrateful wench. One day you will come crawling to me for help."

"Go, Tecwyn! Or I will send for the constable."

"Before I do, I will teach you a lesson," shouted an increasingly incensed male. He took a rapid stride toward Bronwyn and with two hands ripped down her bodice and underlying chemise, revealing her ample and well-formed breasts. His hands moved instantly to fondle both.

Bronwyn bit deeply into Tecwyn's arm and with a free hand managed to reach a heavy pan on the stove with which she hammered her attacker several short blows to the head. He removed his hands from her breasts in order to defend himself, enabling Bronwyn to take a step back and with a mighty swing collected him with a massive whack to the side of the head. He was stunned and fell to the floor.

Bronwyn ran across the room to a low trunk from which she retrieved her late husband's dagger.

As Tecwyn came to, she placed the blade to his throat. "Go and never return! You disgust me." As a token of her determination, she allowed the blade to slightly cut the skin of the cowering would-be rapist.

A still-groggy Tecwyn staggered away, muttering aloud, "I will have you one day. Your sister's magic will deliver you into my bed."

Kynon was frightened of his uncle, and throughout Tecwyn's visit, he hid in the low trunk from which his mother had retrieved the dagger. As soon as Tecwyn left, the boy embraced a shaken Bronwyn, who began to cry.

"What is wrong, Mother?" asked the bewildered lad.

"Son, my mother and my grandmother and her mother before her, going back into the mists of time, had certain powers that with the coming of the English we have kept hidden for fear that we would be accused of witchcraft. Your aunt Dilys foolishly paraded her skills and has paid the penalty. I cry not for what your uncle tried to do to me, but because of what he is about to do. I sense that your uncle is about to embark on a venture that will bring dishonor, if not destruction, to us all."

"Then, Mother, you must stop him!"

Bronwyn was silent for a minute or two. She then made her decision. "I will try. Put on your boots and cape! We must go to the constable immediately."

Huw Cadwallader had just checked on his cattle and was sloshing his way toward his large farmhouse when two figures approached him out of the mist.

Once inside the house, Huw called for food and drink and summoned his son Edwyn to join them in the nook, currently warmed by a blazing fire.

Then he asked, "Now what brings your here in such weather and so late in the day, Bronwyn?"

"You know I have the powers of my mother and grandmother to dimly foresee the future. I have just experienced such a vision immediately following an unwanted visit from my brother-in-law."

Bronwyn recounted Tecwyn's requests and his intention of assisting a late drove through the neighborhood on behalf of an unknown master drover.

Huw was very interested and increasingly concerned. "I agree. This whole enterprise is suspicious. Why would anyone want to drive coastal cattle through this area at this time of year? Our weather would force any right-minded drover to take them much further south. No local would agree to assist a complete stranger in such circumstances. No wonder a desperate Tecwyn needed Kynon to accompany him. What do you think, Edwyn?"

Edwyn Cadwallader was his father's only son and had only recently returned from the Inns of Court. The young lawyer was pedantically clinical. "Goodwife Hedd, you have no evidence to suggest a crime is about to be committed."

Bronwyn riposted, "I did not say a crime was about to be committed. I had an overwhelming feeling of doom. Whatever Tecwyn is up to will bring disaster to all of us."

"I agree with both of you," announced a diplomatic Huw. "We must find out what Tecwyn is really up to. Edwyn, ride to my senior shepherd who knows the track to the Pass better than anyone! Explain what Tecwyn intends to do and have him either follow Tecwyn or make it to the Pass before him. He is not to be seen and must report back as soon as possible."

Edwyn left, and one of Huw's servants escorted Bronwyn and Kynon back to their cottage.

Within the hour, Edwyn returned. He greeted Sir Daffyd Morgan and a group of horsemen who were just leaving his father's farm. He was surprised to find his father in a highly disturbed state.

Huw explained, "I did not say anything in front of the dairy maid, but her intuition is likely to be correct." Huw handed his son a letter. "This is a warning from the high constable of Radnorshire, which Sir Daffyd just delivered, to be alert to the suspected smuggling of goods and disaffected persons from the coast through our county into England. Tecwyn Hedd is a low-class, greedy man of no principles and has animalistic attitudes. He as good as killed his own brother, regularly abuses his own wife, and terrorizes his sister-in-law and a multitude of other women."

Hugh suddenly paled and fainted.

After a few minutes, he recovered but was clearly not himself.

Edwyn was concerned for his father. The normally composed man was still highly agitated. The arrival of an illicit drove or a multitude of vagrants were not sufficient to unsettle him. Something more serious was afoot.

Edwyn's apprehension increased as within minutes, without explanation, Huw left the house. He walked down the drive, disappearing into the darkness. The constable never walked anywhere beyond his farm; he always rode.

Huw was not the only inhabitant of Rhyd to walk out into the night. As soon as his exhausted mother fell asleep, young Kynon Hedd put on an excess of outdoor clothing and left the cottage.

2

The Palace of Whitehall, November 1655

THE PROTECTOR WELCOMED HIS FRIEND, sometime bodyguard, fixer, and secret agent, Colonel Luke Tremayne. Luke was surprised at how easily his leader had adapted to the fineries of monarchical power. The opulence of the apartment dazzled him.

Cromwell spoke, "Luke, I have summoned you here to thank you for your work in Somerset and to acquaint you with the reorganization of my administration in so far as it affects you. For over a decade, I have drawn my personal bodyguard from a company of troops within the national army. Your cavalry regiment, nominally stationed at Dublin Castle, provided it for many years. As Protector, I have now created a permanent bodyguard of veterans, and as a consequence, the companies of your regiment stationed in London will return to Ireland. I have also replaced you as their commander. You have nominally been at Dublin Castle for six or seven years, when in reality you have been in the Americas, in Scotland, in London, in France, and recently in Somerset. The Irish situation demands a resident full-time cavalry commander. I have appointed an old sergeant of yours, now Lieutenant Colonel John Halliwell, to its command."

Luke was shaken. It was bad enough to lose the role of providing protection for Cromwell, but to be deprived of his command after years of long service cut him to the quick. He responded in a faltering but biting tone, "Sir, am I being put out to pasture to help you balance your budget or as a sop to the civilians in your administration?"

"Watch your tongue, Colonel!" warned the all-powerful Lord Protector.

He then smiled and strode across the room, placing his hands firmly on Luke's shoulders.

"Calm yourself! I am offering you promotion. I have divided England and Wales into districts to be controlled by the military. At the same time, the military no longer needs to have separate intelligence agents, as John Thurloe has done an excellent job in servicing that aspect of my government. Nevertheless, I need a special elite military unit ready to act on intelligence reports. It has already been created as a company of dragoons."

"Where do I fit in?"

"Luke, you have a choice, control one of the new military regions or head the new intelligence company, in either case with the rank of major general."

Luke beamed, "Your Highness knows full well that I will accept command of the special company of dragoons, but I reject any promotion. I prefer to remain a colonel. *Major general* is for officers in the field of battle or for administrative governors."

"Thank you, Luke! I also know that you feel deeply the loss of your longtime friend and sergeant, Andrew Ford, a man who despite his rank was your real deputy through many assignments. I have given you as deputy, Captain Evan Williams. His mother is Cornish like you, but Williams is Welsh, as is his native language. He also speaks Gaelic and English. He was an excellent intelligence officer under George Monk in Ireland and Scotland."

Luke would have preferred to appoint his own deputy, but on the surface, Williams appeared a reasonable choice. Time would tell. Luke commented, "During my recent Somerset escapade, I met a very able young officer, John Martin. May I appoint him as a lieutenant in this new unit?"

Cromwell nodded his approval.

"Now, Luke, let us get down to business! The first mission of your new unit is to enter one of the dark corners of the land, Wales. You will be based at Chepstow Castle, just across the English border. As Chepstow has a garrison of regular troops and is likely to house the newly raised militia, your small unit should be able to operate without too much attention."

"What exactly is the mission?"

"In lowland Britain, Thurloe with his brilliant intelligence and the army with its effective force on the ground maintain good governance and security. General Monk has finally brought Highland Scotland under control, but much of upland Wales remains potentially dangerous. We do not know what is happening away from the seacoast and the English border, where our representatives and allies are concentrated."

"What specifically has alerted you to this situation?"

"Wales is predominantly Royalist, with a large Catholic population. The local Papists are not without support from the great Catholic peers in England, and it is rumored that Welsh Catholics have opened up discourse with disaffected Irish Catholics, and both may be assisted with troops from Spain. A Spanish-aided rebellion may be timed to coincide with other uprisings throughout the land.

"The misguided attempt of the Protestant Parliament to bring religious reform by ejecting many the established clergy and spreading the Gospel through itinerant Puritan preachers has backfired and led in places to religious anarchy. Extreme sectarians dominate the more isolated areas.

"Some of these radical communities have been very supportive of the army in the past, but since I have taken the title of Lord Protector, the Fifth Monarchy Men have turned against me and are possibly planning an insurrection.

"A new sect, the Quakers, which General Monk has purged from our armies in Scotland, has no respect for authority and is also sowing the seeds of rebellion."

"With sectarians, the established church, and Papists against you, is there anyone that you can trust?" asked a mischievous Luke.

"Some of less extreme sectarians such as the Baptists and many of the established parishes in which the Puritan clergy of Presbyterian and Independent persuasion have survived offer some support."

"What about the lesser gentry who support you in the rest of Britain?"

"I do not know. Local feuds based on family interests divide the large landowners, and a big gulf exists between Welsh- and English-speaking gentry. I do not have a clear picture. Your mission is to discover whether political, social, and religious dissent in inland Wales poses a threat to our regime, and if so, take steps to eradicate it."

"I will leave for Wales in the morning."

"That is not quite all. Thurloe has received a report from Radnorshire that in Rhyd, a community on the Upper Wye, people, including the local magistrate, have been murdered. Given your excellent work in solving the murders in Somerset, this should be an interesting challenge. Captain Williams has the details of this problem."

Luke bowed to the Lord Protector and left. He had felt more comfortable serving the commander-in-chief of the Parliamentary army than a man who had taken on the trappings of kingship.

Nevertheless, it was the same Oliver Cromwell; and Luke's personal loyalty to the man, if not the position, was as strong as ever.

Chepstow Castle, Wales, a Week Later

Chepstow Castle was a delightful base. The castle overlooked the River Wye just before it joined the Severn. Chepstow was in Wales, but the towns on the other side of the river were in England.

Luke and his new deputy, Captain Evan Williams, rowed across the river to an English alehouse, the White Bull. There they spent the day getting to know each other.

Evan who was a thickly built, almost square framed man of average height impressed Luke. The Welshman had longish black hair, a short black beard, and an olive complexion, which may have reflected his Cornish ancestry. His dark brown eyes twinkled.

Although a knighted member of the Welsh gentry, Evan was, first and foremost, a professional soldier. He had served in Ireland and Scotland under Monk, and it was largely his intelligence work that led to the isolation and expulsion of the Quakers from the army. It was this experience in dealing with religious extremists that had appealed to the Protector. Williams was a hard man and was, like Luke, devoted to the service of Oliver Cromwell. He revealed no religious or personal obsessions and shared with his commanding officer a fondness for Irish whiskey.

After an hour or more of personal chitchat and the consumption of pork pies and roast chickens, the two officers settled down to business.

Luke began, "I have been briefed on the general situation, but understand that you have detail regarding the specific problems of confronting Rhyd."

Evan replied, "I'll put you in the picture. This year, winter came early to the upper valleys of the Wye and its tributaries. The river in this part of the country is the border between the shires of Radnor and Brecon. Cattle that provide the livelihood for most of the locals have long gone from the surrounding hills. Drovers had taken the small black Welsh cattle to the rich English pastures for fattening, while the larger Herefords went directly to markets in London. Those not ready for market were driven from the slopes to winter accommodation in the barns and houses of their owners within the dispersed community."

"So much for climate and cattle, what about politics and people?" asked an impatient Luke.

"Two gentry families vie for control of the area. On the northern outskirts of Rhyd is the large estate of the local magistrate, Sir Cranog Morgan, while several miles downstream stands the fortified manor house of his rival, Sir Conway Jenkins. As the eastern bank of the river is in Radnor and the western bank in Brecon, the authorities have wisely elevated Morgan to the bench in both counties. Midway between the properties of the two local gentry is a ford across the Wye, which gave the community its name—*Rhyd* being Welsh for *ford.* Although in recent times a bridge has been built across the river, its Welsh inhabitants continue to call their settlement Rhyd. On the western bank is a large inn, the Red Kite, and adjacent to it is a blacksmith's forge.

"The bulk of the population is scattered in a multitude of small cottages on the land of the gentry and other farmers for whom they provide labor. There is no compact village, although a row of houses has grown up around the Red Kite, and three or four more near the parish church of St. Brioche some miles south of the inn. Beyond the easy reach of the authorities, a few hardy small holders have isolated hovels on the uplands, where they struggle to make a living.

"The church of St. Brioche, which with the Red Kite had once been the twin focus of this widely scattered community, is now the subject of division. Parliament removed its Anglican rector who was a Royalist and replaced him with a Puritan whose increasingly radical views alienated most of the conservative parishioners. The growing success of even more extreme preachers who hold their services in the barns and houses of their adherents further diminished his congregation.

"This is not the tightly integrated village of their English neighbors further to the east, where houses were adjacent to each other along a road that contained the church and the manors of the local gentry. Nevertheless, their Welshness, family networks, and the loyalty to their social superiors had until recently held the scattered Rhyd community together.

"By mid-1655, this unity was seriously threatened by differing attitudes to the English, the need to defend Welsh values, and the escalating but clandestine conflict between those sympathetic to the king, to the Parliament, or to Oliver Cromwell. The communal unity is also threatened by conflicting faiths. There are Papists, unhappy supporters of the prewar national church, reforming Puritans of both the Presbyterian and Independent ilk, and a host of competing protestant sects, Baptists, Fifth Monarchy Men, and Quakers."

"What about the murders?" asked an exasperated Luke.

"I have just returned from Rhyd. The most important of the murdered men was a likeable opponent of mine in the early years of the war, the local magistrate, Sir Daffyd Morgan."

"The assassination of a magistrate is a serious problem for any government," commented Luke.

"Yes! That is why his son, Cranog, was temporarily appointed to the bench immediately on Daffyd's death, much to the chagrin of the Morgan-hating local rival, Sir Conway Jenkins, the only other gentleman of note in the area."

"So the murders largely involve the gentry?"

"No, the spate of unexplained deaths and disappearances did not begin at that level. It started with the apparent accidental death of a farm laborer, a Mabon Hedd. Some weeks later, his brother Tecwyn boasted of an unexpected drove through the parish and moved into the mountains to join it. The constable, suspicious of this activity, sent his head shepherd to follow Tecwyn. Neither Tecwyn Hedd nor the shepherd returned.

"The then magistrate, Sir Daffyd Morgan, went to investigate. His body was found a day or two later.

"Several other members of the Rhyd community disappeared at the same time, but there is no telling whether they have moved to England for the winter or have been killed. Two or three regulars at the local inn, the Red Kite, are missing, and other gentlemen claim that attempts have been made on their lives and property. Barn burning increases as a popular pastime."

The two officers enjoyed a long midday meal and late in the afternoon returned to the Welsh side of the River Wye.

3

NEXT MORNING, LUKE AND EVAN inspected their new company.

Luke explained to the gathered troops their role. "You have two tasks. The first is easy, to summarily remove threats to the government without recourse to fineries of the law. That is why when on duty, you will have no distinguishing colors and on occasions you will wear hoods. Your second task is much more difficult. Most of you have extensive experience as spies and secret agents for various military commanders and the civilian government. You may be sent into the far corners of Wales to gather intelligence. For espionage purposes, you are divided into ten troops of ten, for your military role, into four troops of twenty-five."

Evan then explained the details their first operation. "We are to investigate a spate of deaths and disappearances in parishes in the Upper Wye valley on the borders of Breconshire and Radnorshire. Our area of concentration is between Rhayader and Builth, the small community of Rhyd. Initially, it will only involve the colonel, three Welsh-speaking troopers, and myself. The colonel and I, as the authorized investigators of the murder of Sir Daffyd Morgan, will stay with various landowners in the valley. The colonel will concentrate on the English-speaking gentry, and I will question the Welsh community.

"Lieutenant Martin, you will move the rest of the company to the small market town of Rhayader, ready to assist us with sufficient force at a moment's notice."

After the larger group had been dismissed, Luke spoke to the three Welsh-speaking troopers. "Stradling and Bebb, you will be my bodyguards and interpreters to the Welsh community. Although I will stay with the local gentry, the two of you will make the Red Kite your home and mix with the local community. What you discover at the inn may be of great importance to our investigation.

"Talbot, Captain Evans has arranged for you to assist the local innkeeper whose husband disappeared sometime ago and attach yourself to the leader of a dangerous religious sect who may be behind much of the trouble. You will leave for Rhyd immediately.

"The task for all of you is very simple. Discover what you can concerning the murdered and missing locals, especially Sir Daffyd Morgan, and unearth anything detrimental to the security of the Lord Protector occurring in the Upper Wye."

Luke marveled at the verdant riverside pastures as he and Evan rode along the bank of the River Wye to Monmouth and then northwest into the uplands until they rejoined the river. They then followed it north through Builth to Rhyd. Snow covered the higher ground, and light sleet tickled their faces.

Darkness began to fall, and Luke asked, "When are we there? I don't fancy sleeping out in this weather or moving any further up this excuse for a highway in darkness."

"Never fear! We are almost there. You can just see the flickering lights of the Priory, the home of Sir Conway Jenkins, on your right. Any minute we should pass the church of St. Brioche on the banks of the river. Further north is the inn, the Red Kite. We can either spend the night there or move up a small valley to Llanandras, the ancestral home of the Morgans. They are expecting us."

"Today?"

"Not necessarily. They were informed that we would arrive before the end of the week."

"Then let's stay at the inn. We may be able to glean some information from the locals. Why do the Morgan's keep a Welsh name for their manor? If they were English, it would be Morgan Grange or Morgan Hall."

"Over the years, some Morgans changed the name, but the locals insisted on referring to it as Llanandras. It reflects the centuries-old history of the place. Before the great sickness, hundreds of years ago, this area was well populated and consisted of two parishes, those of St. Brioche and St. Andreas. At the time of the population decline, the church of St. Andreas burnt to the ground, some sources claim with the living plague victims locked inside. The parishes were subsequently combined, and all worshipped at an enlarged St. Brioche. St. Andreas was never rebuilt because the Morgans occupied the church land and confiscated the material from the gutted church to extend their fortified manor house. *Llanandras* is Welsh for the Church of St. Andreas. Servants at Llanandras claim they have been awakened at night by the screams of the burning victims."

Luke had no time for such rubbish and concentrated on the reality confronting him. "Will anybody speak English at the Red Kite?"

"One man does, the local blacksmith, Garyth Morris. He served with me during the war and spent a lot of time in England."

It was snowing heavily and was dark by the time the soldiers reached the inn. Its door was shut fast. Fortunately, Evan was aware of the procedure and began to ring a gigantic bell that hung beside the door. Eventually, they heard the large wooden bolt being withdrawn, and a young lad surrounded by a group of potentially dangerous drinkers opened the door. The boy asked the purpose of their intrusion while there were mutterings behind him about filthy English oppressors. This background chatter was cut short when Evan burst into Welsh, explaining that they were on the Protector's business to investigate the murder of Sir Daffyd. They sought accommodation for the night.

As soon as they entered the drinking chamber, a muscled giant of a man with a shiny baldhead and incredibly big ears advanced toward Evan with an outstretched hand, "Welcome, Captain, to the Red Kite. At least the authorities had the sense to send a Welshman to investigate Sir Daffyd's death."

This man, whom Luke assumed was the blacksmith, Garyth Morris, then turned to the assembled throng and introduced Sir Evan

Williams as his wartime commander with such favorable comments that one of the wildest-looking drinkers immediately bought each of the soldiers a pint. Before they had finished their drink, a woman emerged from an adjacent room with the lad who had opened the door. "My son tells me you want lodgings for the night. Put your horses under cover! It will snow heavily tonight. There is a barn out the back."

The lad led them upstairs to a small room. Luke then assisted the boy to move their horses from the unprotected hitching rail to the comfort and security of the barn, a barn that appeared more comfortable and warmer than the small room he was to share with his deputy. Luke rejoined Evan in the drinking chamber where they accepted the only food available, beef stew and leeks thickened with oatmeal.

As they ate, the man who bought them drinks approached the table with two more tankards of beer and immediately addressed Evan in Welsh. "Please forgive this intrusion! If Garyth Morris vouches for you, sir, I know you will help me. Do not waste all your time on the problems of the gentry and ignore those of the people! I am Dai Herbert. On the night that Sir Daffyd died, my two sons, Penn and Caleb, disappeared." Evan translated the gist of Dai's request to Luke just as Garyth Morris joined them.

Evan asked Garyth to speak English and introduced Luke as his senior officer and the man in charge of the investigation. Garyth obliged and indicated that while Dai could not speak English, he could understand it reasonably well.

Luke took the opportunity to ask, "Just what happened on the night that Sir Daffyd was killed?"

"As usual on a wet sleety winter's night, most of us were gathered here. Early in the afternoon, that obnoxious varlet Tecwyn Hedd arrived and asked for volunteers to help him lead a drove of cattle from the coast down the dangerous path from the Pass to a temporary sojourn near Llanandras. He was laughed out of the chamber."

"Why?"

"You do not drive cattle at night, especially down the treacherous track from the Pass to here, and Tecwyn was not forthcoming with any details of payment. In fact, he suggested that as we were all indebted to Sir Daffyd, we should offer to help him without reward."

"Did this caitiff Tecwyn speak for Sir Daffyd?"

"No. Tecwyn worked only from time to time and then only for employers who could find no one else. However recently, he has been running errands for Sir Daffyd's steward, Merlyn Gwent. This seemed to be one of those occasions. An hour later, Sir Daffyd and his trusted personal servant Tadd Bowen unexpectedly arrived. Sir Daffyd appeared extremely agitated and explained that there had been developments at Llanandras that were not to his liking and that he needed five or six men to accompany him up the track toward the Pass. I told him that Tecwyn had been here already, trying to get assistance without success.

"Sir Daffyd appeared completely surprised and asked for the details of Tecwyn's request. He gave Tadd a knowing look and announced, 'I know nothing of this drove, and the statement that the cattle are to stay at Llanandras is completely false. I need help to forestall this unauthorized activity.' The innkeeper, two of Dai's sons, and three others volunteered. They have not been seen since."

Luke continued, "How did you find out about the death of Sir Daffyd and the disappearance of the others?"

Garyth replied, "The following evening, Merlyn Gwent with a posse of horsemen arrived and indicated that Sir Daffyd had disappeared and that he wished to augment his troop with as many men who would volunteer. I told Gwent that Tecwyn Hedd had talked about a late drove of cattle from the coast, which he was to meet at the Pass and lead down to Llanandras, and Sir Daffyd's denial of this and his intention to ride to the Pass and forestall the activity. Gwent seemed surprised by both pieces of news and announced that we should reassemble at dawn and make our way toward the Pass."

"And what did the Gwent party find the next morning?" asked Evan. "We found a few fresh cattle prints and the wheel ruts of more than one wagon and a surprising number of footprints. This was a drove with limited cattle and an unusually large contingent of wagons and men."

"Did the tracks lead back to Llanandras?"

"No, they petered out a few hundred yards down from the Pass where we found the partially snow-covered body of Sir Daffyd. It was a ghastly sight. His head had been in large part blown away."

"How did Gwent react?" asked Luke.

"He was shocked. He concluded that Sir Daffyd had come upon the unauthorized drove and was killed, as were his men whose bodies have never been recovered. And that following this tragedy the drovers thought it best to retrace their steps and return to the coast."

"Did the tracks indicate this?" interjected Evan.

"We never had a chance to investigate. Gwent ordered us to bring Sir Daffyd's semiheadless body back home immediately."

Dai commented in Welsh, which Evan translated for Luke's benefit that he hoped that if the drovers had returned to the coast, they had taken the missing men with them; although he conceded it was more likely that as witnesses to Sir Daffyd's murder, they too had been killed.

Just as Luke and Evan were about to climb the stairs to their sleeping quarters, a group of six or seven men who had stood at the back of the room muttering to each other pushed forward in a threatening manner. Dai and Garyth barred their approach to the soldiers. Evan moved forward and asked the leader of the advancing group the cause of their disquiet.

He identified himself as Darryn Lewis. He and his associates had been herdsmen and shepherds for old Sir Daffyd. They lived in the huts on the uplands in summer and cottages in the grounds of Llanandras in winter.

"Why does this cause you to react against our presence?" asked Evan. "You are government men sent here to help our masters. You do nothing for us." His friends constantly repeated the mantra, "Nothing for us."

Evan raised his hands. "Your anger is clear, but why?"

Darryn replied, "On coming down from the mountain at the end of summer, we occupied our cottages as we have time out of mind. Within a week of Sir Daffyd's death, that turd of a steward, Gwent, moved us out without warning. Shepherds and herdsmen on other properties have taken us in, but it is causing difficulties. Make Gwent take us back!"

Evan promised to take the matter up with Sir Cranog and to uncover why out-servants of so many years were summarily evicted without explanation. Luke and Evan were intrigued by what they had heard and agreed that there were several questions that the household at Llanandras, especially Merlyn Gwent, needed to answer.

4

OVER A BREAKFAST OF FRIED black pudding and lard-soaked rye bread, Luke decided to visit Huw Cadwallader, the constable, before they presented themselves to Sir Cranog Morgan.

Luke collected his horse and immediately realized that the shoe on its left front foot was very loose. He led it next door to the blacksmith's forge to be reshod. Garyth Morris greeted him warmly.

While Luke and Evan sat on a bench under cover of the smithy's awning, a young lad arrived. Garyth looked up from his work and pointed to a creamy brown Welsh pony tied to a post at the back of the forge. The boy eyed the two soldiers up and down. His face lit up when he saw Luke's tall sturdy black Friesian stallion. This had been Luke's favorite breed since his experiences in the Netherlands two decades earlier when he fought for the Dutch against the Spaniards.

Evan and boy gabbled away in Welsh for some time, much to Luke's annoyance. After the lad left, Garyth, who had completed the shoeing, commented, "You should have a serious talk to that boy. That's Kynon Hedd. His uncle was the ne'er-do-well Tecwyn who disappeared, and his mother, Bronwyn, midwife and herbalist, is the most powerful woman in Rhyd. She knows more of this community's secrets than anybody else, except perhaps for her banished sister, Dilys, a dangerous practitioner of the black arts. If it wasn't for Bronwyn's close relationship with Sir Daffyd, Dilys would have been hanged as a witch years ago, instead of enjoying a comfortable and profitable exile in a cave near the Pass."

Luke had no time for the mumbo jumbo of alleged magic, satanic, or otherwise; but he was aware that the local herbalists and midwives held valuable information past and present concerning their neighbors. He would speak to both sisters.

As they left the forge and confronted the constant irritation of the misty rain, they saw Kynon leading his pony up the hill above them. He intermittently disappeared in the mist.

Luke suddenly announced, "Let's talk to the lad now!"

The track wound its way up a steep incline beside a babbling brook that flowed rapidly downhill toward the river. In addition to the fog, the bends in the track periodically obscured Kynon from view.

Then two musket shots were heard above the noise of the cascading stream. The shots were so close together that the incident must have involved two separate shooters. Luke assumed that local farmers were killing vermin or putting down injured stock.

Momentarily, the mist cleared. He saw that Kynon had mounted the horse and was galloping upward as fast as he could. More alarming was the sight of two other horsemen. They were not only in pursuit of the lad. They were also firing at him.

Evan commented that their ability to prime and fire a musket while riding at speed reflected some experience.

Luke was worried. "We must overtake these would-be killers before they achieve their end. Why would trained soldiers want to kill a young farmhand?"

Conversation ceased as Luke and Evan concentrated on their riding. Luke was happy that the boy was maintaining his distance ahead of his pursuers who were nevertheless continuing to fire.

Following another shot, the situation changed dramatically.

The boy fell from his horse, but Luke and Evan were almost on the shooters.

Luke primed his carbine.

Rounding the next bend, he heard another musket shot. It grazed his cheek. They were now the targets.

The shots came from behind a large boulder that half blocked the track. Luke and Evan dismounted and threw themselves into a fast-flowing water-filled ditch. There was only open ground between this drain and the rock.

It was a stalemate. Luke and Evan could not advance on the shooters, and they in turn could not disable the two officers, now protected by the contours of the ditch.

Evan intimated that he would take advantage of these contours. He would crawl down the ditch until it emptied itself into the stream. He would then make his way up the stream, which would get him to the far side of the rock. Luke nodded his approval and to distract the shooters put his hat on the barrel of his carbine and lifted it above the ditch's protection. He was not disappointed. Shots tore two holes in his hat. His opponents were not only experienced horsemen; they were also efficient sharpshooters.

Evan found the ditch water very cold. Much of it was freshly melted snow. The force of the water enabled him to partly crawl and partly float downhill. This force was nothing compared with that exerted by the stream. He would have to walk along its edges rather than wade midstream. Luckily, the banks were overhung with willows and alders that provided protection from those above. He eventually reached a small waterfall that forced him to climb the sides of the stream and move through lush undergrowth from which he could observe the far side of the rock. Nobody was there.

Nevertheless, he cautiously made his way to it and signaled to Luke that it was all clear. The enemy had gone.

Their horse prints went a short way up the way and then led down into the stream. They used the stream to conceal their tracks.

Luke suggested they do the same and look for signs of their quarry leaving the brook. They had not gone far when Evan held up his hand and put his finger to his lips.

"I heard a horse whinny."

The two men dismounted. Luke followed Evan in the direction of the sound, both with their weapons primed. There was sudden movement behind a bramble, and just before they fired into it, a young lad staggered forward and collapsed at their feet.

It was Kynon.

The boy had been shot. He had lost a lot of blood, although Luke was sure that nothing vital had been damaged.

Evan offered to carry the boy to Huw Cadwallader's farm, which he thought was only a few hundred yards further up the track, while Luke would continue to follow those responsible.

Within a quarter hour, Kynon was lying on a bed, awaiting the arrival of his mother whose knowledge of healing herbs was unsurpassed. One of Huw's employees had removed the musket ball that had lodged in the upper arm.

Huw was appalled at Evan's account of what happened. "Sir Evan, I am delighted to meet you, although I never anticipated that it would be in such circumstances. I appreciate the government sending you here so promptly. Rhyd seems under threat from an unknown enemy. Sir Daffyd's death was only the most serious of a string of assaults, attempted murders, disappearances, and arson. Why two professional ruffians should try to kill a young lad astounds me!"

A distraught Bronwyn arrived and immediately tended to her son's injuries. She quickly realized that he was not badly hurt, and after dressing the single wound, she sought an explanation. She listened carefully and cursed the unknown assailants.

Evan continued, "Goodwife Hedd, I am here in response to a request from the magistrate to uncover the murderer of Sir Daffyd Morgan and the perpetrators of other abuses in the local parishes. There is a company of dragoons waiting in Rhayader to enforce any actions that need to be taken. After the assault on your son, I will suggest to my commanding officer that the troops be moved here forthwith. Is there anyone who would want Kynon dead?"

"Sir Evan, you are one of us. I see things that have not happened. I receive messages that are clouded in double meanings. I have received an all-embracing vision that we are under threat from an unimaginable evil, and that the death of my husband, and that of Sir Daffyd, and now the attempt on the life of my son are connected. But I do not know how or why."

The boy began to stir and was soon asking for a cheese and leek soup for which Cadwallader's housekeeper was well known.

Eventually, after the boy had two full bowls of the soup and chunks of white bread, his mother asked, "What happened, Kynon?"

"I collected Mr. Parry's horse from the blacksmith as ordered and was leading it back up the hill when without warning someone fired at me. At first I thought it was the two men who looked like horse thieves that I had met at the blacksmith's forge. They were after the creamy Welsh pony.

"Then I realized that neither was riding a black horse, which I had seen at Garyth's place. Then I noticed well below the man on the black horse and his friend were following the men that were attacking me. I rode as hard as I could. I kept ahead of my attackers until I was shot. The pony took me across the stream, but being half conscious, I fell off into a bramble bush. When I came to, I heard the voices of the men I had met at the blacksmith's forge. The next thing I remember was waking up here."

Evan asked, "Do you know these men?"

"No, I have never seen them before. They are not locals."

Luke worked his way upstream. Progress was slow as he had to look at both sides of the brook for traces of emerging horses. After an hour, he found the evidence. A series of hoofprints led up the bank. They were distinctive. They left the imprint of three small ridges on one side of the shoe and four on the other. This would assist with traction. He had seen similar shoes before, but where? He must ask the blacksmith.

The prints disappeared on the harder rock of the track as it climbed upward.

Luke continued up the path, assuming his quarry had done likewise. He was soon well above the misty rain of the farming valley and battling the sleet and snow that dominated the uplands. Eventually, he reached the peak of the small mountain that he had been climbing, and as the snow momentarily cleared, he looked down toward the valley of the Wye.

In the distance, two horsemen were making their way back toward the river down a small valley further to the west. Luke was anxious. These men were not leaving the area. Were they remaining to try again? If they were remaining, where were they staying? And to where did that western valley lead?

Luke made his way back to Cadwalladers where Evan introduced him to the constable. The three men discussed the situation. Cadwallader could throw no light on the identity of the shooters but explained that the valley that Luke saw the men descending made its connection with the Wye to the north and west of Llanandras. The only habitation in that area was the manor house of the Morgans and the cottages of their workers.

Luke muttered to Evan, "The Morgans require an immediate visit."

On their way to Llanandras, Luke and Evan dropped in on the blacksmith, Garyth Morris. He was appalled to hear of the attack on young Kynon. He had no explanation. Luke then asked, "These men rode horses with distinctive ridged shoes. Have you made any such shoes?"

"I know of the shoes you mention, but I have neither forged nor fitted such shoes to anybody in Rhyd."

"Damnation! I hoped that the shoes might bring us quickly to the culprits, but it would appear that they are not local. Nevertheless, horses need regular shoeing. Every horse rider would need to visit you regularly."

"Not necessarily. As a cavalry man, you would have learnt to reshoe your own horse, or at least your troop would have someone capable of doing so. Similarly, the large estates—the Morgans and the Jenkins—have servants who maintain the shoes of their horses without bothering me. Mr. Vaughan, the local horse breeder, also has one or two servants who are able to efficiently shoe and unshoe their animals. In this rural community, my main role with horses is to manufacture the shoes, not necessarily to fit them. Those shoes could have been purchased from anywhere and fitted and refitted as the need arose by a host of people."

Luke was not happy.

5

LUKE AND EVAN WAITED IN the hall of Llanandras for a considerable period. Evan was furious. "This is a deliberate snub. These old Royalist families have not learnt the lesson of the last decade and a half. They lost the war."

"Calm yourself! If the Morgans wish to play it this way, they are stupid. We hold the upper hand," advised Luke.

Evan was not placated.

"This is not the hospitality I expected from the Welsh gentry. Socially, I outrank these people. If they cannot respect an officer of the Protectorate, they should at least extend common courtesy to a knighted member of their own class and race."

They were finally admitted into the presence of Sir Cranog, his wife Lady Glynnis, and the steward Merlyn Gwent.

Sir Cranog was a small thin sickly-looking man whose gaze did not rise from the floor. His mousy hair was exceedingly long, and his lace collar and cuffs were exceedingly wide. His dark gray doublet did nothing to enhance his image.

His wife was the opposite. She was a well-proportioned black-haired beauty that soon revealed an engaging personality and ample breasts that were only partially concealed by an emerald green bodice. Her green eyes bored into Luke as he stared transfixed at her heaving bosom.

Cranog mumbled a welcome, which was taken up by his wife who spoke perfect English, "My husband and I are delighted that you have chosen our humble abode as the base for your investigation into Sir Daffyd's death and the other mysterious events of that night. He would be delighted that one of the investigators is one of us. In fact, Sir Evan, your great uncle married a Morgan."

Evan now joined Luke as a victim of Glynnis's charm.

Merlyn rudely interrupted the reverie of the two soldiers. "I endorse her ladyship's welcome, but it may be more convenient for you to stay at the Red Kite, where I gather you have already received an interesting welcome."

Luke could not resist, "No, Mr. Gwent. If we are unwelcome here, we shall move immediately to the Priory. The Lord Protector is about to draw up a new list of magistrates. If we report that we received little cooperation from Sir Cranog, I am sure the new list will replace him with Sir Conway Jenkins." Lady Glynnis glared at Merlyn and smiling seductively at Luke replied, "Don't take offense, Colonel! Merlyn is only thinking of your comfort. We have had a few accommodation problems at the manor house. A servant will show you to your rooms. Your troopers will sleep in the servant's quarters."

"Not necessary, your ladyship. When they arrive, one or two will stay at the Red Kite, and the rest will sleep in your barn or stables. They prefer to be close to their horses."

As Luke and Evan followed a servant out of the room, they heard both Glynnis and Merlyn cajoling Cranog for his failure to respond strongly to the government men.

Cranog was a figurehead. The real power at Llanandras was with Glynnis and Merlyn.

The soldiers met the rest of the small household at supper. Cranog had clearly been urged to take a more active role in the conversation as he introduced his stepmother, Sir Daffyd's second wife, Lady Alis, and his cousin Lady Rhoslyn. A regular guest, Lord Kimball was currently in London; and a full-time resident and chaplain, the former Anglican rector of St. Brioche, Arwin Arnold, was in Chester.

Luke indicated that he would talk to the household individually over the next few days, and if the discussions went to plan, Evan and he would leave Llanandras by the end of the week.

Glynnis frowned; Merlyn smiled. Luke was bemused.

When Luke and Evan arrived next morning for their scheduled meeting with Cranog, he was accompanied by Glynnis and Merlyn. Evan boiled and in Welsh let forth an oath-laden diatribe, which had the wife and steward scurrying from the room.

Luke tactfully explained, "Sir Cranog, it is more productive for our inquiry if we interview everybody alone. Please accept my condolences on the death of your father and my congratulations on the work you have done in the short time you have been a magistrate. The government rejects the rumors spread by your enemies that you have been particularly harsh on the lower orders, religious sects, and those who do not speak Welsh."

Luke's relaxed and flattering approach slowly gained the confidence of the timid Cranog, whose independence was stifled by the strong personalities of his wife and his steward.

"Gentlemen, the household looks down on me as an abject failure when compared with my father. I don't want to be a magistrate. I don't want to be lord of this manor. Let me withdraw into the poems and legends of our forefathers! I pleaded with Sir Daffyd to name another as his successor and allow me to be absorbed into the life of a Welsh bard. I have already written a ballad dedicated to the life and achievements of my late father."

"Sir Cranog, the body of your father was brought down from the mountain and buried immediately without a doctor or the coroner examining it?" asked Luke.

"Yes, Merlyn said that his head had been largely obliterated. I could not look on what remained. As a consequence, I forbade the household from viewing the corpse, and Merlyn arranged for its immediate interment in the family crypt."

"What happened on the fateful night?" questioned Evan.

"Father became highly agitated when Tadd Bowen, his valet, interrupted dinner, an unusual occurrence, and whispered to him. Father went red in the face and shouted for Merlyn who had not dined with us that evening, another unusual event. Gwent could not be found, and Father and Tadd left Llanandras immediately. I later found out that they had gone to the Red Kite to recruit men to forestall an illegal drove."

"An illegal drove that was to have rested here at Llanandras," added Evan.

"A lie. Merlyn says it was a deliberate falsehood to destroy my father's reputation. Sir Daffyd was meticulous in dealing with the community. He would never have engaged any drove without involving the local parishioners."

Luke felt sorry for Cranog. "Sir, your life is not made easy by the conflict between your wife and your steward. Have you made any attempts to resolve it?"

"No, Colonel. My wife is a strong woman whom I love dearly. She creates a private world where we can both be soft and loving. I would die without her. On the other hand, I have no experience or desire to run an estate. Merlyn keeps Llanandras viable, and I leave everything regarding the running of the house and the estate to him. Glynnis and Merlin come into conflict over issues that each considers belongs to their own world, such as how to cope with your visit. I need them both, and I cope by appearing indecisive and timid. I am not as weak or confused as I pretend. It is my way of handling the situation."

Evan changed the subject, asking, "Sir Cranog, what can you tell us about your mysterious lodger, Lord Kimball?"

"He is my stepmother's mentor. He has visited here regularly since Father married Lady Alis. He is her cousin. He is a peer whose estates straddle both sides of the border between England and Wales but who is often absent from the area in London and Europe on undisclosed business. Given his anecdotes over dinner, he spends a lot of time in France and Germany. He is a courtier of long standing and has spent considerable time recently at the Royalist court-in-exile. He also seems very knowledgeable about New France. Father largely ignored him, but he spent a lot of time with Merlyn."

"Did your father and Lady Alis quarrel?" asked Luke.

Cranog bristled, "I do not see how my late father's relationship with his second wife has anything to do with his death."

"Was Lady Alis having an affair with Lord Kimball?" added the more direct Evan. Cranog was genuinely shocked. Such thoughts had never entered his head.

He responded, "Lady Alis made the last decade of my father's life comfortable and enjoyable. In over a decade, I only heard one cross word between them, and that involved religion. They stopped the argument when I entered the room. And Kimball is not the sort of man who would have an affair with the wife of his host."

Cranog turned to Evan and asked, "Sir Evan, would you like to hear my ballad in honor of father and my Morgan ancestors?"

Luke nodded approval in Evan's direction. Luke did not understand a word of the poem but was impressed with the emotion and obvious love, devotion, and adoration that Cranog expressed for his father. At its end, there were tears in the eyes of both Welshmen.

Luke thanked Cranog for his open and honest discussion.

Luke ignored Glynnis and Merlyn who were hovering in the antechamber and asked a servant to inform Lady Alis that he sought an audience with her.

The servant did not return, but Lady Alis presented herself within minutes.

Lady Alis was in her early forties, perhaps a decade younger than her late husband. She was a short plump strawberry blonde with pale blue-gray eyes and a striking orange bodice highlighted by slashings that revealed lemon undersleeves and a shortened dress showing a lemon-colored petticoat.

"Your ladyship, forgive us. Our message was not intended as a summons."

"No problem, Colonel! I am free at the moment. I am delighted that the government has seen fit to send one of its most able investigators to examine the murder of my husband. My cousin Lord Kimball knows of your work, Colonel, and tells me that you are an intimate of the Lord Protector himself. Daffyd would have been honored."

"You are too kind, my lady. I have not had the pleasure of meeting Lord Kimball. Apart from visiting his cousin, does his lordship have any other reason for spending time in what is an isolated manor house?"

"You have not only met him, you have worked with him. He usually goes by his English title of Lord Stokey."

Luke was dumbfounded.

Stokey and he had both played a part in solving several murders and saving missing English treasure falling into the hands of French criminals.

Luke regained his composure. "Simon Lord Stokey is one of Charles Stuart's most trusted courtiers. My question is therefore even more relevant. What is the king's confidante doing in Llanandras?"

"He doesn't come that often. He routinely visits his many estates. He has several manors on the borders, a townhouse in London, and spends months in Europe."

"Is he due to visit in the near future?"

"I don't know. He usually avoids our harsh Welsh winters. He has invited me once the period of mourning is over to stay with him in London, an invitation that I am likely to accept."

Evan took up the questioning, "Lady Alis, your stepson seems an unfortunate lad who is not suited to the task entrusted to him, exacerbated by the conflicting advice he receives from his wife and steward. Was Sir Daffyd aware of this problem?"

"Yes, it troubled him greatly, and he had planned to solve it. Daffyd was still a relatively young man and in robust health. He did not consider his succession an urgent priority."

"But what did he intend?" asked Luke.

"With Cranog's agreement, he would legitimize one of his many illegitimate sons. During his youth and the early infertility of his first wife, Daffyd populated the neighborhood with a dozen or more bastards."

"Do these bastards know of their illustrious paternity?" continued Luke. "No, part of the agreement with their mothers was that if they wanted continued assistance from the Morgans, Daffyd's paternity was never be revealed, except by Daffyd himself. Although given his hair color and physical abnormalities, it was glaringly obvious in a number of cases."

"Has he revealed any of this information to others?"

"Only to Cranog who knows these half siblings exist, but not their identity. He certainly pressed his father to take action to free him from the succession. Cranog could be one of Wales's greatest bards."

"Cranog speaks highly of you. Praise from a stepson is unusual. Did you take his side against his father?"

"No, Colonel! Daffyd was initially disappointed in the boy but gradually came to respect the scholar and poet in him. So much so that in recent years he allowed the young man to spend his time in such pursuits and failed to train him in the art of estate management and political survival."

"Was there conflict between Daffyd and yourself?" asked Evan.

"Only over one issue, and after that initial altercation, we decided not to refer to it again."

"Religion?"

Alis hesitated, "Yes, but I will not break my promise to Daffyd and open up the issue to you. Religious faith in this day and age takes many forms and can have fatal consequences."

6

EVAN CONTINUED THE INTERROGATION. "ON the night of Daffyd's death, did anything unusual happen?"

"Two things stand out. Tadd Bowen, a servant, interrupted the evening meal, and Merlyn Gwent was absent. Daffyd was clearly upset by what he had heard from Bowen and screamed for Merlyn as if he were to blame for some calamity. Daffyd and Tadd immediately left the manor at breakneck speed."

"Did Merlyn appear that evening?"

"No, he later claimed that he received news of vagabonds entering the county and had gone to arrest them."

"On what authority?" asked Luke.

"His own. He is an overseer of the poor for this and a number of adjacent parishes. He sees his role as removing as many poor from the area as possible and so prevent a drain on rates, which only the gentry and a few wealthy yeomen pay."

Luke thanked Lady Alis for her assistance.

All three adjourned to the dining hall for the midday meal.

Later that afternoon, at the invitation of Lady Rhoslyn Morgan, Luke and Evan took a stroll with her in the manor's extensive gardens.

When well away from the house, she explained, "Gentlemen, I did not wish to discuss intimate matters with you indoors. That horrible Merlyn Gwent has servants eavesdropping behind every door. He will already have a detailed account of all the questions you asked Sir Cranog and my aunt, and more disconcerting, the answers that they gave. My aunt and Sir Daffyd kept that ambitious varlet in his place, but now, despite the efforts of Lady Glynnis, Gwent rules. He threw a dozen or more loyal herdsmen and shepherds and their families out of the cottages on the estate. He has banned the entire household from entering those now deserted cottages and the West Field in which they are located. He has brought in builders from London to erect more cottages and large outbuildings in the very area from which we are all banned."

Evan asked, "Surely this is not unusual? Builders do not like people wandering over their sites, often stealing valuable items."

"Maybe, but something strange is happening in the West Field. My bedchamber was at the back of the house on the second floor, and from my window I could see over the boundary wall and monitor the activities in that field. Strangely, little happened during the day when you would expect the builders to be flat out, but at night, there were many lanterns moving about, and I am sure that several of the cottages are still occupied."

"The new occupants are probably the builders. Did you ask Gwent about it?" probed Evan.

"Yes, but he sidestepped the question by suggesting that if this nocturnal activity disturbed me, I could transfer to a larger bedchamber on the ground floor at the front of the house. Even though I did not consent, I arrived back from a three-day trip to Hereford to find I had been moved."

Rhoslyn's answers to a string of questions confirmed the general picture drawn by Cranog and Alis concerning the nature of the household and the events of the night on which Daffyd died.

Evan asked, "Lady Rhoslyn, you are Sir Daffyd's niece?"

"I was a baby when both my parents were drowned. My father was Daffyd's younger brother. Daffyd and his then wife took me in and brought me up as their daughter. Subsequently, my stepmother, Alis, has continued to nurture and protect me."

Luke, Evan, and Rhoslyn sat on a low stonewall that separated the manicured garden from a small field. Luke tentatively asked, "Being a favorite of such a powerful and popular man as Sir Daffyd, are you promised in marriage to any of the wealthy neighbors and does his death alter any such arrangements?"

Rhoslyn's face lit up with a mischievous smile. "Colonel, are you implying that my feminine allure as well as a substantial dowry make me an irresistible magnet to a host of simpering males?"

Rhoslyn giggled and moved her body seductively to highlight her undoubted charms and continued, "Nothing was finalized before Daffyd's death. Stepmother wanted me to marry her friend, Lord Kimball, who is at least twice my age. All of Daffyd and Alis's plans would in any case have come to nought."

"How come?" asked Luke, who took over the questioning.

"I love Edwyn Cadwallader, the son of the constable. And he feels the same way about me. Edwyn and I were about to announce our betrothal weeks ago, but Daffyd's death put the household into formal mourning. Any such felicitous news now has to wait several months. Daffyd's dowry no longer applies, but even if Cranog does not replace it, Edwyn and I will still marry."

Luke continued, "Is this relationship common knowledge?"

"Quite the contrary. Nobody, not even Daffyd or Huw Cadwallader, was told. Please keep it that way!"

"If no one knows of this, are you pestered by other suitors?"

"Yes, Daffyd enjoyed the politics of my potential marriage. A grandson of the marquis of Worcester, a poverty-stricken bishop, and Ned Jenkins the eldest son of Daffyd's local rival, Sir Conway Jenkins, have shown interest. Then there is the sly and frightening attention and suggestions that are made to me by Gwent. During Daffyd's lifetime, he would not dare to consider me as a marriage equal. Now he hints that he is the real ruler of Llanandras and given his ancestry being a descendant of the powerful Gwents who ruled this area until recently, he would be a perfect husband."

"Have you told anyone of this harassment?"

"Only Edwyn."

"Thank you, Lady Rhoslyn. Merlyn Gwent has a lot to answer. Have you discussed with Edwyn the general situation in this household and surrounding parishes?"

Rhoslyn gave another gentle laugh. "Come, Colonel, you must be very old. The short time that Edwyn and I have together in Hereford or London is not wasted on boring politics or religion. Following my latest confrontation with Merlyn Gwent, Edwyn did say that his father did not trust our steward and that Daffyd had been informed several months before he died of several of Gwent's misdeeds."

Luke concluded, "Did the death of Sir Daffyd alter any of your long-term plans?"

"No, but the abdication of Cranog will. He has no heir, and I have no brothers. If Cranog resigns, I inherit Llanandras, unless he legitimizes one of Daffyd's bastards. Although it is clear legally that a father may in certain circumstances legitimize one or more of his illegitimate offspring, Edwyn does not believe that half brothers can achieve the same end."

"Maybe this is why Daffyd did not proceed with his plan to legitimize a bastard. If Cranog resigns, you become heir, and your husband, Edwyn Cadwallader inherits Llanandras, and the Morgan wealth and power. From what you have implied, Daffyd would have been delighted with that outcome."

"Yes, but he was never told of that possibility."

After supper that night, Luke and Evan made their way into a darkened area of the second floor to discover what they could see in the West Field from the window of Rhoslyn's original bedroom.

The door was locked, but the combined weight of both men was sufficient to force an entry. The room was pitch black. To prevent discovery, neither men had brought candles.

Luke stumbled to the window and cursed quietly. "Damn your Welsh mist, Evan! I cannot see anything through it. We must visit the building site itself, now."

Determined not to be seen by any of the servants, they carefully descended from the second floor. As they approached the main exit from the house, a servant confronted them. Luke turned toward him, "Good man, can you open the door for us? My horse has not been well, and I wish to see him before I retire."

"No, sir. Once the main door is latched and bolted in the presence of the steward, it cannot be opened without Mr. Gwent's express orders."

"Must my horse suffer until morning?"

"No, sir. If you come with me, you can exit and return through a half-door that enables the stable hands and kitchen staff to enter the house and find their sleeping quarters in the attic."

"I thought stable hands slept in the stables to be near the horses," commented a surprised Evan.

"They used to, but since the builders have been working in the West Field and in other outbuildings near the stables, Mr. Gwent forbids anybody to be out of doors after dark, except for the kitchen staff."

Luke and Evan made their way past several servants who no doubt speculated as to what the government men were up to, especially without Mr. Gwent's supervision. Luke surmised that the steward would soon be informed. The two soldiers left the house and found themselves on a paved section of a courtyard that separated the house from the stables, several outbuildings, and a large kitchen. Llanandras continued the medieval safety precaution of cooking in a separate isolated building. While the stables were in darkness, the kitchen was alight with tapers as the scullery maids battled to clean dozens of dirtied utensils.

Behind these outbuildings was an expanse of grass terminated by a tall stone fence. The misty rain was interspersed with sleet, and Luke questioned his judgment. What did he hope to find? He followed a well-worn track across the grass verge to what he expected to be a gate in the fence. The gate was gone, and the gap was almost filled in by a continuation of the stone fence. The masons had not quite completed the task.

The soldiers were about to clamber over the unfinished wall when they heard an Irish voice exclaim, "Did you hear that?"

"Did I hear what?" asked another with a Welsh accent.

"The dogs that guard the kitchen and the stables are making a lot of noise. There may be an intruder."

"Don't worry, Sean. The kitchen maids have probably just finished for the night, and the dogs know when to bark for the scraps of food they leave them. Even if there are intruders, they cannot enter the house. The one small half-door is well guarded, and no one can penetrate this enclosure. There are armed guards every few yards."

"Not that our muskets will be of any use in this sleet."

"I prefer to use my dagger should any fool try to force his way past me."

The sleet was replaced by snow. Luke signaled to Evan to follow him along the stone fence to the end of the West Field. Every few yards they saw men who clearly guarded the enclosure.

Evan was curious. "Are these guards keeping people in or keeping them out? Let's get to the other side of the field."

They clambered into an adjoining field and were amazed to notice that a tall palisade had augmented the stone fence that originally divided the two fields.

"What a waste of time and effort! Modern cannon could smash it down at the first salvo," commented Luke.

"Its main purpose is not to keep people in or out. It is to hide what is going on within," surmised Evan. "Its purpose is not defense. It is concealment."

After reaching the far end of the neighboring field, they could then track along the far side of the West Field. It too had stretches of palisades, and where they had not been completed, tall hurdles filled the gap.

Some of the hurdles had been drawn aside, and Luke heard the lash of a whip and the cursing of a wagoner. Emerging through a hole in the fence was a wagon drawn by oxen followed by two armed men on horseback. The hurdles were replaced, and the wagoner broke into a tirade of cursing. Why was he forced to a drive through the snow at night and on a hardly used track? Luke did not hear the response of the horsemen, but they were clearly determined that the wagon reached its destination.

Evan was perplexed. "The wagoner has a point. Where is this wagon going? Why is it using a sheep track up into the hills? It leads nowhere. The main road passes in the front of Llanandras and through to the Red Kite."

After a quarter hour, the cold began to have an effect. Nothing could be gained by following the wagon and the horsemen on foot. Luke would confront Merlyn Gwent on the matter in the morning.

They returned to the house.

Luke and Evan squeezed through the half-door and were confronted by the servant who had let them out. "Gentlemen, I was about to send out a search party. You were not in the stables, and you have got yourselves very wet. There is still a fire in the servants' hall. Come, dry off before you retire for the night!"

Luke's pleasant surprise at such hospitality was quickly soured. He saw through the open door of the hall the friendly servant in deep conversation with Merlyn Gwent.

7

WHILE TAKING BREAKFAST WITH CRANOG and the ladies of the household, Luke received a letter. It was an ultimatum from Mr. Gwent. The steward had urgent business in Rhayader. If Luke wanted to question him, it had to be within the next two hours, or they need to wait for at least three days. Luke barely concealed his ire as he addressed the servant who had brought the letter, "Tell Mr. Gwent to be in the library an hour before noon!"

On reflection, Luke decided to take a gentle approach with Gwent and leave it to Evan to ask the difficult questions.

Merlyn arrived dressed for travel and left no doubt as to his eagerness to be on his way. Luke pandered to his wishes. "We will not keep you long. We already have a full picture of the events on the day Sir Daffyd died and the situation within the household since."

Gwent was a tall man with long curly brown hair worn defiantly in the Cavalier style. His full sky blue cape half-concealed his dark blue doublet. His rugged face and graying beard suggested that life had not been kind to Merlyn Gwent, yet there remained a dignity and a presence.

While Luke sat quietly, Evan's questioning rose in intensity. "Because of this picture, we give you a chance to defend yourself against several serious allegations that have emerged against you."

Gwent bristled, "I had to take over on Sir Daffyd's death. Sir Cranog is incapable. I have ruffled a few feathers, especially among the ladies of the house, but they should commend me, not undermine my position by their lies."

Luke intervened with his more gentle approach, "Merlyn, don't take offense! Our task is to assess your role as steward and inquire into the personal tensions within the household, only as far as they relate to the death of Sir Daffyd. What exactly did you do on the day and night of his murder?"

"The day before, an acquaintance of mine who was traveling from Aberystwyth to Hereford stayed overnight. He mentioned in passing, knowing of my role as an overseer of the poor, that a band of vagrants were not far behind him on course to enter our parishes. Next morning, I rode up to the Pass to investigate."

"Alone?" questioned Evan.

"Yes, I intended to assess the situation and then return here to organize an appropriate reception for them."

Evan continued, "What options did you have?"

"Three, but only two were politically feasible. Our religious sectarians would have me welcome them into our community and assist them in their hour of need. Our ratepayers would have none of that. I would either have to turn them back at the Pass or hurry them through our parishes into England."

Luke asked softly, "And which did you adopt?"

"Neither. There were no wandering beggars anywhere near the Pass. I took so long checking a number of lesser-known tracks in search of them that I could not make it home that evening, especially as snow had begun to fall. I spent the night in a shepherd's hut halfway down the slope.

"I reached Llanandras late morning the next day. Daffyd's absence was initially not a cause of worry, but when he had not returned by nightfall, I sought information at the Red Kite."

"You would not have been too popular there," muttered Evan.

Gwent ignored the comment. "There I was told that Sir Daffyd had headed toward the Pass the night before. Heavy snow continued to fall, so I delayed any search until the next morning."

Luke asked quietly, "And what did you find?"

"The snow concealed whatever had happened near the Pass, but one the men found Sir Daffyd's almost headless body in a ditch partly protected from the snow by some overhanging branches."

Evan was unconvinced. "If the body was virtually headless, how did you know it was Sir Daffyd?"

"I recognized the clothing as his, and on one hand was the family ring worn over generations by the head of the Morgan family, the ring that now adorns Sir Cranog's finger."

Evan continued, "Did any of the women of the house gain by Daffyd's death?"

"Lady Alis lost a devoted husband, and Lady Rhoslyn her lifelong protector. The latter became Cranog's heir, until he has children of his own. They both lost by the old master's death."

"What about Lady Glynnis?"

"Apart from the obvious that she became lady of the manor, I see little gain. She has a major task assisting Sir Cranog carry out his duties. The lad wants to resign. It is just not done. The best thing for the house of Morgan is that Cranog begets a son. The heir can succeed with a guardian appointed until he reaches maturity."

"And who would be the guardian?" asked Luke.

"Nothing is gained if it were his parents. Frankly, if such an heir is to inherit a viable estate on his maturity, a joint guardianship involving Lady Alis and myself would be the most effective way of ensuring it."

"And a marriage to Lady Rhoslyn would enhance your chances!" Evan commented.

Gwent blushed. "You have uncovered some of the personal secrets of this establishment. Lady Rhoslyn currently shows no interest, and I have not discussed the matter with Sir Cranog, who would need to give his permission."

"If you are trying to increase your influence at Llanandras and within the Rhyd community, why did you evict the herdsmen and shepherds from their winter quarters here on the estate when you are actually building even more cottages in the West Field?" probed the relentless Evan.

"To be more precise, Mr. Gwent, why is the West Field being turned into a fortified enclosure?" added Luke.

Gwent gave a long sigh. "I had hoped that you would not have noticed the extraordinary precautions I am taking there. The eviction of our people is in their interests."

Gwent went to the door of the chamber, opened it, and peered into the next room. He shut the door and resumed his seat across the small table from Luke and Evan. He leaned across it and murmured, "Gentlemen, I am trying to prevent a disaster. If the truth leaves this room, there will be panic across the county."

"What can be so catastrophic that you evict your servants, build more cottages, and enclose an area like a fort?" asked Luke.

Gwent whispered, "The plague."

The soldiers gasped, and Luke asked, "Explain!"

"Just before his death, Sir Daffyd misguidedly planned to give all the servants of the estate a cottage for themselves and their families, and to provide smaller abodes for the retired and aged who had served him well. As most of the local labor was engaged in their pastoral pursuits or employed in the various droves into England, Sir Daffyd was forced to employ a group of builders from England to erect these additional edifices.

"Almost coinciding with his death, several of the builders went down with what at first I thought was a fever. It spread through the builder's camp, and several of the men died. It was then that I saw the lumps under their arms. It was the plague, the dreaded Black Death.

"I immediately evicted my servants from their cottages and closed off the West Field. I put guards on the perimeter to ensure that no one left or entered the premises. I kept my own men clear by telling them that one of the builders had leprosy, and I was just taking precautions."

"What did you do with the bodies?"

"As the builders died, their bodies were bundled onto a wagon by the surviving workers and taken up the trail at the back of West Field to near a quarry where they were cremated—clothes and all—and their ashes buried. "When all the itinerant builders are dead or have recovered, I will dismantle the enclosure and invite the shepherds and herdsmen back to their cottages. Until then, I cannot risk the panic that will occur if these facts are known."

Evan was livid. "Do you really care about the safety of this household and the surrounding community? Despite your precautions, people could inadvertently enter the West Field and catch the deadly disease. A thirsty builder might wander across to the Red Kite."

"Unfair, Sir Evan! The guarded enclosure prevents men from coming in and out. It is the only way to contain and defeat this disease."

Luke was silent for some time and then surprised Evan with his comments.

"Merlyn, you have done an excellent job in containing the disease and in concealing information about it. Nevertheless, it would be wise if the household moved away until the situation improves. Perhaps the lie about leprosy will convince Sir Cranog and the ladies to leave for a month or two."

A wide smile appeared on Gwent's face. "An excellent idea, Colonel! To have the household out of the way would enable me to solve the problem more efficiently. I saw the advantages of such a move myself, but Sir Daffyd's death has not created an atmosphere conducive to such a suggestion. You may be able to help me persuade the women to leave."

Gwent rose and moved to the door. He called for a servant. It was the man who had let them out of the house the night before. Gwent turned to the soldiers, "This is my nephew, Tudor Gwent. He is my personal valet and in my absence becomes acting steward. If you have any questions during my absence, ask Tudor!"

The Gwents left the room without further ado, leaving the soldiers lost for words. They stared at each other in contemplative silence.

Luke broke it. "If we take Gwent at face value, he is a hero, and his behavior on the night of the murder, the subsequent eviction of his servants, and the enclosing of the West Field are all explained. Perhaps I have misjudged this unlikeable but efficient man. He may not be pleasant, but is he a murderer or a conspirator against the government? We have no such evidence."

"We lack evidence only if we believe him. We must break into that enclosure. If it is not as Gwent claims, we have a case against him," argued Evan.

"Not on our own! Has Gwent left yet? Delay him if he is still here. I will pen a coded letter for Lieutenant Martin at Rhayader."

Evan returned a few minutes later with Gwent.

Luke asked, "Could you deliver this letter to the officer named. He is staying at the Old Dragon in the center of the town."

Gwent seemed anxious to assist the soldiers whom he no longer viewed as a threat to his current or future operations.

Only Lady Glynnis of the senior household remained to be interrogated. Luke suggested, "Let's leave that until tomorrow. We shall ask her ladyship to choose a time that suits her. I notice that unusual as it is in this God-forsaken place, the sky is blue. There is no mist, rain, sleet, nor snow. Let's look through Lady Rhoslyn's former window and see if there is any evidence we can gather concerning the West Field."

The surveillance of the enclosure revealed nothing suspicious. All was in accord with Gwent's picture. A few healthy builders were at work, and the soldiers assumed the sick and dying were in the cottages. Several empty wagons stood in one corner of the enclosure. Luke had seen enough and made to leave the room when Evan called him back. "Luke, look who is making his way from hut to hut, obviously not worried by the plague."

Luke scurried back to the window. A figure was walking through the enclosure, putting his arm around others, shaking hands, and even engaging in a playful wrestling match.

It was Tudor Gwent.

8

NEXT MORNING, LUKE ASKED THE blacksmith, Garyth Morris, if he could find two men experienced in the Welsh uplands to guide Evan and himself up the three main valleys that led down into Rhyd.

Garyth replied enthusiastically, "I will be one, and the other is Darryn Lewis, one of Sir Daffyd's evicted shepherds forced to sleep in the barn of the Red Kite. I will ask him immediately and meet you in the inn in a few minutes."

The four men gathered in the inn.

Luke explained, "Since we have been here, two of our suspicious characters have escaped up into the mountains, following narrow valleys that all eventually pour their water into the Wye, not far from the front door of this inn. The men who attacked young Kynon Hedd disappeared up the valley that goes past the Cadwallader farm, and an unexplained wagon disappeared up the valley at the back of Llanandras. I want to move up both of these and the main road from the Pass to Rhyd to see if we can find anything that will help with the investigation."

Evan translated for the benefit of Darryn.

Darryn responded in Welsh, which Evan interpreted for Luke.

"Darryn says that three valleys begin, very close together, near the Pass. The streams that dominate them start from springs only yards apart from each other along the same ridge. If you are at the Pass, you only need to move along the ridge a small distance to enter the

Llanandras valley and about the same distance again to that of the Cadwallader."

Luke clarified a situation. "So an illegal drove or group of vagrants could avoid the main track from the Pass and eventually rejoin the Wye valley through either of the other valleys?"

Garyth answered, "Theoretically maybe, but it would be almost impossible for wagons to use either of those secondary tracks. If they came up the highway from the coast and wished to avoid the main road into Rhyd, the wagons would have to be manually lifted along the ridge until they reached the beginning of the other tracks. In many places, these are too narrow for a wagon. It would be possible in the right weather for man and horse to take advantage of them, but it would increase the distance considerably. To go up the track past the Cadwalladers would take more than twice as long as following the highway along the Wye itself to the Pass. These minor trails are little more than sheep tracks. No one would risk their cattle or horses up and down such treacherous routes. Sheep and vagrants are a different proposition."

Luke surmised, "It would therefore be possible for the men that attacked young Kynon to reach the top of the Cadwallader valley and come back down that which runs along the back of Llanandras, or they could use the highway."

Garyth was aghast. "Is someone at Llanandras involved in the attack on Kynon?"

Luke shrugged his shoulders and asked the Welshmen, "How long does it take to go up and down these valleys?"

Garyth and Darryn conferred for a minute or so. The former then affirmed, "It is impossible to do the three valleys in a day. We could easily climb the Llanandras valley and back down the highway in a day. On the second day, we could climb the Cadwallader valley but would need to overnight in one of the shepherd huts and return down the highway or the Llanandras valley the next day."

"Let's start immediately!" ordered an enthusiastic Luke.

"No way, Colonel!" Garyth quietly interjected. "It is too late in the morning, even for the shorter Llanandras valley, and the mist is beginning to descend. We need an early start and reasonable weather.

Darryn thinks we should leave the lower reaches of the Llanandras vale while it is still dark. He has used it many a time to take sheep to the uplands."

The men agreed to meet an hour before first light across the fence at the northwest corner of the West Field.

Luke changed the subject. He quietly asked Garyth, "What has happened to my trooper Rhun Talbot whom you found employment for at the inn? I have not seen him at the Red Kite since I arrived."

"The news is very good or very bad. Talbot made an immediate impression with Gwyn Jones, the Fifth Monarchy leader, and is traveling the countryside with this charismatic but dangerous man."

Luke was pleased.

On returning to Llanandras, Luke was informed that Lady Glynnis would answer his questions over a shared meal in her antechamber that early afternoon.

She welcomed him with a provocative remark, "Haven't you noticed the change? With Mr. Gwent away, the household is relaxed and happy."

Luke, ever the diplomat, concurred, "And a perfect opportunity for you to tell us all you can about that man, the rest of the household, and the events on the day your father-in-law was killed."

The seductive Glynnis seemed to have a different priority.

She immediately disconcerted Luke. Her bodice was cut so low that only a transparent gossamer chemise covered her breasts.

She had placed Luke beside her on a padded bench and began to rub her leg against his.

Luke, hoping to change the developing atmosphere of the meeting, said, "Perhaps you should invite Sir Evan to share this meal?"

Glynnis giggled.

"You are a man of the world, Luke. You come from a wealthy landowning family in Cornwall and only recently rejected the opportunity to marry the richest woman in England. Sir Evan is one of us, the rather impoverished Welsh gentry. What I want to suggest to you is so personal that it is better encompassed by a relative stranger."

With those comments, she took Luke's hand and whispered, "Do you find me attractive?"

Luke's spontaneous answer was to take Glynnis's face in his hands and to kiss her in a lingering and passionate embrace. Glynnis moved Luke's hand onto her left nipple that to Luke's enjoyment was long and large. He buried his face into Glynnis's breast.

After several minutes of mutual groping and kissing, Glynnis surprisingly drew away and announced, "Later, Luke, when I will explain my behavior. For now let us calm down and enjoy the meal.

"There is lambs stew, vegetables and leeks, and roasted Welsh lamb glazed and marinated in honey.

The three flagons on the table are Sir Daffyd's favorite Bordeaux red, Welsh ale brewed in our kitchen, and a very sweet braggot, a cross between mead and ale."

Luke still found it difficult to focus on his roast lamb and ale, while the enticing lady of the manor consumed the stew and drank the braggot. After an hour, Glynnis intimated that Luke might wish to start his interrogation, after which she would like to make a proposition to him. Servants brought in additional nibbles of Welsh rarebit and Glamorgan sausage. Luke enjoyed the latter, a cheese mixed with breadcrumbs and egg.

Luke, still finding it difficult to concentrate, began his questioning. "In the weeks before his death, did Sir Daffyd change his behavior or express opinions that might offend people?"

"Sir Daffyd and I were not close, so I can only answer that question with regard to Cranog and myself. Daffyd in recent months came around to accepting Cranog's desire not to be his successor as lord of Llanandras. I gave up trying to persuade Cranog not to pursue such a self-denying path, but I continued to disagree strongly with Sir Daffyd as to the details of the succession."

"In what regard?" asked Luke.

"Daffyd sired several illegitimate children in his younger days. This activity stopped the moment he married Alis. Almost every aspiring young man in the village claims to be Daffyd's bastard, much to their mothers' chagrin. Daffyd decided to legitimize the most able of the males and legally designate him as heir. He would be brought into Llanandras and be educated by Daffyd into his future role. Cranog and I would leave the main house and live in a large new edifice that he would build in the West Field. He and Cranog had worked on the plans, and builders from London were hired for the job."

"You opposed this plan?"

"Yes, I argued that the Morgan line should be continued through a legitimate son, which Cranog and I would produce in time. Daffyd was not impressed, but Cranog was slowly beginning to see some virtue in my approach."

Luke apologized for any indelicacy. "My lady, you and Cranog have been married for some years, and there is yet no child. Is pregnancy a viable option in your case?"

Glynnis blushed. "Yes, I have had problems conceiving. For years I took a ghastly tonic prescribed by the doctors in Hereford. Recently, I talked to the local cunning woman, Bronwyn Hedd, who advised me that the tonic was useless. She has replaced it with an herbal mixture, which she claims will have me fertile in no time. She also assured me that Mr. Gwent was not out to murder me."

"How does Mr. Gwent get into this story?"

"Some months ago, he noticed my general ill health, probably caused by the Hereford tonic. He suggested that I take a special concoction of his late mother. He assiduously sends a vial of it to my room, daily. I did feel much better, until Rhoslyn suggested that Gwent was trying to poison me."

"Why would Gwent want you dead?"

"Again, it was Rhoslyn who drew a frightening scenario. If I failed to produce any children and Cranog resigned his position, the current heir would succeed as Daffyd's plan to legitimize one his bastards died with him. The current heir is Rhoslyn. She claims that Gwent has made advances to her and even hinted at marriage. I am frightened, Colonel. If Gwent married Rhoslyn, he would take over Llanandras on Cranog's abdication. I must have a child to thwart such a plan."

"You must send Gwent's tonic to the authorities," suggested Luke.

"I already have. I took it to Bronwyn. She put my mind at rest. It did not contain any fatal poisons, but it did contain strong ingredients that might inhibit pregnancy. Gwent was making sure that I did not produce a child, which gives some life to Rhoslyn's more dramatic picture."

Luke was quite appalled at Gwent's behavior. "Lady Glynnis, the attempted intervention of Gwent in the most intimate relationship between husband and wife must give Cranog an excuse to dismiss him. This man is acting well above his current station in life. He may be efficient and Cranog feels that he could not manage without him, but there are plenty of able young lawyers of impeccable backgrounds that could replace him. Why not young Edwyn Cadwallader?"

Glynnis recoiled in astonishment. "Amazing, Colonel! You have only been here a few days and you repeat a statement I heard three years ago from Rhoslyn. She was clearly annoyed with Mr. Gwent at the time and she muttered to me, 'That varlet will get his just rewards when young Edwyn Cadwallader returns to Rhyd.'"

"Did Gwent fear that Daffyd would replace him with Cadwallader?"

"I don't know, but Daffyd and Edwyn's father were the closest of friends and the most loyal of allies. On the other hand, Daffyd was very conscious of Gwent's ancestry. He gave Gwent some land to begin his reemergence as a property owner and encouraged him to invest his earnings in accumulating a number of small estates, which brought Gwent into conflict with the Jenkins's aligned land-hungry predators, Price, Griffith, and Vaughan."

"Now what was the proposition you wished to put to me?"

Glynnis rose from the bench, and as Luke did likewise, she drew him close and nibbled his ear. "This, and what went on earlier is not the lustful physical yearnings of a wanton woman. I needed to know if you could and would respond to my allurements."

"What is this about, Glynnis?"

"The cunning woman told me that the most likely reason for me not producing a child was that Cranog was sterile. I want you to give me the child that he can't. To the outside world, the Morgan dynasty must continue."

9

Next morning before dawn, Luke, Evan, Garyth, and Darryn started up the sheep path that wound its way up the valley behind the Llanandras estate. The recent damage done to the track by wagon wheels was increasingly obvious.

Luke commented, "These ruts are very deep. The wagons were heavily laden. A wagon loaded with the bodies of four or five men could not cause such indentations. And further, several of these wagons needed to be drawn by oxen or more than one horse."

"So the wagons were hauling something much heavier than a few bodies for cremation!" exclaimed Evan.

Luke asked Garyth what could have been hauled in the wagons to cause such deep indentations.

His answer was disappointing. "Building materials! To cut costs, you would need to fill the wagons with the maximum load and beyond. The local slate quarry is halfway up this valley. Nothing sinister, I'm afraid. These wagons were hauling slate for the floors and roofs of the new and renovated buildings in the West Field."

As they climbed the increasingly steep track, Luke and Evan looked unsuccessfully for ruts leading off the path to an area where bodies could be cremated. Eventually, they reached the slate quarry where all wheel tracks ceased. Garyth's interpretation was probably right.

Luke was increasingly frustrated.

As they neared the summit ridge, Garyth let out a string of Welsh curses. "The upper reaches of this track have been widened since I was here last. That could only be for one purpose, to make it accessible to wheeled vehicles. The ruts finished at the quarry, but the path since then has been on solid rock. Wagon wheels would leave little trace. Someone nevertheless has been bringing goods down from the summit to the quarry."

On reaching the summit, the group carefully guided their horses along the ridge until they came to the valley that contained the highway leading down to the Red Kite, clearly indicated by a gap in the ridge, the Pass.

"There is no way that wagons full of heavy goods from the coast could have reached the Pass and then been diverted down the Llanandras valley to Gwent's enclosure across such a rugged ridge," pontificated a disappointed Luke

No one commented as the men ate their bread and cheese. During this break, Darryn walked several yards down the track toward the coast and then the same distance toward the Red Kite. He was clearly bemused and spent a considerable time talking to Garyth. Then both Welshmen walked back along the ridge to the beginnings of the other two valleys.

Luke, content to sip on his warming flask of Irish whiskey, closed his eyes and nodded off. Half an hour later, the two Welshmen returned, displaying the broadest of grins.

An excited Garyth woke Luke. "Colonel, you were wrong. You will be delighted to know that heavy goods were brought from the coast by wagon, manhandled across the ridge, and reloaded onto different wagons waiting at the top of the Llanandras valley. Darryn walked beyond the beginning of that valley and noted that the fragile plant life there was thriving, whereas between the Pass and Llanandras, it had been trodden almost into extinction. There were also several piles of human feces and many discarded cuds of well-chewed tobacco. We also found this hat, which was probably blown away by the very fierce winds that are common here and then concealed from the owner by the fog or snow."

"Well done! Evan and I will need to find the wagons used in the Llanandras valley and identify the goods they contained."

Luke carefully perused the hat. "I have seen hats like this before with a slight bend in the brim. The Irish Confederates wear them. There was an Irishman guarding the enclosure at Llanandras. Is there an Irish connection?"

Evan gloomily mused, "Maybe the so-called London builders are Irish troops being gathered for a Papist uprising against the Protector. Gwent is an overt Papist, as is Lady Alis and Lord Kimball."

As darkness fell, the group reached the Red Kite where they ate and drank well into the night. As they were heading out at first light up the much longer Cadwallader valley, the soldiers decided to stay at the inn. Luke's aides, troopers Stradling and Bebb, had finally arrived; and Luke added them to the climbing party.

Next morning as the four soldiers ate a breakfast of bacon, eggs, black pudding, and fried bread, Garyth arrived and reported some disturbing news. "After you all retired last night, Tudor Gwent arrived here and managed to wheedle out of some of the more intoxicated drinkers the general gist of our activities yesterday and our plans for today."

"I am sure Merlyn ordered his stooge to monitor our movements," mused Luke.

They approached the Cadwallader farm, and Luke decided to inform the constable of their intentions.

As Luke made his way to the house, he was surprised to see young Kynon Hedd carrying feed to the barn.

Luke quickly outlined his plans to Huw and brought him up-to-date on the progress of his investigation.

"If I were a younger man, I would come with you. Be careful, especially as you near the summit. The track degenerates into a winding ditch that has been carved between the rocks by the water constantly cascading down it for centuries. After a heavy rain, it becomes a dangerous water course."

Luke as he left commented, "I see young Hedd is working for you. I thought he was employed by Rowland Parry."

"He was, but his mother felt that his future would be more assured if I apprenticed him. Parry is facing problems and may sell out."

Huw suddenly smiled, struck by a good idea.

"Luke, take the boy with you. It would be good experience. He can handle a horse and, despite his recent injuries, is a fit lad."

The boy was delighted to ride with the English colonel and his greatly admired black Friesian stallion.

The journey was slow with many twists and turns, but the morning climb was in clear weather. In the early afternoon, fog descended and reduced their visibility to a few yards. Luke assessed that they must be near the summit as the track transformed into a narrow ravine with large rocks on either side. The group could only progress in a single file. Darryn led the way followed by Garyth and Evan. Kynon was next, and Luke brought up the rear with Bebb and Stradling.

Luke suddenly stopped. He heard a rumbling noise that rapidly increased in volume, and then Darryn shouted in Welsh. Luke saw Kynon jump from his horse and push himself against the sidewall of the sunken track. Screams of horses and men filled the air as several large rocks bounced down the track, crushing and trapping the climbers. Luke had dismounted but was hit by a glancing blow and rendered unconscious.

When he came to, he was pinned to the ground by a branch, as were Bebb and Stradling. The branch was itself held firmly in place by a large rock. After some time, young Kynon emerged from the mist, leading Luke's Frisian. This encouraging sign led Luke to call out in English. "Is anyone alive?" He repeated it several times at regular intervals.

After what seemed an eternity he received a response from Evan who faintly replied, "Thank God, Luke, you are still with us. Garyth and Darryn are dead, as are all the horses. My left leg is a mess. There is much blood. I can see the raw bone, but I am still mobile, just."

A few minutes later Evan crawled out of the mist and was delighted to see Kynon. The two of them could not free Luke or the troopers.

Evan assessed the situation and turned to Kynon. "Lad, ride the colonel's horse back to Mr. Cadwallader and tell him what has happened. Do not rush! None of us is dying, and it is important that you get through to raise the alarm. Sadly, nothing can be done for Garyth and Darryn."

After Kynon had left on the big black stallion, Luke spoke to Evan, "Not all the horses are dead. I can hear them. Crawl back and put them out of their misery! Take my carbine as well."

As Luke lay pinned to the track, he heard three shots.

Evan eventually returned with tears in his eyes, "That mare has been with me for five years. The rocks broke her back."

As black clouds rolled in from the coast, the mist gave way to heavy rain. The track was quickly transformed into a fast-flowing drain, washing over the trapped soldiers. Evan struggled to place small rocks in place to divert the main thrust of the temporary stream away from the soldiers' heads. Most of the water passed harmlessly over their legs.

Sometime in the middle of the night, the rain stopped, and the temperature dropped. Coldness began to numb much of Luke's body, which Evan countered by placing his own great coat over his commander. Help could not be expected at the earliest until the next afternoon.

Evan felt that talk would make the time pass more quickly. "I am distraught to lose Garyth. He and I went through horrendous times together. To think he survived all that to die in an avalanche that hit us in the only place on the track where we could not avoid it and where mist and terrain hid its approach."

Luke muttered, "This is no accident. Those rocks were dislodged long before the downpour began. Someone just tried to kill us all."

"Surely not," commented a less suspicious Evan.

"Our enemies at Llanandras could have reached this summit up their own shorter valley in plenty of time to place the rocks on the edge of this sunken part of the track and then push them down at the very moment we approached. The random direction and bouncing of the boulders largely missed you and I, young Kynon, and my horse. Two men were killed, four were injured and one unharmed, six horses were killed, and there was one survivor. If I was the field commander of our unknown enemies, I would be quite pleased with such a result. Our would-be killers must be rejoicing."

"Not if the sole purpose of the exercise was to kill Colonel Tremayne and Captain Williams," riposted Evan.

"True. They must have been after us. There was no reason for anyone to kill Darryn or Garyth, and nobody knew the boy would be here."

"And as we have discovered nothing up this track, our activities up the Llanandras valley yesterday, or our interest in the enclosure, must have them worried."

"And *them* could only be the Gwents," pontificated Luke.

"But Merlyn has been in Rhayader these last few days."

"But his nephew knew of our movements today," Luke replied.

Cadwallader had just finished his early morning chores when Bronwyn arrived with some freshly baked cakes for her son.

Huw explained that Kynon was not there. "Yesterday he left with the soldiers and Garyth Morris to explore the upper reaches of the valley. They are not expected home until this evening."

Bronwyn expressed her dismay that Cadwallader had allowed the boy to undertake such a dangerous activity.

Huw responded, "Bronwyn, you sent him here to prepare for a brighter future. This experience will hold him in good stead. Not many Welsh lads will be able to claim they rode with the Protector's most feared colonel."

Then they both froze. Galloping across the nearest field, which was a shortcut from the road, they saw Kynon riding the colonel's large horse at breakneck speed. The beast thundered into the courtyard, and Kynon pulled him up beside Huw's hitching rail and slumped forward.

Huw grabbed the exhausted boy and lifted him from the horse, and summoned the relevant servants to look after horse and lad.

Kynon was still conscious and pushed his would-be helpers aside and addressed Huw, "Mr. Cadwallader, I am on an urgent mission for Colonel Tremayne."

He explained what had happened in the clearest detail and then passed out.

Bronwyn was very proud of her son.

10

Huw ORGANIZED THE RESCUE AND retrieval party. Kynon was unhappy. He wanted to return with Huw, but his mother was adamant that he should remain behind.

Huw eased the boy's disappointment. Colonel Tremayne's horse needed regular monitoring after the shock of the rock fall and the treacherous and demanding ride home. The colonel, having entrusted his steed to Kynon, would expect the boy to stay with him.

Kynon went happily to the stables, and Bronwyn accompanied Edwyn Cadwallader to inform Goodwife Morris of her husband's death. Darryn had no known family.

Huw with six servants and six extra horses set out for the rescue. They took the much shorter route past Llanandras. They would traverse the summit ridge and come down into the head of the Cadwallader valley.

They reached the stricken party early in the afternoon.

The rescuers soon removed the rocks and the branch that pinned Luke and the two troopers who had now regained consciousness. Apart from a few bruises and temporary loss of feeling in their extremities, none were seriously injured. Evan was lifted onto a horse, which was led by a servant down the main highway to Rhyd.

Huw and Luke walked to the top of the sunken part of the track and made their way along its edge, one on each side. Huw called across to Luke, "This is no accident. There has been extensive digging around where a number of boulders have originally rested. It would have needed several men to push them to, and then over the edge."

"The same on this side. There must have been six or seven men involved," concluded Luke.

Suddenly, one of Huw's servants cried out from the track. "Morris is alive."

Huw and Luke climbed down into the track. Luke placed the blade of his dagger against Garyth's mouth.

"He is still breathing, but it is very faint. Given the massive bleeding and bruises on his head, I hope he is dead. I have seen too many men hit by cannon balls who survive, but as imbeciles."

Darryn's body was strapped across the saddlebags of a horse. The comatose body of Garyth was placed on a makeshift stretcher that Huw had brought with him.

Huw sent one of his men ahead to prepare Goodwife Morris for another shock, news that her husband was not dead but severely injured and unconscious.

It was well into the night when the rescue party reached the Red Kite and its neighboring cottages. They carried Garyth into his house where his wife assisted by Bronwyn and two or three other women were ready to nurse him.

Evan and the two troopers were taken straight to Llanandras.

Huw and Luke adjourned to the Red Kite where the rest of the rescue party had taken the body of Darryn Lewis.

Huw spoke to a number of Darryn's fellow shepherds and offered to pay for the funeral of the impoverished victim. He also sent one of his servants back to Morris's house for one of the women there to come and prepare Darryn's corpse for burial.

As they drank, a giant of a man burst through the inn's door.

"Here's trouble," Huw whispered to Luke.

Within minutes, half of the Red Kite's customers moved into the antechamber where Darryn's body lay. Immediately, they heard a booming voice reciting in Welsh passages from scripture. This was interspersed with periods of absolute silence followed by the same booming voice haranguing the mourners.

Huw explained. "The big man you hear is Kendric Lloyd. He is a shepherd who in recent years has become a Baptist preacher. He has a considerable following among the herdsmen and shepherds that work for the Morgans and many of the tenant farmers."

"What about those who work for the Jenkins?" asked a curious Luke.

"No, religion is the major divide among the animal herders. Morgan's people are Baptist, but those employed by Jenkins are Fifth Monarchy Men, as is their master."

"Why did you say 'here's trouble' when Lloyd entered the room?"

"Tomorrow Lloyd and his supporters will take Darryn's body in procession to the church for burial. The current rector of St. Brioche is of the independent variety of Puritan with strong Fifth Monarchy inclinations. He will refuse to accept the body for burial in holy ground and will have instructed the sexton not to have any grave dug in preparation. He will seek aid from Sir Conway Jenkins who shares his views to prevent the Baptist invasion. There will be a major affray."

"Can't you prevent it? You are the constable."

"Unfortunately, any men I can muster would be overwhelmed by the combined Baptist and Fifth Monarchy contingents, and it will take too long to get troops from Hereford or Chepstow."

"Never fear, Huw, I should have a welcome surprise for you. In any case, I will escort the body from the Red Kite to St. Brioche. The presence of a government official may have some effect. Sir Conway does not wish to alienate me. Send one of your men to the Priory now and inform Jenkins that Cromwell's representative in the area will personally escort the body of Darryn Lewis to the church and expects that rector and sexton to do their duty."

Luke eventually returned to Llanandras and looked in on Evan who had finally fallen asleep after a liberal amount of Irish whiskey imbibed, according to Glynnis, to dull the pain of his damaged leg.

Next morning, Luke, concerned for his deputy, dispatched a trooper to Chepstow for a military surgeon.

Then with troopers Stradling and Bebb, Huw, and six of his men, he escorted a group of mourners to the churchyard. Some twenty men walked behind a wagon on which Darryn's now enshrouded body had been placed. An equal number of wailing women followed ten yards behind the men. Ahead of the body-bearing wagon walked the immense frame of Kendric Lloyd.

On arriving at the church, all looked well. A freshly dug grave was visible, and a nervous rector Morgan Derfel greeted the procession at the church's gate with studied civility.

This normality did not last long.

Kendric pushed past the rector and headed for the church door. He would claim the pulpit and preach the sermon. His adherents almost crushed Derfel as they followed their leader inside.

Derfel turned to Huw. "Stop this outrage! I consented to allow the burial to oblige Sir Conway. I did not agree to riffraff taking over the church. Lloyd is an illiterate shepherd. He has no authority to preach, let alone conduct a burial service."

He then addressed Luke. "Colonel, you represent the government of our Lord Protector. Enforce his regulations regarding the church!"

"That would be difficult in the current circumstances. The Protector believes that any man who has the love of the Lord Jesus within him has a right to worship in the churches supported by the state. You surely would not claim that these Baptists are not Christian."

"Colonel, in England, it may not be a problem. Most Baptists spurn the established church and have set up conventicles of their own. Such clashes do not occur. Here the Baptists wish to use the established churches for their unauthorized services. Sir Conway, Jenkins will not permit it."

"But the Parliament that appointed you, Mr. Derfel, might," commented Huw. "Sir Conway has no authority in church matters. It is the Parliament or the Morgans who have that power."

As Luke, Huw, and Derfel argued, a large group of cudgel and staff-wielding persons entered the church yard by its back gate and made their way to the freshly dug grave. One of them took up the shovel that the sexton had left in the soil and began to fill in the hole. The rest of the group cheered.

Huw hastened inside the church to warn Lloyd that troublemaking Fifth Monarchists had gathered outside and had already filled in Darryn's grave. Huw then returned to the mob of seething agitators and asked them to leave peacefully, indicating that Sir Conway would not be pleased with their behavior. This was not well received.

Their leader, a Gwyn Jones, responded haughtily, "Constable, you and Sir Conway represent a tainted man-made authority that has strayed from the paths of righteousness. The Lord is about to return, and we have a duty to defy evil authority and replace it with the rule of the godly. Usually, Sir Conway stands with the Lord, but on this matter, the satanic Englishman who stands beside you has coerced him to do the Devil's work."

Jones had a weather-beaten face with short gray hair and bushy eyebrows. He was clean-shaven and wore a shepherd's smock and brown gray jerkin. He was a small man, at least a foot shorter than Luke and had a deep resonant bass baritone voice that kept the crowd enraptured. Luke was intrigued with the musical Welsh lilt of his speech, although he did not understand a word of what was being said.

Stradling summed up the tirade for Luke as pure Fifth Monarchist drivel.

At that moment, Lloyd and three of the largest and strongest of his flock left the church. Another group carrying a plank, on which the shrouded corpse lay, followed them into the churchyard. The bulk of the mourners began to gather two deep around the body. Without any warning, Jones and his fanatics charged the gathered Baptists.

Huw withdrew his men and advised Luke to do the same. They were no match for over fifty cudgel and staff-wielding combatants. Luke saw those carrying Darryn's body place the plank on the ground in order to defend themselves.

This was too much for Luke. He remounted his horse and forced it through the combatants followed by Stradling, Bebb and two of Huw's men. They all dismounted and with swords drawn surrounded and protected the body.

Both sides accepted their neutrality but continued the affray.

The confrontation continued unabated for many minutes.

Luke then heard a familiar sound, a cornet.

Coming up the way from the direction of the Red Kite were several troops of dragoons. On reaching the churchyard, their officer, Lieutenant Martin, had the cornet sounded again. Confronted by twenty to thirty dragoons with primed muskets, most of the combatants stopped their activities.

A few continued, and Martin ordered his men to ride them down.

All but one man stopped. He charged maniacally at Lloyd.

Martin shot him dead.

Huw then addressed the subdued throng. "These soldiers will enforce law and order. Any troublemakers will join this idiot who did not know when to cease. Kendric Lloyd, complete the burial of brother Darryn!"

Luke turned to Huw. "I said I had a surprise for you. Gwent on his current visit to Rhayader gave a message to my lieutenant who was stationed there to move here immediately. Can you house and stable them on your farm for a few days? They can assist you in your duties as constable. I will have them transferred to Llanandras as soon as I can arrange it."

Luke left a small group of troopers to oversee the burial, while another supervised the withdrawal of the troublemakers. Martin led the rest of his company up the track to the Cadwallader farm.

Luke returned to the Red Kite and after the return of the mourners enjoyed the wake for the departed shepherd.

Luke was surprised when Lloyd approached him and even more so when he spoke in English.

"Thank you, Colonel, for your help today. You did well in the sight of the Lord. Do not trust the Fifth Monarchy vermin. Some claim loyalty to the Protector, while secretly they all accuse him of usurping the role of the Lord Jesus. If there is plot against the government in this area, look no further than that nest of vipers and their protector, Sir Conway Jenkins."

11

LUKE WAS ANXIOUS TO MOVE out of Llanandras. Glynnis disconcerted him. He had no qualms about accepting the sexual advances of attractive women, but her ladyship's proposition worried him at two levels.

As an officer accepting the hospitality of Cranog, it would be dishonorable to have an affair with his wife.

More important in Luke's value system was his devotion to the concept of family dynasty and rightful inheritance. He could not bring himself to be part of a plot to distort the heredity succession of a noble Welsh family such as the Morgans. He was appalled at Merlyn's attempt to keep Glynnis infertile. Would he be any better in creating a fake paternity? In particular, he found it offensive to deprive the legitimate heir Rhoslyn and her future husband of their rights. For the same reason, he was sickened by the late Sir Daffyd's plan to legitimize a bastard and make him heir.

On the other hand, he was strongly attracted to Glynnis.

Luke's planned absence would give Glynnis time to reconsider her offer. He diplomatically left the recuperating Evan to complete the investigation at Llanandras.

Luke moved to the Priory to examine the contribution of Sir Conway Jenkins and his allies to the malaise and tension that appeared to dominate Rhyd.

The Jenkins were relative newcomers to the neighborhood and had strong English connections. They represented the new capitalist approach of the reforming English landowners with little regard for tradition or Welsh sensitivities. Sir Conway ingratiated himself with the Cromwellian regime by overtly supporting the Protector and displaying a religious attitude that dovetailed with Oliver Cromwell's personal beliefs. This was a man who claimed, with some truth, to have provided the Protector's only support in Royalist mid-Wales.

Luke remained skeptical. Jenkins was probably another scheming opportunist who would turn against the government as soon as it suited him. The man had all the makings of a political trimmer.

Luke for the moment had the initiative. Jenkins's immediate objective was to obtain a favorable report from Luke and be appointed magistrate in place of the ineffectual Cranog Morgan.

Luke deliberately made an exaggerated show of openly assessing Sir Conway Jenkins's loyalty to the government and his influence in local affairs.

Unlike the reception at Llanandras, the Jenkins's household provided a lavish welcome. Luke was allocated a magnificent bedchamber and was immediately invited to the early afternoon meal for which Sir Conway had assembled both his household and important neighbors. The meal that Luke enjoyed was English. There was no place for Welsh food on this menu.

Ten persons sat around the table with Luke. Conway welcomed him effusively. "We are delighted that his highness should send his most trusted officer to visit us. Assure the Protector of our absolute loyalty to his cause, although it has been a difficult and hazardous position for us to take in this unenlightened and dangerous neighborhood. I tried to stop the affray at the church yesterday. Unfortunately, those Baptist scum provoked my people. I am delighted that there are now dragoons here to assist us maintain law and order."

He introduced those around the table with a brief biography for Luke's edification. There were two women, Conway's wife Lady Mary and his daughter Elizabeth.

His three sons, who after considerable experience in their allocated professions, now lived at the Priory and played a major role in their father's affairs.

The eldest and heir, Captain Ned Jenkins, had fought for Parliament in the Civil Wars and until recently had commanded a company of Welsh infantry that contributed to the garrison at Hereford.

The second son, Lawrence, had trained at the Inns of Court and had been a steward on an English estate for some time. He had also recently returned to the Priory to become his father's legal adviser and steward.

The youngest son, James, had trained at Cambridge as a clergyman. He advocated extreme Puritan views. His nominal independent position had accommodated most of the more radical views of the Fifth Monarchy Men, many of whom had turned against the Protector. This radicalism had led to his ejection from several parishes, and he now found himself reduced to chaplain to his family's household. He could not be made rector of St. Brioche as that gift lay in the hands of the Morgans.

The remaining four guests intrigued Luke. Two were wealthy farmers who shared Conway's view of the world—Anthony Griffith and Emlyn Vaughan. Conway made it be known that if he became magistrate, Emlyn would be his choice as constable.

Conway remarked that Emlyn was the area's largest and wealthiest horse breeder, and if the army needed more mounts, they could do worse than approach Emlyn.

The third guest was Conway's business partner, William Price. Price was dressed in dark brown clothes with narrow lace collar and cuffs. He wore no jewelry. He had deep-set dark eyes, which he used to intimidate those he looked at. They seemed more menacing as they were set in a face that was of a sickly pale complexion. Luke could think of no better description for this man than *a living corpse*. He had made his fortune in the last decade. He had been a penniless English drover who accumulated so much wealth that he was now an extensive landowner and banker.

He acknowledged Luke with a nod of the head but remained silent throughout the meal.

The final guest dressed in the black of the clergy was the local rector, Morgan Derfel, another independent Puritan whose extreme views paralleled those of James Jenkins.

Luke was certain that Sir Conway would take steps with Parliament and the Protector to replace Derfel with his own son, although their radical views were identical. Both men in Luke's eyes were close to being subversive.

The ecclesiastical situation in Rhyd was complex. For centuries the right to appoint the rector of St. Brioche had been in the hands of the Morgans. A Committee of Parliament had removed their last appointment, high Anglican Arwin Arnold and appointed Derfel. Arnold remained in the parish as chaplain to the Morgans and lived at Llanandras. There was an annual battle between him and Derfel when the tithes were to be collected. Because of some legal omission by the Parliamentary Committee, Derfel was appointed to preach. No reference was made to the right to collect the tithe and other ecclesiastical fees. In practice, those who sympathized with the Morgans delivered their tithe to Arnold, and those that supported the Jenkins brought it to Derfel.

Looking around the table, Luke felt sorry for Cranog Morgan. With this array of ambitious talents Jenkins arrayed against him, he would struggle to maintain the Morgan's local influence. To even compete, he needed the ruthlessness of Merlyn Gwent.

Luke outlined to the dinner guests that his mission was threefold—to investigate the death of Sir Daffyd Morgan, to uncover any antigovernment activity, and to make recommendations regarding the local government of the region. To facilitate the inquiry, he would speak to each of them alone over the ensuing week.

Given the affray between the two groups of radical Puritans, the Baptists and the Fifth Monarchy Men, Luke arranged to talk to Reverend James Jenkins immediately after breakfast the next morning.

Luke did not pull his punches. "Explain the last few years of your life, especially your association with the Fifth Monarchy Men and their treacherous ideas! On the surface, you do not appear to differ very much from the hundreds of subversives I have imprisoned."

James pompously complied, "After I left Cambridge, a Parliamentary Committee appointed me to a populous London parish to replace a corrupt high church Anglican. At that time, I was a radical Puritan agreeing with the army and its leader Oliver Cromwell that each parish should decide its own form of worship. My parish was close to Blackfriars, which had been taken over by the Fifth Monarchy Men who preached that the current authority was invalid and that the Lord Jesus was about to return to recreate his earthly kingdom. The Saints must help prepare the way for the new kingdom by removing the existing satanic authorities. I accepted most of these ideas."

Luke summarized what he had just heard. "You were originally an ardent supporter of Cromwell and the army in their removal of such disgraced institutions as the monarchy, the bishops, and the Rump Parliament. You saw Cromwell as doing Christ's work and preparing for his coming. But since he became Lord Protector, you have turned against him, now claiming he is the Antichrist."

"Not true, Colonel! In London and North Wales, some of our people do hold such views, but many others, including myself, do not. In mid and south Wales, our brethren still accept the Lord Protector as the harbinger of the Lord. Here we remain his strongest supporters."

Luke continued his criticism. "That may be true of you and your family, but the inferior sorts are more persuaded by anti-Cromwell rhetoric. Does that mob, which descended on the church the other day, agree with you and your father, or are they fanatical enemies of the Protector? And where does the Reverend Derfel stand?"

"Gwyn Jones is a troublemaker and delights in using his charismatic influence to counter the views of Derfel, my father, and myself. He has not openly supported the Cromwell-is-Satan view, but he does raise questions among the local brethren as to the Protector's continued fitness to be viewed as Christ's forerunner. He frequently travels into northern Wales and consults our rabid anti-Cromwellian brethren who thrive in that area."

"Why should I believe you that while most of the Fifth Monarchy sect, especially in Wales, have turned against the Protector, you and your family resist the trend?"

"Colonel, be practical! My father and brothers are ambitious men. Their only hope of climbing the social ladder, and ruling this part of Wales is in alliance with your government. In addition, my father's views are very close to those of the Protector himself. Would our family really jeopardize our record of loyalty to the Protector and our bright future in his government by siding with his radical opponents?"

"Words, James! Can you point to any activity of the Jenkins that would convince me?"

The cleric thought for a while. "You are a government man, and I have some hesitation in revealing some of the potentially treasonable acts of my brethren. There are very few Fifth Monarchy Men in positions of influence. Major General Harrison who led the movement resigned from the army and is now under house arrest. However, the army still has many Baptists in key positions. There is a campaign by the Fifth Monarchy Men, started when Cromwell created the Protectorate, which has been continuing since, to convince Baptists to reject the government of Oliver Cromwell. From the beginning, Father and I have used our influence to prevent the two Puritan factions from uniting. We have been helped by Gwyn Jones, who whatever his political views are cannot stand the local Baptists as you witnessed yesterday. His concept of unity would be to thrash every Baptist into submitting to his views."

Luke sensed that there was not much more to be elicited on these issues. He thanked James for his cooperation, noting that "the attempt of Fifth Monarchy Men to subvert the Baptist movement into opposing the Protector is of great concern. To this point, it has largely failed. Any such converts in the military have been immediately dismissed."

Luke moved to another topic. "The government is now very concerned with the Quakers. Are there any in this area?"

"No. Last summer, a couple of them were in Rhayader but were driven from the town. They then spent weeks in the uplands above the Wye, preaching to the shepherds and herdsmen. Gwyn Jones organized a group to harass them. They spent some time recovering from their severe wounds somewhere in the area and then appeared again and attracted a group of women along the river near St. Brioche. This time, Father had them arrested. They were again severely beaten and then placed in pillories that were erected just outside the Red Kite. Someone freed them overnight and burnt the pillories to the ground."

Luke dug deeper. "So while there are no overt Quakers in the area, there are secret sympathizers who may be people of considerable rank. Do you suspect any local landowners of harboring these fanatics and sympathizing with their views?"

"Only Parry. He employs the dangerous witch, Bronwyn Hedd, and has been known to express inappropriate ideas."

"Enough about the religious tensions in the area. Tell me about your family!"

"As the youngest son, it is not my place, nor would it be honorable, to discuss family matters with a stranger."

12

"RELAX, JAMES! I WILL PRY into family secrets only as far as they are relevant to my mission. You're not involved in the death of Sir Daffyd nor in plotting to overthrow the government of the Protector. I accept that your family is determined to become part of that government.

"Consequently, my probing is directed to that part of my assignment concerned with the family's suitability to dominate local government.

"Why did you leave London?"

"My congregation openly opposed Oliver Cromwell's creation of the Protectorate. The government arrested many of them and put me in prison for a week or so. At the same time, Father asked me to return here, eventually to minister to the locals."

"Does Derfel know that his days as rector are numbered? But even if Sir Conway becomes a magistrate, he does not have the advowson of St. Brioche. That would still rest with the Morgans. That family is not likely to appoint a man of your extreme Puritan views."

"True, but Father hopes that when he is a magistrate, he may be able to influence Parliament to override the Morgans and appoint me in place of Derfel."

"How does Derfel feel about this?"

"He is quite happy. Father has offered him a wealthy living in Hereford where the Jenkins do hold the advowson."

"Your eldest brother Ned has proved his loyalty to the Protector over years of soldiering. Why did he resign his position in the

Hereford garrison?" "Father wanted him to return home and lead a local militia that he anticipated Cromwell would create and at the same time take up some of the responsibilities as heir."

"I noticed at the dinner table that apart from your mother and sister, there were no other women present. Are none of the brothers married?"

"Lawrence and I have never married. Father is still planning for a perfect match for us both and the family's future. Ned did marry, but that is a complex story."

Luke was intrigued. "Surely your father is concerned that his heir has no heir. Any variation from father-to-son inheritance can create difficulties."

"Father is not worried. Lawrence and then myself are in line to lead the family should our older brother die. We are both young enough to marry and sire lots of children when the need arises."

"My point stands. None of you have children at this stage. The Jenkins dynasty is secure for one generation only. I am surprised that such an astute man as Sir Conway has not planned further ahead in this vital area. What happened to Ned's wife?"

"He returned from a routine patrol and found his wife gone. She just disappeared without trace. The authorities investigated but remained as mystified as Ned."

"Your brother Lawrence has been at the center of political activity in London for some time. Did he show overt support for the army and the Protector in that period?"

"You are mistaken. Lawrence left London several years ago to take up a position as steward to a Cromwellian colonel in Essex and then later to a Protectorate-supporting aristocrat in Shropshire. He has proved his support for the allies of Cromwell."

"Why did he come home?"

"For the same reasons as Ned and myself. Father summoned him." "For any particular reason?"

"Yes, Father has been accumulating property not only in this area but also in England. Our longtime family steward died, and it appeared logical to replace him with someone as experienced as Lawrence."

"But does this not this cause friction with Ned? A younger brother currently controls the properties that Ned will eventually inherit?"

"They will share the inheritance. Father will leave some of his newly acquired English properties to Lawrence, but Ned will receive the Welsh lands and the title."

"What about yourself and your sister?"

"I will be left the growing number of advowsons in Wales and England. I will eventually appoint myself to one of them and derive a considerable income from the others, which will be ministered to by lowly paid curates. After Father dies, I will certainly not remain here but reside in one of the wealthy English parishes on the Borders."

"And your sister?"

"Poor Elizabeth. She is a pawn in Father's attempt to gain local dominance."

"Details?"

"The obvious obstacle to Father's dominance in the area are the Morgans and the independent yeoman farmers such as Cadwallader, Parry, and Davies. He thought he would control the Morgan possessions through the son that would be born to Cranog and my sister Elizabeth. Father was thwarted when Cranog Morgan married Glynnis Kyffin. He is now working on an alliance with Cadwallader by suggesting that the constable's son Edwyn would be a fitting wife for Elizabeth."

Luke knew that such a solution was most unlikely. He ended his meeting with James.

Ned Jenkins and Luke immediately established a rapport. They discussed their mutual experiences in the military service of the Parliament and the Protector. Luke was convinced of Ned's loyalty. He had none of the overt ambition of his father or the radical Puritanism of his brother James.

Ned indicated that during his period in the Hereford garrison, he had periodically purged its ranks of enemies of the government—Levelers, Presbyterians, Baptists, and Quakers. He hoped to do the same for Rhyd, but it would be difficult as the local landowners depended for their essential labor on men holding potentially subversive ideas.

Luke probed deeper. "Do you share any of the Fifth Monarchy views of your father and brother James?"

"Yes, I share all the views of the Fifth Monarchy Men, except one. I still accept Oliver Cromwell as the Lord's deputy until His coming, a return that I doubt is imminent."

"Ned, what happened to your wife?"

"I knew my brothers would have raised that episode with you. While in the garrison at Hereford, I regularly led a three-day patrol along the Severn. I returned from one patrol and found my wife gone. She and I lived in a large townhouse that Father had leased for me. She took none of her personal possessions, and none of our servants saw her leave. Both my personal inquiries assisted by some of my troops and those of the authorities found not a single clue."

"Was she troubled by anything? Was your relationship good?"

"We were very happy. Eleanor had just discovered she was pregnant."

Luke whistled, "Did anyone else know of this development?"

"Only Father. I thought it appropriate that he should know that I had done my bit for the succession."

"Was he pleased?"

"He was initially delighted but became concerned about my wife's pedigree. Such matters are of prime importance to Father. My wife talked little about her parents. She claimed to be the estranged daughter of a peer, but whenever I pressed her for details, she changed the subject or got angry and walked out of the room. Until she could provide satisfactory details, Father thought I may have been duped by some gold-digging harridan."

"Your father must now be worried that you and your brothers have no recognizable heirs?"

"I cannot remarry until my wife is legally declared dead. And I do not know if her pregnancy resulted in a living child. Father has tried to speed up the legal process without success. He has prevented my siblings marrying until my position is clarified."

"Do they resent this?"

"James has no interest in women, and Lawrence is a cold fish. I do not know what my lawyer brother thinks. Neither have had affairs. After all, we are a moralistic Puritan family, at least where it relates to drink and women."

"You have reservations regarding other Puritan credentials of your family?"

"Father and Lawrence are obsessed with material and social aggrandizement. The accumulation of property drives both of them, and they appear willing to adopt any methods to achieve their ends. At least the Morgans under Sir Daffyd were concerned for their servants. He was a much beloved master. I have heard many of our servants compare Father unfavorably with his late rival."

"Would your father be happier if Lawrence was his successor rather than yourself?"

"Enough, Luke! Our intimate family tensions have nothing to do with the purpose of your inquiry. In fact, Lawrence would be a much more obvious supporter of the Protectorate if he were lord of the manor than I. He has impeccable credentials as a trusted friend and steward of high-ranking Cromwellians."

"Would you relinquish the succession?"

"No! Even if I did and Lawrence replaced me, the law is not likely to agree. The English system protects the rights of the eldest son except in cases of madness and treason. For Lawrence to succeed to Father's estates, I would have to be dead."

"When you eventually take over as lord of the manor, would you alter much?"

"Yes. I am disgusted with my family's unrelenting search for greater and greater wealth, and with the disruption of the local community that this causes. I would emulate the late Sir Daffyd in looking after my workers. Daffyd built cottages for them. I would do the same. Despite Father's Englishness, this is Wales, and I am Welsh. We must preserve our traditions."

Next day, Luke's plan to interview Lawrence had to be put on hold. The lawyer had left before breakfast for Rhayader on family business.

Instead, Luke sought and obtained a meeting with Conway.

Luke began with a statement. "Sir Conway, in terms of my mission, your household has no relevance to solving the Sir Daffyd murder, and you and your sons have an admirable record in support of Parliament and Protector in an area where our enemies have dominated. My questions therefore are directed toward the future administration of the region. In addition, many suggest that the area is suffering from a general malaise, which I would like to understand and interpret, and assess its relevance to the government of Oliver Cromwell."

"Colonel, surprisingly, I can contribute a little to your murder investigation. One of my men was riding back from the coast at the time and says he passed a drove of more wagons, more men, and less cattle than anyone would expect. His horse went lame not far down on this side of the Pass. He decided to wait for the drove to borrow a horse or obtain a ride on one of the wagons. It never appeared. That would support the generally held view that Sir Daffyd heard of an unauthorized drove and went to investigate. The drovers resented his appearance, killed him, and then retreated back the way they had come."

"Yes, that appears to be the accepted version of events. My colleague Sir Evan Williams is following up a few loose ends."

"Why are eldest sons such wimps? That a man such as Sir Daffyd should be succeeded by Cranog, the poet," exclaimed Sir Conway.

Luke was caught unprepared. He slowly responded, "Your own eldest son's record surely destroys such a generalization. He has fought nobly for our cause. His battle honors are impeccable."

"Ned is a courageous soldier, but the wars are over. In business, he is soft-hearted if not soft-headed. He is too concerned with the consequences of our business dealings on the inferior sort."

Luke changed the subject. "Although there has not been the slightest rumor that you had anything to do with Sir Daffyd's death, you would not deny that his demise has greatly lifted your presence in the area and your chances of becoming a magistrate and possibly a member of Parliament?"

"No doubt! I would never have been able to compete with Sir Daffyd, despite his reactionary views. Even my own servants admired him."

Luke knew he was being totally unfair, but the fact that one of Sir Conway's men was in the area of Sir Daffyd's murder was interesting. He moved on.

"Sir Conway, I have two concerns regarding the future of this area and your role in it. I can see three divisive issues that may undermine your ability to carry the Protector's colors in this region. Your attitude seems to inflame the religious division. Will Derfel go quietly when your son replaces him? Has James the temperament to heal the religious divisions in the area? Second, will your preference for Lawrence undermine Ned's position and divide your household? Third, will your continued economic expansion cause a major rift in the community among the lower orders?

"The Protector would be looking to a united household that would use its influence to create harmony both in religion and in society in general. Ideally, would you as the Protector's agent destroy the malaise that pervades the area?"

"Colonel, I reject many of your assumptions. You have been listening to Ned. My business expansion will create work for the lower orders, James will enforce a religious uniformity in line with the Protector's views, and Ned will lead a group of militia to enforce Cromwell's orders.

"To achieve all of these, there are occasions when you have to be cruel to be kind."

13

WHEN LUKE FINISHED HIS INTERROGATION, Conway invited him into an adjacent chamber in which a large fire was burning and a small table groaned with a cold collation. He summoned Ned and James to join them.

The group talked informally about Luke's adventures as they sipped their mulled wine and nibbled on pieces of chicken, pork, and lamb.

Luke took advantage of the relaxed atmosphere and casually asked, "What annoys you most living in this isolated part of the Upper Wye?"

Conway was direct. "Misinformation."

"In what regard?"

"First, official information comes through the local magistrate and constable, and is promulgated in the church. In Daffyd's day, it was not a problem. Now Cranog and Cadwallader either don't pass any news on, or Derfel refuses to accept it. If we did not have family and business links in England, we would be largely ignorant of political events. That is why we prize your visit, Luke. It is the closest I have ever been to accurate political knowledge."

"That is hardly misinformation," Luke observed.

"Agreed. The real misinformation floods into our parishes, and the sources are usually impossible to uncover, although traveling tinkers and itinerant religious preachers play a major part. A number of times we have heard that there has been a rebellion against the

Protector and that he is either dead or a prisoner. All false! In Rhyd, there are two centers of community interaction, the Red Kite and St. Brioche. They are both hot beds of unsubstantiated rumor and gossip."

"Surely the extended households of the large landowners are another source," posed Luke.

Ned joined the conversation. "Very true. You touch a sensitive nerve. Gossip among our servants is usually baseless and often harmful. The Morgan servants and farmworkers are just as bad."

Conway returned the conversation to his point. "Knowledge of the facts is a vital weapon in any political society. Without knowledge, you are severely handicapped. All the little uprisings against the government fail because the rebels do not have the facts. The Protector would face real danger, if his enemies were properly informed."

James muttered disparagingly, "Is it not part of your job, Luke, to deliberately mislead the opponents of the government. This is John Thurloe's specialty as master counterspy and propagandist for Cromwell. Only he knows the truth."

"It may be Thurloe's civilian approach, but it is not mine. My job is to discover the truth. I agree with Conway that political success depends on having the facts. That is why I am here. Is Wales about to rise against the government? Will the threat come from the covert Papists, the parliamentary Presbyterians, or the Puritan radicals? If it is the last, will it be Fifth Monarchy Men, Baptists, or Quakers?

"What role will you, the dominant local gentry, play in any such move?

"James, do you agree with your father that the main disadvantage of living in the isolated Upper Wye is the lack of factual political information?"

"Only in part, more serious is the lack of law and order."

"The Welsh have a reputation for disorder, but surely that is an English prejudice. I have seen absolute anarchy in many parts of the country. By comparison, your parishes are relatively law abiding," Luke replied.

"I don't agree. Was the murder of Sir Daffyd Morgan law abiding? Was the appalling display of Baptist rioting in the churchyard law abiding? Are the affrays and assaults that regularly emanate from the Red Kite law abiding? Was the attempt to kill young Hedd and the avalanche of rocks that killed a shepherd, incapacitated the area's only blacksmith, and nearly killed you signs of a law-abiding community?"

Luke was taken aback by the James's passionate outburst, which he attempted to placate. "Part of my mission is to try and explain these abnormal outbursts. The area survived for decades under Sir Daffyd's leadership with nothing worse than a bit of cattle rustling.

"What about you, Ned? Ignorance of the true political situation and the lack of law and order have been advanced as the major issues confronting the Rhyd community. Do you agree?"

"No, change, especially the attempt to Anglicize everything, is far more destructive. My own family is leading the charge. Welsh traditions must be revived. For example, ignore the technicalities of English law and accept a man's word and a handshake."

The warmth of the fire and the mulled wine was having its effect. Conway drowsily commented, "All this talk is making me sleepy. Feel free to doze."

Conway took his own advice and within minutes was asleep, soon to be followed by Luke and Ned. James was not amused at such a waste of time and left the room.

Conway, Ned, and Luke slept for almost two hours and were eventually awakened by Conway's valet.

The following morning, an excited Elizabeth Jenkins with three of her maids gathered in the hall to be questioned by the handsome colonel. The bevy of beauties, among whom the mistress was the most striking, impressed Luke. She was a tall girl with curly dark brown hair tied behind her head by an array of very dark red ribbons. Her bodice and skirt were of a similar hue. Her collars and cuffs were very tiny, and she wore no personal adornments. She was the dutiful daughter of a Puritan father.

She had an outgoing personality and immediately asked Luke to tell of his adventures. It was great for his ego. It was some time before Luke put an end to the diversion.

"Ms. Elizabeth, I am trying to lay bare the tensions within the local community, both to understand the death of Sir Daffyd Morgan and to better recommend measures to assist the government's standing in the area. Relationships within the landed classes are an important part of the scenario. You as an attractive woman with a sizeable dowry are a major player in this scene. Are you betrothed?"

"No, Father has forbidden any such commitments by my brothers or myself until Ned's wife is declared legally dead. He has a master plan to marry us all to important English nobility. My wishes will play no part in any negotiations."

"He has no any interest in betrothing his children to his Welsh neighbors?"

"The only locals of equal status are the Morgans, and the only person of marriageable age is Lady Rhoslyn. She is likely to succeed to the Morgan estates if Sir Cranog dies without children. Father probably has her under consideration for one of my brothers. A grandson who would inherit both Morgan and Jenkins lands, and power would be Father's ideal vision of the future. The only possibility for me would be Edwyn Cadwallader."

Luke assumed that this young gentlewoman had little significance to offer and hastily announced, "Thank you, Ms. Elizabeth. I have no more questions as you are isolated from the day-to-day tensions within Rhyd."

"Don't be so patronizing! Yes, Father shields me from the gossip and rumors that sweep through the community but with no success. My maids keep me very well informed."

"How can that be? This is a well-disciplined household. Your father would not let your maids consort with the outside world."

"True, but these girls are locals. They visit their families on one half-day each month. Occasionally, I send them outside the house on errands. They have parents, siblings, and friends who pass on the latest news circulating in the Red Kite and within rival households."

"And what do they report as the latest gossip?" asked Luke with renewed interest.

"Ask them directly! They have very difficult Welsh names, but Father renamed them Faith, Hope, and Charity."

Luke was amazed at Conway's arrogance and asked the tallest of the girls her real name. The girl looked embarrassed and commented, "Please, sir, the master will dismiss us if we use our birth names or speak Welsh under his roof. I am Faith."

"When you last visited family and friends, what was the latest gossip?"

"You, sir. They think you are here to make Sir Conway the new magistrate and help him control his rivals. They hope you will find Sir Daffyd's murderer and think whoever was behind the murder tried to kill you, an attempt that did kill Darryn Lewis and incapacitated Garyth Morris. The Baptists applaud you for forcing Mr. Derfel to allow Darryn's burial in the church grounds, and many of the Morgan shepherds and herdsmen have confidence that you will persuade Mr. Gwent to let them return to their cottages."

Luke turned to the small plump girl who answered to *Hope*. "And what has your family been discussing?"

"Kynon Hedd." The other girls giggled, suggesting that Kynon was a potential heartthrob of one or more of them.

"What did your parents say about Kynon?"

"That he is the illegitimate son of a powerful landowner, and the current heirs are trying to kill him."

"Which landowner is his real father?"

"My family is divided. Kynon's mother, Goodwife Hedd, was very close at the relevant time to Sir Daffyd Morgan, Mr. Huw Cadwallader, and several other gentlemen."

Charity interrupted, "My relations would not agree. They think Kynon discovered something that is happening in the community now, and the perpetrators want to silence him. Ask Kynon directly!"

Luke thanked the maids and turned to Elizabeth. "Tell me about Bronwyn Hedd."

"When I was little, I was scared of her mother Adara Bithel, who was repeatedly accused of witchcraft by the rectors over several decades. Sir Daffyd and Huw Cadwallader who prized her ability to cure sick animals protected her. She had two daughters.

"The eldest, Dilys Bithel, inherited the dark side of her mother's abilities and has constantly been cited as the cause of marital disputes, poisonous potions, and debilitating curses. She is a troublemaker who has much of the community terrified of crossing her. Many still go to her to purchase love potions, and some claim, poisons with which to kill their husbands, wives, and enemies.

"Adara's younger daughter, Bronwyn, is the opposite. She was and is a very attractive woman who, it is claimed, slept and still sleeps with many leading men of the community. She used her magical powers to help them achieve their success both in bed and in the wider world. It is rumored that she has children by many lovers.

"The community takes its problems, personal and medical, to Bronwyn. She has used her magic to help people find lost animals, and many of the youths of the parish resort to her to find their true love. She is Rhyd's most experienced and respected midwife and as such knows the most intimate secrets of the community.

"Her mother married her off to the saintly Mabon Hedd a few months before she gave birth to Kynon.

"Among the lower orders, she is a very powerful woman.

"Father says that as soon as he is appointed magistrate, he will have Dilys Bithel hanged as a witch and Bronwyn Hedd exiled from the community, but many farmers could not survive without Bronwyn's ability to cure sick animals."

"Let me return to the danger of bastards suddenly being legitimized. This would cause considerable unease among the landowning families of Rhyd, especially those that have an uncertain succession. A stranger might suddenly appear to claim his share."

"That's what Father says."

Luke rose to leave, but Elizabeth dismissed her maids with orders to prepare and provide refreshments for her and Luke.

"Please, Colonel, stay a while. Father keeps such a keen eye on my behavior that I rarely have an attractive male to myself. I often wish I were one of my maids. They seem to spend every spare moment being with or talking about their sweethearts. Are you married, sir?"

"No, as a professional soldier for nearly two decades, I have been on the move. I have never been in one place long enough to call it home and create the proper environment for a wife."

The serving girls returned with plates of food and some freshly mulled red wine. After half an hour of pleasant conversation and refreshment, Luke made another attempt to leave. Elizabeth grabbed his hand and pressed it tightly. "Colonel, please visit me again."

Luke took his leave and left the Priory for a head-clearing walk in the direction of the Red Kite. He was halfway down the main drive when a horseman galloped toward him at unnecessary sped. He was surprised.

It was Merlyn Gwent.

14

MERLYN PULLED HIS HORSE SO rapidly that it nearly fell. The rider just managed to right it. He screamed at Luke, "Follow me back to the house. There has been another murder."

Merlyn dug in his spurs and headed for the main door of the Priory. Luke ran after him, eventually entering a reception room in which the family was gathering as Merlyn regained his breath.

Sir Conway asked, "What is it, Mr. Gwent, that brings you here in such a state?"

"Sir, I bring you the worst of news. Your son Lawrence is dead."

Conway sank to his knees and held his head in his hands.

Lady Mary screamed and began to sob uncontrollably.

Elizabeth sighed continually.

Ned and James remained silent and immobile. Then the latter began to pray aloud.

Finally, Ned probed, "What happened?"

"Lawrence and I were in Rhayader on similar business. A judge of the Assizes was informing stewards across the county of changes that the Protector has introduced in the administration of estates. We stayed in the same inn and breakfasted together every day, including this morning.

"My party set out for home immediately after breakfast, but Lawrence said he had one last item of business to settle before he left.

"Halfway between here and Rhayader, Lawrence caught up with us and then trotted ahead. He said the rest of his group was following, but he needed to get home as quickly as possible. Ten minutes later, I heard two shots and put it down to local hunters. Five minutes after this, I rounded a bend in the track and saw a body lying on the verge. It was Lawrence. He had been shot in the back and in the back of the head.

"My men are bringing the body here."

Luke knew this was not the time or the place to conduct an inquiry. He would question Gwent in the morning. He offered his sympathy to the family and walked to the Red Kite.

Word of Lawrence's murder had already reached the inn, and the drinking chamber was alive with a myriad of theories discussed in Welsh, not a word of which Luke understood.

Fortunately, Evan limped into the room and was updated on the latest development by Luke. Evan moved about the chamber and was cajoled for some time by a gray-haired dwarf with a muscled upper body and rough calloused hands.

Luke was getting frustrated and filled in his time by consuming vast quantities of the scarcely palatable Welsh ale, while glancing apprehensively in Evan's direction.

At last Evan returned to his comrade. "Very interesting. That dwarf is Baden Carew. Until a year ago, he was a tenant farmer on land owned by an English absentee and was making a reasonable living. The Englishman sold the land to Lawrence Conway. Rents were tripled, and he was evicted from the cottage on the property, which had been the family's home for generations. Baden struggled on for a month or two but was told that unless he left immediately and formally relinquished his tenancy, no one would buy his stock. He refused. Then his few cattle and horses were fatally poisoned."

"How does Baden relate this to Lawrence's death?"

"He says that he is not the only one treated by Lawrence Jenkins in this way. He drank a toast to the murderer, claiming that if he were not such a coward, he would have killed the rack-renting dispossessing landlord himself. "Few here will mourn him. In essence, Lawrence Jenkins bought up properties across several parishes between here and Rhayader, and forced the poorer farmers off their land by means illegal and immoral."

"What did Jenkins do with these forcibly vacated properties?" asked Luke.

"He filled them with sheep, which require very little labor. Most of these properties were along the road to Rhayader. Carew is convinced that one of the dispossessed farmer shot Jenkins."

"It certainly creates a picture of Lawrence Jenkins I did not obtain by talking to his family, and it certainly offers a plausible explanation for his death. Where was Carew earlier today?"

"Returning from Rhayader."

Luke sighed.

"And he possesses on old musket, which I asked him to bring to me tomorrow," added Evan.

"Good, I don't know yet any details of the weapon used against Lawrence. The Jenkins have sent for their family doctor in Hereford. Is the army surgeon that came to look at you still here?"

"Yes. He dresses my wound every morning."

"I will send him to the Priory. Between them, the two doctors should be able to tell us something useful. Tomorrow I'll question Gwent and then visit the site of the shooting."

Next morning, Merlyn received Luke most cordially. "I thought I had got rid of you and that now you were annoying those uppity Jenkins."

"Yes, I was happy to leave any further inquiries here to Evan, but then you go and stumble onto a murder. You are making a habit of it."

"Apart from listening to the judge, which I imagine was a sideshow for busy stewards, why was Jenkins in Rhayader?"

"Lawrence was legally consolidating a large number of holdings that he had recently purchased and removing any encumbrances that they might carry."

"Was this widely known?"

"Yes, a large group of jeering farmers gathered outside the courthouse and pelted Lawrence with filth."

"Did he give you any hint as to what delayed him the morning of his death?"

"He was highly agitated over breakfast and again when he trotted past us. Whatever had happened in Rhayader that morning, he was anxious to tell someone back here about it as soon as possible."

"Did you see anybody ahead of you on the road, or did anyone come in the opposite direction and pass you after you heard the shots?"

"Yes, within seconds of hearing the shots, I passed five men who had tied their horses to the branches of a tree and were slumped against a low stone wall, drinking from leather flasks."

"Could they have fired the shots you heard?"

"Initially, I thought so, but finding Lawrence's body much further along the road destroyed that assumption. They could not have fired the shots that killed Lawrence. They were too far away, and there was no time for them to move from the murder site to where I saw them."

"Maybe there was a sixth man. He shot Lawrence and rejoined his friends after you had passed. What can you tell me about the men you saw?" continued Luke.

"I didn't take much notice except that I had a passing impression they were well armed. I saw sword blades flashing in the sunlight, and across the saddles of several of horses I saw muskets."

"Could they have been highwaymen?"

"My god, they could have been. I was lucky to have so many men with me. There would have been good pickings along the Rhayader road yesterday for such men with traders and lawyers returning with their pockets full of money."

"Did you examine the scene of the murder in any detail?"

"No, I rode immediately to the Priory, and my men brought home the body. One of them can take you back to the scene."

"I will accept that offer, but the evidence suggests a dispossessed farmer is our most likely suspect. That is certainly the gossip in the Red Kite. The murderer may even be one of their regular customers."

"Whoever was responsible was very lucky to ambush Jenkins."

"What do you mean?"

"Until breakfast time, Lawrence did not intend to return home that day. He planned to go into England and complete family business near Ludlow. If this killing were planned in advance, the assassins would have been waiting on the wrong road. The murder was an opportunistic killing. That creates a real mystery for you, Colonel."

"It certainly does. If it was an opportunistic killing, then a sixth man attached to the group you saw might be the perpetrator.

"I will meet your man at the Red Kite in half an hour."

On his way to the inn, Luke met Huw Cadwallader heading for Llanandras. Ned Jenkins had informed him of the murder. Luke brought Huw up to date, and Huw offered to accompany him to the murder site.

Huw was immediately concerned that Merlyn had deliberately made things difficult. Their guide, Adda, was known throughout the community as Addled Adda. The boy was a half-wit. It made little difference to Luke. The boy only understood and spoke Welsh.

He nevertheless completed his given task.

He led Luke and Huw to the site of the murder. Luke found small deposits of congealed blood on the verge and traces of spilled gunpowder behind a low stonewall. Footprints indicated that the perpetrator had then escaped across a ploughed field and rejoined the main road. This road almost encircled the field, making it possible for the shooter to wait until the Gwent party had passed and return back down the road unobserved. It could have been a man associated with the group Merlyn had passed.

Adda became agitated and waved his hands about, pointing to his head. Huw listened carefully to the unfortunate boy and eventually turned to Luke, "This boy may be slow, but he is very observant. He has come up us with an amazing possibility."

"Get on with it, Huw."

"The boy says he saw the body of Mr. Jenkins yesterday. The wound to the head was the same as that to the mangled head of Sir Daffyd."

"Come on, an experienced soldier such as myself finds it difficult to distinguish what causes wounds. How can this stupid lad know anything?" commented an insensitive Luke.

"Nevertheless, the lad says much of the head of both cases was blown away. He has seen hundreds of shot animals, and the ammunition has rarely exploded. The wounds to Daffyd and

Lawrence were much larger than those caused by normal musket fire."

Luke was quiet for some time. "The boy could be on to something. There is an explanation for such wounds. It happens when you use lead that is too soft. The ball shatters when it meets its target, causing an extensive wound. It can be made worse if the musket ball is combined with lead shot. But no one deliberately manufactures such poor-quality lead balls. They make a mess of any game you shoot. It would be inedible."

Huw appeared inexplicably nervous and noted, "Does it suggest that the person who murdered Daffyd was the same man who shot Lawrence?"

"It's a possibility. Have there been complaints about soft lead musket balls?"

"I've heard nothing in the Red Kite, and I have not received any complaints officially. Most people here make their own musket balls. William Price supplies ammunition to those few who do not make their own. Nobody would admit his own shortcomings. There are numerous musket ball molds that former soldiers purloined during the recent conflicts. If you could retrieve the ball from Jenkins's head, it may reveal some peculiarity of the mold, and then you could track down the maker."

"Normally, yes, but if the ball shatters as it has in both these cases, it can't be done."

Huw was suddenly more relaxed. "If the same person killed Daffyd and Lawrence, you only need to find a common motive. What possibly could it be? Where do you start?"

Luke smiled. "With the person who found both bodies, Merlyn Gwent. Perhaps Merlyn and Lawrence were partners in some illegal or immoral scheme and were meeting in Rhayader away from both the Morgans and the rest of the Jenkins family. Did they spend much time together in Rhayader?"

"We will get some further information from my son Edwyn. As my steward, he went to Rhayader to hear what the judge of the Assizes had to say. He will be home tomorrow."

15

A SMALL GROUP GATHERED IN the chapel of the Priory to formally examine the body of Lawrence Jenkins-Huw Cadwallader, the Jenkins's family physician from Hereford, the army surgeon from Chepstow, Ned Jenkins, and Luke. The medical men confirmed Luke's assumption that a musket ball had fragmented in the victim's head, creating a larger than usual wound. Ned revealed that family servants who had prepared the body had removed not only many fragments but also quite a lot of lead shot.

There was no mystery. An unknown assailant firing both shot and ball from reasonably close range had killed Lawrence Jenkins.

He would be buried later that day in the floor of the family chapel. His brother James would conduct the service with only the immediate family in attendance.

Huw invited Luke back to his farm for a late breakfast and to question Edwyn who had arrived home late the previous evening. Luke was continually impressed by the young lawyer and could see why he was the heartthrob of the two most eligible genteel spinsters in the community.

"Edwyn, your father has undoubtedly already raised these questions with you last night. Can you tell me anything about the movements of Merlyn Gwent and Lawrence Jenkins during their stay in Rhayader?"

"Certainly. There was considerable public hostility to Lawrence. A crowd gathered outside the court, and when he arrived, they hurled abuse and buckets of filth at him. The mob included a number of locals whom I have seen at the Red Kite."

"Any names?"

"Yes, they made no effort to hide themselves. They actually appealed to me to join them. There was Alwyn Bonner, Baden Carew, and Kendric Lloyd. I thought I also recognized Rowland Parry."

"And the basis of their grievance against Jenkins?"

"They all claimed that Jenkins was using the law to deprive them of their rights as tenants, following his purchase of the properties. They believed that Jenkins was in Rhayader to close any legal loopholes that may have existed in their favor."

"Would any of men be capable of killing Jenkins?"

"Definitely, given the atmosphere that existed outside the court. The hatred was so infectious I could have shot Lawrence myself."

"Apart from this demonstration against him, did you see Jenkins on other occasions?"

"There is only one decent inn in Rhayader. All of the lawyers, including Jenkins, stay there. He never ate alone. He had breakfast with Merlyn Gwent and his other meals with a friend and business partner Anthony Griffith. "More important with hindsight is whom he did not openly meet with. On one occasion to clear my head, I left the inn and found a rowdy alehouse. Sitting in a corner deep in conversation was Lawrence and one of his family's wealthiest allies, William Price.

"I did not think they saw me.

"When Price left, he was disguised with a big floppy hat, long topcoat, and a cape that half covered his face.

"What is more intriguing before breakfast yesterday, I saw Price leave our inn by the servant's quarters. A few minutes later, I met Lawrence who looked quite distraught. My intention of chatting with him was curtailed by the arrival of Gwent who swept him off to breakfast."

"Great! Edwyn you have provided us with a missing link. Gwent admitted that Jenkins was not himself that morning, and whatever had happened, he changed his mind about continuing into England.

He suddenly decided to hurry home. Now we know that it involved William Price."

"That's not all, Colonel. I have left the most interesting facts until last."

Luke smiled in anticipation.

Edwyn continued, "After breakfast yesterday, in the darkened corridors of the inn, I was set upon by two ruffians. The taller of the two assailants pushed me toward the balustrade of the stairs and threatened to push me over."

"What did they want?"

"They delivered a gentle and simple message. Mr. William Price was not in Rhayader and did not meet Mr. Jenkins. Mr. Price did not want the good people of Rhyd to know of this liaison, and there was nothing to be gained by me in passing on any information regarding the meeting."

"Did they threaten you with what to expect if you did tell anyone?"

"No, but I don't think they needed to," replied the pragmatic Edwyn.

"Tell me about Price!"

Huw answered, "He's everything we Welsh detest. He is English born and English based, but pretends to have Welsh ancestry. He has turned Rhyd upside-down and in the process created much misery to many in our community while making himself a fortune. Rhyd, from the Morgans and Jenkins down, rely for survival on the sale of their cattle at the English markets. Their profit depends on the ability to get those cattle into England in good condition and at the right time. For generations, the Davies family has been the recognized master drovers for the Upper Wye. Up until five years ago, Nye Davies organized and conducted all our droves."

"What happened five years ago?"

Edwyn took up his father's narrative. "Sir Conway, on the advice of his son Lawrence, then steward to an English notable, brought Price into the community as his new drover. The Jenkins used their influence to persuade or force many of their tenants and some independent farmers to use Price instead of Davies."

"What force was used to make them change?"

Huw intervened, "I wouldn't make too much of that aspect. Price had a major advantage over Davies. It was in everybody's financial interest to change to him."

"Why was that?"

"Money. Davies, as had been the custom for centuries, collected the cattle and issued a note promising to pay for them when he had received money from their sale in England. The family was meticulous in meeting their obligations to the people. Price, who has unlimited funds, buys the cattle outright at the farm gate. The farmer receives his money months earlier and is protected against the vagaries of the English market. It is Price that bears any risk."

"How has Davies been able to compete?"

"Only with the support of the Morgans. Sir Daffyd, and consequently all his tenants, stuck with Davies. He is Welsh, one of us, and had served us well through good times and bad. Sir Daffyd made it clear he did not approve of English money destroying the unity of the community. Unfortunately, since Daffyd's death, several farmers have put their financial interests above community spirit and Welsh tradition and have agreed to offer their cattle next season to Price."

Luke followed the directions that Huw had given him and found William Price's home farm, which covered most of the lower reaches of a small stream to the south of the valley that contained the Cadwallader's land. The farmhouse had been greatly extended. Recently built barns and animal pens and fences were evident.

A surly-looking servant ushered Luke into a lavishly renovated antechamber. He informed Luke that Mr. Price was paying his respects at the Priory but was expected home at any time.

Luke readily accepted a mug of Kentish beer and had just emptied it when William Price entered the room. He greeted Luke warmly and to Luke's relief spoke English.

"Mr. Price, I need to question you on the general state of this community. I would appreciate the opinion of a man who knows it well yet can see it through the eyes of a rational Englishman. But I come today on a specific matter, the death of Lawrence Jenkins."

"I have just come from the Priory. A tragedy. How can I help?"

"Why were you in Rhayader? Why did you hide yourself from the many locals that were visiting the town to the point of wrapping yourself in a large cape and concealing your face? Why the attempted concealment?"

"It was not in my business interests to have been in Rhayader last week."

"Why?"

"Apart from my own business ventures, I have conducted others in collaboration with a partner whose behavior has caused me some distress."

"Lawrence Jenkins?"

"Yes."

"You went to Rhayader specifically to see Lawrence?"

"Yes. Lawrence had used coercive methods and twisted the law to alienate a number of people from properties that we had jointly purchased. He was in Rhayader to finalize these acquisitions. I wanted him to change his mind and give the people who were now our tenants a chance to survive."

"On what precise issues did you disagree with Lawrence?"

"All of the properties we purchased grazed cattle. I make my living organizing and executing the big droves of these cattle to the English markets. Lawrence was forcing the cattle farmers off the land and replacing their stock with sheep. Why would I be happy with that?"

"Why the disguise?"

"Most of people Lawrence forced off the land are droving clients of mine. They do not know that I am Jenkins's partner. I did not want them to see me in Rhayader talking to Lawrence."

"And is that why you had two of your men threaten Edwyn Cadwallader?'

"Colonel, I would never formally confess to such a deplorable act. The young Mr. Cadwallader had the misfortune to see me talking to Lawrence in a seedy alehouse. I simply reminded the young gentleman that it would not be in anyone's interest to report such a meeting in Rhyd. It is clear that my gentle suggestion has been totally ignored, but I would prefer it if you did not broadcast it across the community."

"When did you last talk to Lawrence?"

"The morning of his death, before breakfast."

"What was discussed?"

"What I have just explained."

"Our reports suggest that Lawrence left that meeting quite disturbed and changed his plans to go into England. What upset him?"

"I told him that if he did not reconsider, I would inform his father of some dubious deals that Lawrence had entered into in his father's name. More precisely that he had mortgaged some of the family's traditional lands to raise finance for somewhat suspect purchases."

"Thank you, Mr. Price. You have been straightforward with me. What you have said confirms other information that we have. What happens now in regard to your partnership with Lawrence?"

"I don't know. Everything rests on his will and testament?"

"Did he have a will?"

"I hope so. We will all be in a mess if he didn't."

Next morning, Luke returned to the Priory and sought out Ned. Luke mentioned the question of Lawrence's will. Ned was ignorant of any such document. Lawrence had only recently persuaded Conway to update his. Ned agreed that he and his father would look through Lawrence's papers to see if a will could be found.

Later that day, Ned reported that they had not been able to find a will but that Conway was very disturbed by some of the material he had uncovered.

"So much so that he wants Edwyn Cadwallader to assist me in sorting out the mess. We found no will, but we did find two letters that referred in passing to a will. There is a will, but where is it? Father is distraught. He was completely unaware that Lawrence had developed business interests of his own outside those of the family. If you have time, I would like you to assist Edwyn and myself sift through the papers."

16

THE THREE MEN SPENT TWO days reading the documents.

Edwyn was meticulous. He looked initially at every item and then passed those of family importance to Ned and those pertinent to Lawrence's murder to Luke. He kept those whose content concerned financial and estate administration to himself.

On the second evening, they summarized their findings over supper in a room adjacent to the Priory's library.

Ned was pessimistic. From what he had read, Lawrence did not always distinguish between his activities as the family steward and lawyer, and those of his own and his various partners' business interests.

Edwyn was more positive and claimed that by a careful analysis of the legal documents, he would be able to separate most of the family possessions and rights from those recently acquired by Lawrence for himself or in partnership with others.

There was no doubt that his major partner in recent local acquisitions was William Price. Unfortunately in most of these, the share of each party was left vague. It would be a legal nightmare trying to prevent Price from claiming more than he was perhaps entitled to unless a detailed will was recovered.

There was one letter, which stunned all three readers. It was four years old and from lawyers whose name and location had been torn from the top of the document. It reminded Lawrence that he had been tardy in his payments, and their client was not happy.

Ned was disconcerted. "For what mistake was Lawrence paying?"

Luke was more buoyant. "Gentlemen, this letter proves to me that there is a significant part of Lawrence's archive that we have not recovered. This is the only letter of a personal nature we have recovered. Similar letters must exist but have been filed somewhere else. Ned, you thoroughly searched the library and Lawrence's office?"

Ned nodded.

Luke continued, "Did you notice anything different about the library and the office since Lawrence became steward?"

"I have no idea. I hardly entered either of these rooms until we conducted this search. Father might know."

Ned left the room and returned a few minutes later with Conway.

Luke asked, "Sir Conway, when Lawrence became steward, did he alter anything in the library and in the room from which he worked?"

"Yes, he replaced my father's old cabinet with its secret drawers and writing easel with the large flat table desk you see. I was not happy."

"Where is that desk now?"

"It is in James's bedchamber."

Ned spoke, "James is in Builth for a few days. Follow me!"

The four men entered the bedchamber, and Ned opened and shut the many drawers of his brother's cabinet. He found nothing that was relevant to Lawrence.

Conway smiled. "Ah, Ned, you did not find the secret drawers. My father told me how to open them just before he died."

Conway fiddled underneath one of the drawers and removed it entirely, revealing a hidden niche that contained carefully bundled letters, tied by ribbons and organized according to the period of time covered. By these dates, it was clear that Lawrence had access to his brother's cabinet up to a week ago and had continued to hide his personal mail therein.

Additional candles were brought; and Luke, Edwyn, and Ned settled down with mugs of Irish whiskey and began the mammoth task of reading the personal letters. There were cries of amazement and grunts of disappointment.

The amazement related to the many letters that referred to an enclosure that was regularly forwarded to a mysterious client through a firm of Ludlow-based lawyers, Ridges and Robb. On a number of occasions, the enclosure contained legal documents, making the recipient a partner in some of Lawrence's business adventures.

Lawrence had a mystery partner in addition to William Price.

The grunts of dissatisfaction followed the discovery that key passages in some letters were in code. Luke offered to use his experience and that of his men to decode the letters. Edwyn raised an additional problem that might thwart the English would-be code breakers. The encoded material may be in Welsh.

Luke brought the meeting to an end in the early hours of the morning. "We have obtained all we can from these letters until parts are decoded. I intend to set out in the morning for Ludlow to question the lawyers, Ridges and Robb. Do either of you wish to accompany me?"

Both did.

The three men arrived in Ludlow two days later. Ned accompanied Luke to protect the family interests; and both felt they needed another lawyer, Edwyn, to deal with the Ludlow attorneys. Ned knew the thriving market town well, having spent periods there with a detachment of his Hereford garrison, when from time to time they supplemented the Ludlow defenders against potential Welsh insurgents.

Luke, ever cautious, armed with the Protector's special authorization, made himself known to the current garrison commander and indicated that he may need the assistance of a troop of horse.

After spending the night at the Three Cows, they made their way to the chambers of Ridges and Robb. The clerk informed them that Mr. Ridges was dead, and Mr. Robb had retired. The active attorney was Mr. Robb's nephew, Geoffrey Rudd, who was currently very busy and did not see anybody without an appointment.

Luke intimated that they were on the Protector's business and required Mr. Rudd to present himself immediately.

The clerk left and after a considerable time returned with a presentable tall younger man. "Sorry for the delay. My clerk tells me you are on the Protector's business. How can a poor regional lawyer be of assistance to the government?"

Edwyn spoke, "You acted for Mr. Lawrence Jenkins. Mr. Jenkins has been murdered, and we suspect it may have had to do with some business you were conducting on his behalf."

Rudd was visibly shocked. He groaned and put his head in his hands. "Murdered? Lawrence was my friend long before he became my uncle's client. Lawrence was steward to a wealthy aristocrat in this region for five years, and I was his deputy."

Ned introduced himself. "I am Lawrence's eldest brother. I know that he made regular payments through you to a third party who also appears to be his partner in several business adventures. Who is this party?"

"I don't know."

"That is hard to believe," commented Luke.

"Do not question my integrity, sir!"

Edwyn interceded, "Tell us, Geoffrey, how the monies and documents are passed on to your client."

"Every month a servant of my client collects the material received from Lawrence. You are in luck. He is due here tomorrow at noon to collect the latest. Lawrence must have sent it before his murder. It arrived today."

"Great, we will return then and follow the man. Do not inform him of Lawrence's death. We shall do that personally to his master," instructed Ned.

Luke asked more gently, "As his friend, do you know why Lawrence was so close to this person or so in debt to him that he sent a regular payment and associated him in many property and business deals?"

"I asked him as much when he first approached my uncle to act for him. He said he had done a very silly thing and then compounded it by an unforgivable act for which there was no absolution. When I asked him whether he was being blackmailed, he said that the law may look at it in that way, but he preferred to see it as paying for his sins and hopefully regaining redemption."

Ned exploded. "I knew it! Lawrence was being blackmailed. That explains his strange out-of-character behavior. And it probably explains his murder."

Edwyn, anxious to discuss developments in private, thanked Geoffrey for his cooperation and indicated that they would return to follow the client's servant.

Edwyn was about to close the door on the lawyer when Geoffrey calmly asked, "Do you have a copy of Lawrence's will?"

Ned replied, "No, unfortunately, we have not been able to find it."

"Your search is over. Lawrence left a copy of it with us. I will fetch it."

Luke swore, "Typical lawyer!"

Geoffrey left the room and returned several minutes later with a large parchment, which he carefully unrolled and read.

"Lawrence divides everything he owns equally between his eldest brother Ned and another party whose name appears to be encoded. There is a codicil on the bottom that states that this party on being informed of his death will present us with the code that he, Lawrence, has countersigned."

Geoffrey handed the will to Ned.

He was overwhelmed, and a tear ran down his cheeks. "Why me? Lawrence and I were never close. If anybody in the family was to a beneficiary, I would have expected it would have been Father or James."

Luke said nothing, but already he was wondering whether Ned and the unknown partner shared Lawrence's estate because his mistake had hurt both of them. At the right time, he would ask Ned if Lawrence had ever done anything that seriously harmed him.

Just before noon the next day, the three men gathered in the vicinity of the lawyer's chambers. A number of people entered and left the building, but it had been prearranged that Geoffrey's clerk would accompany the relevant servant several yards down the street. To confirm the identity of the courier, the clerk would scratch his own head.

Eventually, a hair-scratching clerk walked out of the chambers and along the street with a medium-sized middle-aged man. Their target walked a hundred yards along the street and then mounted a chocolate-colored Welsh pony that he had tethered outside the Golden Head.

The courier led the three sleuths out of Ludlow, heading west toward the Welsh border. He soon turned north along a minor track that climbed into the low hills. Finally, he went through the main gates of an estate on which stood a magnificent manor house.

Luke cautioned the others not to confront the inhabitants of the house until they had more information.

Ned saw several laborers renewing a hedge. He dismounted and engaged them in conversation. "What is the name of that magnificent house?"

"Barton Oak, sir."

Ned gasped. That was a name recorded in Lawrence's papers as a property, which he had owned and had subsequently leased. Luke and Edwyn who had now joined him were equally impressed.

Luke asked, "My man, who is the master of such a fine house?"

"It has no master," answered another of the hedgers.

"It is run by a steward then on behalf of an absentee landlord?" interjected Edwyn.

"No, sir."

"Is it property which the government has sequestrated?" asked Ned.

"Enough of your sport, lads! For whom do you work?" demanded Luke.

"Lady Penelope Abbott."

Luke nearly fell from his horse as Edwyn expressed the general surprise. "Lawrence's partner and constant beneficiary is a woman."

Ned was obsessed. "We must see Lady Penelope, now."

The door of Barton Oak was opened by an elderly servant supported by two men whose hands were close to the hilt of their swords. The servant inquired as to their names and the purpose of their visit. One of the armed men made it clear that Lady Penelope did not receive strangers, especially those who appeared unannounced.

Luke indicated that he was on the government's business and that Lady Penelope could assist his inquiry considerably.

Ned added that they also brought bad news for her ladyship. Her friend Mr. Lawrence Jenkins had been murdered.

The servant replied, "I am sure her ladyship will be delighted to receive you, and I will forward to her your sad news regarding Mr. Jenkins. Unfortunately, she is currently staying with friends in Shrewsbury. She will be home in two days. If you are staying locally, I can contact you when she returns and arrange a time for you to meet."

The three men looked at each other, and Edwyn told the servant that they would stay at the Three Cows in Ludlow until they heard from Barton Oak.

17

MEANWHILE, EVAN CONTINUED HIS DISCREET surveillance of the West Field and the track that led up to the Pass along the Llanandras valley. He placed his men at concealed locations at appropriate intervals up the dale.

He had retired for the night when one of these men burst into his chamber.

"What is this, trooper?"

"A wagon passed me going up toward the Pass, presumably carrying the bodies of deceased builders. An hour later, the wagon returned but was having difficulty in the heavy conditions. It became bogged on a number of occasions within my line of sight. It was carrying heavier material downhill than on its outward journey. If we hurry, we could confront the bogged wagon and offer our assistance."

"And take a peek at the cargo. Good work, trooper!"

Evan collected three more of his men as they moved up the track. The five soldiers were delighted to see in the pale moonlight the wagoner and his two escorts trying to dig their wagon out of the mud.

Evan adopted a relaxed friendly approach as he reached the wagon. "It's your lucky night. The weather is worsening. If the rain starts to fall, you will be stuck until morning. Let's help!"

The wagoner mumbled his thanks, but one of the guards wanted to know what the troopers were about.

Evan replied, "Given the problems that have engulfed this community, the colonel ordered night patrols along all the main ways of the parish. With what have you overloaded this wagon?"

The wagoner replied, "I told the lads not to load the last few bundles of slate. It was the last straw." He giggled at his use of words.

One of the guards quietly placed his shovel on the ground, carefully primed his musket, and fired into the air.

A startled Evan turned on him, "Why did you do that?"

Before he could answer, the other guard fired another shot and hastened to explain. "We have orders from Mr. Gwent that if we strike trouble along the track and are within hearing distance of the manor, we should fire two shots. He will then send us help."

Evan was suspicious. He whispered instructions to a trooper who immediately moved to the far side of the wagon. Instead of digging under the wheel to free it from the mud, he furtively loosened its connection to the axle. As a result, minutes later, when all of those involved put their weight behind the wagon and pushed it forward, it toppled over on to one side as the tampered-with wheel collapsed.

The wagoner let out a tirade of abuse and accepted that he was stuck there until morning.

He immediately suggested that because of this eventuality, Evan and his men could resume their patrol.

Evan, without warning, lifted an edge of the cover but had only time to glimpse a large metal cylinder before the wagoner pulled it back and secured it even more tightly.

Evan's men resumed their patrol, heading uphill away from the manor. He was determined to discover where the wagon had come from with its overload. The ruts were easy to follow, and they led as expected to the quarry.

During an occasional burst of moonlight, Evan noticed an anomaly. There was no sign of recent activity around the piles of slate, and the wagon had been parked at the other end of the quarry to where the split slate had been stacked.

He would return in the morning to investigate this anomaly.

He did, with John Martin and a full troop of dragoons. By noon, their assiduous searching had been rewarded. What looked to be a solid cliff face proved to be a movable rock, which had been cleverly balanced to permit easy shifting.

When pushed aside, it revealed a vast cavern, which contained three empty wagons and several barrels of gunpowder. There was a broken box that Evan recognized as identical with those used to transport muskets. Overall their finds were disappointing, but Evan was convinced that the cavern had been a staging post for the supply of weapons and gunpowder to Llanandras.

John disagreed. "There is nothing here that you would not expect to find at a quarry, gunpowder for blasting and wagons for cartage."

Evan nevertheless doubled the surveillance on the West Field.

On his return to Llanandras, he was informed that he would be expected at supper as the household was entertaining an important visitor.

Lady Alis introduced Evan to her cousin Lord Kimball. Kimball observed the Welsh captain for some time and mused, "Looking at you takes me back a few years to my adventures in France. My friend and companion in that period was Colonel Tremayne's then deputy, Harry Lloyd. For a short time, I worked with Tremayne himself. He was knee-deep in solving a string of murders, which Alis tells me is his major role here. If anyone can solve Daffyd's death, it will be Luke. Where is he at the moment?"

"He is in Ludlow following several leads. I have no idea when he will return."

"I shall still be here when he does," commented Kimball. "He knows me by another of my titles. To him I am Simon, Lord Stokey. In England I use *Stokey*, in Wales *Kimball*."

Evan looked around the table and then asked Cranog diplomatically if a servant could locate Merlyn as he had a few urgent questions to ask the steward. Cranog's valet returned ten minutes later, quite agitated.

Cranog made his excuses to the ladies and asked Simon and Evan to follow him. The valet led them to Merlyn's quarters.

The room had been trashed.

Merlyn lay unconscious on the floor.

The valet who had found him minutes earlier suggested that he had been cudgeled severely but was breathing normally.

Merlyn was carried to his bed, and two female servants were called to dress his wounds. There were a few cuts, but the injuries were mainly massive bruises, already appearing in a variety of hues. His face had been hit, and several teeth had been displaced. He was passing in and out of consciousness.

Merlyn was in no state to answer questions. Evan would stay in the room overnight to prevent any further attack. In the morning, he would assign dragoons to protect the steward.

Next morning, Merlyn was either still too ill to answer questions or deliberately avoiding the experience by feigning his condition. His condition so worried Glynnis that she sent for Bronwyn.

One thing that Evan had fortuitously discovered during the night spent in Gwent's room was that the chimneys in this part of the house acted as sound channels. You could clearly hear what was being said in the room below.

This gave Evan an idea.

Merlyn may not talk to him, but he may do so to others. While a soldier would stand guard at the door of Merlyn's chamber, another would spend time in the room directly above, crammed into the fireplace with his ear to the chimney.

During the morning, many members of the household visited Merlyn but said very little.

Evan took his turn eavesdropping in the upper room just as Simon, Lord Kimball, entered the steward's bedroom. Evan was entranced as the conversation progressed.

Simon said, "Merlyn, my dear man, what happened? Who assaulted you?"

"There were two of them. They extinguished the tapers as soon as they entered the room. They were workmen from the West Field."

"What did they want?"

"That I turn a blind eye to the removal of the special goods that I have accumulated for you."

"All our good work, and these thugs wish to benefit," pontificated a very annoyed Simon.

"It is even worse. They want to utilize the material immediately in some hare-brained scheme, which sadly I think is planned and led by my own nephew Tudor."

"Was it Tudor that coshed you?"

"It could have been."

"We must thwart their plans immediately."

"I have no men. Those whom I could call on in the past I have alienated by evicting them from the cottages. The only armed forces in the area are the government troopers under Tremayne and Williams, but they would not help us, unless we reveal our secrets, which would destroy two years of work."

There was a long silence, and Simon finally spoke, "Where is the material stored?"

"In the special concealed cellars under the vast new barn I have almost completed building."

"Excellent. Let's tell Sir Evan the truth. In these troubled times, you have been building up an arsenal that you have securely sealed in those cellars. You have become aware that potential insurgents are planning to seize the material and probably use it against the government. All this is absolutely true, and I am sure Sir Evan will be willing to help. When he returns, I will confess to Luke Tremayne our exact role in this. It is imperative that we inform Sir Evan at once and ask for his immediate help."

Evan scrambled out of the upper room and ran to his own chamber. He had just got himself settled when there was a knock on the door. "Sir Evan, may I come in? I have solved the Gwent assault and need your assistance."

Evan listened to Simon outline the situation. The peer was sure Tudor Gwent was behind the planned theft and the assault on Merlyn.

Evan asked, "Lord Kimball, what were you doing importing arms and ammunition to this isolated community?"

"I know the import and distribution of weapons is against the law, but if rural gentry do not have the means to protect themselves, they will be victim to every form of uprising. Well-armed gentry are in a position to assist the government put down rebellion. Daffyd refused to take part in this operation, but I convinced Alis who converted Merlyn to the scheme. He began planning the transport and concealment of weapons months ago."

"Luke is convinced that the importation of something occurred on the night of Daffyd's murder. Were your men responsible?"

"Daffyd was my friend. None of those involved in the transport of the arms and ammunition killed Daffyd. My men tell me a lone horseman and then a little later a group of about four or five others were in the vicinity of the Pass at about the time of Daffyd's death."

Evan trusted Simon. What he had told him openly was identical with the private conversation Evan had overheard. Although the movement of arms was a major offense and one, which his unit was especially concerned with, allies of the government did need to be armed.

Merlyn briefed Evan as to the routine within the West Field enclosure. He admitted that he had handed over that project to his nephew Tudor who appeared to have misdirected it to his own ends. The thieves would need four of five wagons to remove the arsenal. Merlyn suggested that Evan and his men surround the West Field in hidden locations and wait for the wagons to appear.

Later that night, Evan began to doubt the wisdom of his decision. Nothing had stirred within the enclosure. An hour before dawn, he was alerted by the arrival of three wagons that had come down the track from the quarry. They entered the enclosure where two more carts appeared close to the unfinished barn.

Suddenly, the enclosure was alive with people, but their absolute silence created an unreal atmosphere. The wagons were assembled in line and moved forward out of Evan's vision into the barn and close to the hidden cellar.

Evan and Simon had agreed that the first wagon would be allowed to depart, and John Martin with a small group of men would follow it. They wanted to know who would benefit from the theft.

Life was made easier for the government soldiers as the wagons were loaded one at a time, and moved out of the enclosure some five to ten minutes apart. This enabled John to follow the first cart, while the subsequent vehicles were seized well away from the West Field and in such a manner that the following wagons were not aware of any trouble.

As the neighborhood had no jails and none of the landowners had secure-enough cellars to incarcerate the dozen men arrested, Evan had them returned to the West Field and placed in the very cellar from which they had just removed the arms and ammunition.

His interrogation revealed little of value. Most of the men were the builders originally hired by Sir Daffyd who had been offered money by Tudor Gwent to assist in removing the armaments. Another group was Irish laborers who had been recruited by Merlyn or Tudor to supplement the original building workers. They all thought they were carrying out the orders of their master and had no idea that Tudor was acting against the wishes of Merlyn and the Morgans.

Evan then asked the assembled prisoners, "Was Mr. Tudor Gwent among you this night?"

A man replied, "Yes, sir, he drove the first wagon. He has escaped your net."

Evan smiled to himself.

He would await John Martin's return.

At least one mystery had been solved.

There was no illness—no leprosy and no plague. Merlyn later confessed with Simon's approval that the story was a ploy to expand accommodation and build new structures including a secret arsenal without the danger of prying eyes. After completion of the new buildings and the concealment of the arsenal, the evicted shepherds and herdsmen would have been invited back.

18

JOHN MARTIN AND TWO COMPANIONS followed the first wagon at a discreet distance. They were led past the Red Kite and beyond the turn off to Cadwalladers. As they climbed a low hill, John was aware of complete silence ahead. The wagon had stopped.

John dismounted and cautiously walked up the track toward the wagon. He heard voices. He climbed over the low stone fence that edged the track and crawled, concealed by the wall, to a position adjacent to the disabled wagon.

Tudor Gwent was furious. The wagon had been overloaded, and as a result, one of the wheels had come off.

John mused that maybe it was the same wheel that Evan's patrol had sabotaged.

A wagoner was not optimistic. "Sir, we will have to unload most of the cargo. That wheel will only hold if we massively lighten the load."

"And where do we hide the goods we have unloaded? This is not a pile of sheepskins or rounds of maturing cheeses," answered Tudor sarcastically.

"Then we wait for the other wagons. We can redistribute our cargo among them."

"An excellent idea!" proclaimed a relieved Tudor.

John was anxious. He knew that no other wagons would appear. How would Tudor react when this became evident?

Tudor became agitated. He approached the stonewall and urinated, a yard or two from John's position,

Tudor then angrily turned on his wagoner. "Even the last wagon should have made it here by now. Are you sure you left the knotted handkerchief at each crossroad to direct them?"

"You saw me do it. If they are lost, it is your fault. You should have told each driver their destination."

"The man who bought the weapons did not want the destination revealed."

"But we will all know that when we deliver the goods."

"If that's the case, the purchaser will shoot us all," joked Tudor.

The wagoner froze.

He suddenly realized that in the circumstances, that was a distinct possibility. Why did he volunteer for this escapade?

Tudor laughed. "Don't fret, my man. How would I complete the building project in the West Field if all the men on this adventure died? We leave the wagons in a designated field, and the purchaser's men will collect them long after we have gone.

"Only I know the identity of the buyer."

The wagoner breathed more freely and chided Tudor on his black humor. "What do we do now?"

"Unload the wagon and conceal the cargo behind that stone wall. We can cover it with bushes I saw back along the track. I will tell the buyer where to find it."

For John, it was time to retreat. He walked back to his men, and the three of them returned to Llanandras.

Next morning, Simon, Evan, John, and Merlyn met over breakfast to evaluate the situation.

John reported that he had already sent a detachment with a wagon to collect the hidden weapons.

Merlyn seemed relieved that his nephew was just a vicious, unscrupulous, money-grubbing animal and not a dangerous religious fanatic.

Simon brought the group back to order. "We must nevertheless arrest Tudor and interrogate him as to the identity of his purchaser. The purchaser is undoubtedly a dangerous revolutionary."

"And how will we do that?" Merlyn asked.

Evan answered, "It won't be too difficult. Tudor will be anxious to discover what went amiss. He can only discover that from those in this room or the men in the West Field.

"By midday, all of our men will have left the Cadwalladerfarm and have taken up quarters in the West Field, which will be our barracks for the near future. John, you will ensure that our men take control of the West Field and that no one leaves the enclosure and no one enters. This will force Tudor to try and intimidate his uncle for any information he seeks."

"When will Tudor come?" pondered Simon.

Before Merlyn could answer, a soldier entered the room and announced calmly that Mr. Tudor Gwent was without and wished to speak to his uncle.

There was a gasp of astonishment. Evan expressed the general reaction. "The arrogant bastard. He does not know that we know he was behind the robbery. Let's keep it that way and with that exception tell him the truth."

Tudor entered the room. He was taken aback to find Simon and Evan were present.

Simon seized the initiative. "Where have you been, Tudor? We could have done with your help last night."

Tudor calmly replied, "I was visiting a young lady who lives on the way to Rhayader. She persuaded me to stay the night. Why? What's happened?"

Simon continued, "By sheer chance, Sir Evan's patrol ran into a convoy of wagons heading past the Red Kite. They were loaded with the weapons and gunpowder that we had concealed in the cellar of the new barn. The men said they were paid to move the arsenal. They thought they were carrying out your uncle's orders."

Tudor turned toward the bed-ridden Merlyn, "Given your condition, I will take over all your duties. I will look into this fiasco. I will immediately get work in the West Field back on track."

Merlyn surprised everybody and rose from his bed. He turned toward his domineering nephew. "I am sorry, Tudor. Things have changed. I will reassume all my responsibilities as from now. The

West Field is now the garrison for a company of dragoons. They will impose discipline on any recalcitrant workers, including yourself."

"What do you mean, Uncle?"

Tudor turned toward Evan and Simon and snarled, "Did the beating cloud the old man's mind?"

Simon responded, "No, it actually cleared it. He can see you now for the treacherous knave that you are."

Evan called in a couple of troopers and then turned to the truculent Tudor, "As a dealer in weapons, I arrest you in the name of the Protector, and given the absence of gaols in this area, you will be secured by fetters in one of the West Field cottages and later escorted to the military prison in Chepstow."

A troubled Tudor turned to his uncle. "Do something for your brother's sake! You promised him you would look after me."

"Lad, your assault on me and your betrayal of this household renders null and void all of my obligations to you."

Evan nodded to his men who took away a stupefied Tudor.

He then turned to Simon and Merlyn. "Gentlemen, we have been allies to this point, but I cannot ignore your importation and storage of arms. A small amount sufficient to defend the manor house would have been acceptable to the authorities. But we have recovered enough munitions, including three cannons, to sustain a major rebellion."

Simon responded, "I can assure you that while technically illegal, our importation of arms and ammunition was not aimed at undermining the government."

"Where did you get the arms?"

"They were smuggled from Spain, landed near Aberystwyth, and transported up to the Pass by local smugglers supervised by a small detachment of Spanish soldiers and then by Merlyn's men to the quarry.

"You still imported arms from a country with which we are at war. And why did your import so much?"

"Luke knows my background. I am a Papist who suffered greatly for my faith in our civil conflict. As this part of Wales is increasingly overrun by fanatical Protestants who show no respect for other variants of Christianity or for the landed classes, I took it upon myself to arm the Catholic gentry of mid-Wales. Our enemy is not the government of Oliver Cromwell, but the fanatical followers of Vavasor Powell and George Fox. If Daffyd lived, given his views, none of these arms would have stayed at Llanandras."

"My lord, that is a very plausible story, but it is hard to believe. For months there have been rumors that the Catholics of Wales were about to rise against the government, supported by Spanish and Irish troops. The Spaniards who escorted the arms here were probably an advance guard that for some reason have not been augmented as expected. Even if I accepted your story, I am not sure whether it makes the situation much better. Armed Catholic gentry would scare a lot of people, including the government. I could make a strong case to the Lord Protector that we have uncovered a major Papist plot."

"Then I will have to convince Luke and your superiors, including Major General Berry, that any force we Papists can muster is an ally of the government and not an enemy. What Luke and you should uncover as soon as possible is who bought our arms. The real plot to destroy the Protectorate involves the would-be recipient of those weapons, not us."

"Before Tudor leaves for Chepstow, I will question him on that key point," promised Evan.

He wasted no time and was soon questioning the prisoner.

"Tudor, your only hope of avoiding hanging is if you help us. I could then advance an argument that you are no rebel, but a simple thief."

"That is exactly the case. I am only a thief. It is Uncle Merlyn and Lord Kimball that should die as traitors. They imported the goods from our current enemy Spain, and Kimball is a known Papist extremist and Royalist courtier. If Sir Daffyd were alive, none of this would have happened. Please save me!"

"I can only save you if you help me. To whom did you sell the arms?"

"Sir Evan, you are a man of the world. There is no way I can reveal the name. I would be dead within hours. Even here I am not safe. I took a lot of money and did not deliver."

"In that case, give us a name, and we can remove this threat to your life."

"No. Get me out of here immediately! I will be safer in Chepstow."

"I agree. I hope that once safely inside the military prison, you will tell your interrogators the name."

Evan returned to the manor house, having given instructions that Tudor and two troopers were to leave immediately for the south. He made his way into an antechamber to enjoy drinks with Cranog, Simon, and the ladies of the house. After an hour, he thought he heard gunfire from outside. Perhaps his men were having musket practice, or the farmhands were removing vermin.

A few minutes later, Cranog's valet arrived accompanied by John Martin. "What is it, man?" Cranog asked.

Lieutenant Martin answered, "Ladies and gentlemen, Mr. Tudor Gwent has been shot dead, and a trooper is wounded."

All the men left the room, and John Martin explained to them, "Gwent and two of my troopers left the West Field by the back gate and intended to head south. They were not even through the gate when three shots rang out. Tudor fell from his horse. The two troopers, one slightly wounded, headed up the track in the direction of the shots. They saw three horsemen well ahead of them heading for the Pass. The wounded trooper fell from his horse. By the time I reached the scene, further pursuit was futile."

Evan retraced the last minutes of Tudor's life. He located the place from which the assailants had opened fire. Then he saw an important clue. The horses used by the assailants had ridged shoes. Were these the same men who had tried to kill Luke and himself at the source of the Cadwallader valley?

19

Meanwhile in Ludlow, Luke, Edwyn, and Ned received a message that Lady Penelope was at home and anxious to see them. On arrival at Barton Oak, her valet ushered the men into an antechamber and indicated the Ned should remain there. The servant then led the others into an adjoining room. Draped over a long lounge was a very beautiful woman, perhaps past her youth. She revealed much more of her body than befitted a noblewoman interviewing male strangers. Luke was surprised.

Penelope immediately asked for details of Lawrence's death. She listened intently to Edwyn who studiously looked out the window rather than gaze on the tempting female flesh confronting him.

She then coldly asked, "Why is the government interested in a series of murders in upland Wales? It's a natural pastime for the Welsh to kill each other off."

Luke recovered his equilibrium and answered, "My lady, the government is concerned with national security. I need to establish that the current disorder in Wales is no more than that traditional Welsh lawlessness. I need to confirm that the murders of Sir Daffyd Morgan and Mr. Lawrence Jenkins in no way threaten the security of the regime."

Edwyn asked, "My lady, forgive this question. You appear to have no husband, yet you claim to be referred to as lady. Are you the daughter of a peer?"

"A lawyer's question. I had a husband, but he was not titled. Indeed, my title rests on being the daughter of a peer."

Edwyn continued, "If you are a peer's daughter, why did you rely for your upkeep on the generosity of Lawrence Jenkins?"

Luke interjected, "To be more specific, what exactly was your relationship with Lawrence?"

Penelope replied, "He was my first husband."

Both men were speechless.

Luke recovered and offered his condolences to her ladyship.

Edwyn did the same but could not restrain his curiosity, "Why did you not live together?"

"Circumstances changed, and we fell out of love."

"If that was the case, why did Lawrence continue to support you and make you a partner in some of his enterprises?" asked Luke.

"It is a long complex story."

"We need to know all," Luke stated awkwardly.

Penelope called for refreshments.

"As a young teenager, I was seduced by a neighboring gentleman who refused to marry me. He convinced my father that I was to blame. Father refused to enforce the nuptials. Instead, I was exiled to London to live with an impoverished and lecherous relative who on most nights tried to take advantage of me.

"My parents had stormy a relationship. When Mother helped me with a small allowance, Father became enraged. He ejected my mother from her home, claiming she had committed adultery. He took legal proceedings against us both.

"One of our London lawyers was a young Lawrence Brown. Because he believed that the Welsh were discriminated against, Lawrence Jenkins used the Brown alias.

"We became lovers and in the heady atmosphere of London, and in my relative freedom, we married without any parental approval. Father and Mother reconciled, but they refused to recognize me as a member of the family. I was cut off without a penny."

"Young lawyers make little money. How did you and Lawrence survive?" asked Edwyn who had experienced the vagaries of a lawyer's income.

"With great difficulty. Lawrence decided that his future lay in becoming a steward to wealthy landowners. After a short but pleasant experience in the eastern counties, which I enjoyed, he accepted a very well paid position in Shropshire. Unfortunately for me, his new employer did not want the steward to be accompanied by a wife. He feared it would tempt his lascivious and apparently uncontrollable sons."

"So what happened to you?"

"Lawrence found a townhouse for me in Hereford.

"In the beginning, he visited me regularly, but these visits became less and less. Eventually, they ceased altogether.

"I became very lonely and was increasingly attracted to a mature officer in the Hereford garrison.

"Lawrence was so unconcerned when I wrote to him about my new lover. He did not even ask the man's name. The situation developed so rapidly that I married the officer."

"But you were already married?"

"Yes, but as the officer wanted to keep our marriage a secret from his family—only his father was told—and as Lawrence showed no further interest in me, it was easy to ignore my earlier marriage."

"What went wrong in your second marriage?" asked a sympathetic Luke.

"Two things occurred almost simultaneously.

"I got pregnant.

"Second, Lawrence discovered the identity of my bigamous husband. "He went berserk and threatened to kill me, and then himself. He was overcome with guilt and remorse."

"What could have been so horrendous to provoke such a reaction?"

"My second husband was his own brother, Captain Ned Jenkins.

"That is why I wanted to talk to you first and hope you will help me break the news to Ned."

"Is that why you left Ned without warning and disappeared completely from his life?" uttered an incredulous Luke.

"Yes, Lawrence and I did not wish to hurt Ned. Rather than a messy, harmful, and disharmonious explanation, we agreed on a plan. I would disappear, and Lawrence would maintain the unborn child and me. These payments were not blackmail. Lawrence saw them as portion of his penance for his part in such a sordid affair."

"My god!" exclaimed Edwyn who appeared stunned. "How are we to tell Ned?"

"Does he still love me?" asked Penelope.

"I don't know," replied Luke.

Edwyn addressed Luke, "You and I must tell everything we have just heard to Ned. If he then wishes to see Lady Penelope, so be it. On the other hand, he may not want to see her, at least initially. This way, he will have time to properly comprehend the situation."

The two men returned to the antechamber. Ned rose to his feet and headed for the door they had just come through. "My turn now. You took a long time. What's our lady of the manor like?"

Luke grabbed Ned by the shoulder and propelled him back to the chair he had just left.

"What is this, Luke? You and Edwyn look as if you have seen a ghost."

"You may well be right," said Edwyn.

Luke began the long narrative. As soon as he reached the part where a young woman falls in love with an officer, Ned saw the truth.

"Heaven preserve me! Lady Penelope is my missing Eleanor."

Luke completed the story.

Ned remained silent and absolutely still for some time.

Edwyn began to fidget, and Luke began to assiduously fondle a piece of silver on the table.

Ned seemed to lack emotion of any sort. He was not angry. He was not elated. He seemed to have been frozen to his chair.

Eventually, he spoke, "I need to be alone. I am going for a walk. Wait for me here!"

He left.

Luke turned to Edwyn. "Should we leave him alone? He may harm himself or Lady Penelope?"

"I don't think so," replied the lawyer.

"Nevertheless, I will follow him. Tell Lady Penelope what is happening!" requested Luke.

Ned walked through the manicured gardens of Barton Oak and crossed over into the nearest field. He followed the hedge to the road where the hedgers of several days earlier were still working. Ned questioned them intently on their mistress.

Luke hid on the other side of the hedge, until Ned made his way back into the garden.

Just then, a young boy bounded out of the house followed by his nanny. The boy saw Ned and raced up to him, "Is that sword very sharp, sir?"

Ned was transfixed. He finally answered, "Yes, my boy, it is very sharp. What's your name?"

"Edward, but Mother calls me Ned, after my father who died in battle."

Ned turned away, and he began to sob. He moved into a maze, and Luke was unable to follow him effectively.

As time passed, Luke became more and more anxious.

Much later, Ned emerged from the labyrinth with a spring in his step and a smile on his face. Luke scrambled to reach the antechamber before Ned.

Ned greeted his friends, "I am twice blessed this day. Given the death of Lawrence, I am legally married. I have a legitimate wife. Second, I have a fine son and heir. Father will be delighted. I want to see my wife and son."

Edwyn intervened, "Just as Lady Penelope gave you time to absorb her horrendous news, I think I should forewarn her of your attitude to the turn of events."

"By all means. But hurry up."

Edwyn left the room, and Ned and Luke finished off the flagon of ale that stood on the table.

Sometime later, Edwyn returned. "Ned, Lady Penelope will see you now. She has spent some time preparing to receive you. Follow her servant!"

Ned leaped to his feet.

"If you do not appear in an hour, Edwyn and I will return to the Three Cows and head for Rhyd first thing in the morning," shouted Luke.

Within twenty minutes, Ned returned to the antechamber. "Friends, I will remain here with my wife and child for some time. Please inform Father that I have found my wife and have a child, but do not tell him of Lawrence's role in this affair."

Luke and Edwyn had just reached the Three Cows when a trooper who had obviously ridden hard for some time approached Luke. "Colonel, I have an urgent dispatch from Captain Williams."

Luke took the sealed letter. He read with increasing amazement. Eventually, he told Edwyn.

"The situation at Llanandras has been volatile. Evan has uncovered a gun smuggling racket organized by Lady Alis and an old friend of mine, Simon, Lord Stokey, who in Wales uses his other title Lord Kimball, to arm the Papists of the Upper Wye. Apparently, Tudor Gwent assaulted his uncle and stole the Catholic arsenal, which he aimed to sell to an unknown person. Before he could reveal the buyer's name, he was shot dead. There is no leprosy or any other illness in the West Field, which has been taken over by my troopers."

Edwyn concluded, "I have a lot to tell Father, and your workload has increased. You now have three murders to solve, Daffyd, Lawrence, and Tudor Gwent."

"Yes, I hope this latest murder helps with the others. Find someone who had to get rid of Daffyd, Lawrence, and Tudor and I have our murderer."

On arriving at Rhyd, Edwyn and Luke went straight to the Priory where Luke asked Conway to gather the family in the library because he had some very happy news to relate.

When the family gathered, Luke spoke. "I will not waste words. I have nothing to report regarding Lawrence. My good news refers to Ned. He has found his wife Eleanor, whose real name is Lady Penelope Abbott. Sir Conway, you have a grandson and ultimate heir, another Edward also known as Ned."

Luke and Edwyn left the room, partly to allow the family to take in the news alone but also to avoid any awkward questions that might arise. Captain Ned could explain in full when and if he returned.

20

LUKE JOINED THE LLANANDRAS HOUSEHOLD for breakfast. Simon, Lord Kimball, rose from his seat and shook Luke's hand. The peer announced to the assembled group that he and Luke had worked together to bring two notorious French criminals to justice.

Luke responded, "All this is true, but I have no personal recollection of it. I lost my memory, accomplished all the meritorious deeds that his lordship refers to, and with the return of my memory cannot recall any of it. I do know that Simon pulled off an amazing feat and rescued a vast treasure from the greedy paws of the English and French governments, the exiled Charles Stuart, and conniving French malefactors.

"Whatever happened to that hoard?"

"Despite my fears at the time and my suspicion of the English army, since the creation of the Protectorate, all that treasure has been returned to the rightful owners."

"And have you heard of your clever accomplice, Mother Evangeliste, in recent years?"

"Yes. Sadly, savages attacked her mission in New France, and she was killed in a most brutal way. The heathen crucified her to the cross that stood before her convent. I deeply regret that during our adventures together I could not persuade her to give up her vows and marry me."

Tears rolled down Simon's cheeks.

Luke also was moved by the news.

He changed the subject. "Are you back in England permanently, or are you still a courtier to the young Stuart?"

"I have left the court for good. I continue to represent Royalist and Catholic interests in the Welsh marches and in Wales itself, and I am in regular contact with his majesty. However, I have made it clear that all this is done in cooperation with the government of the Protectorate.

"To my amazement, Catholics find the security that Oliver Cromwell, that arch-heretic, has brought to the country most reassuring after the horrible experiments with fanatical sectarians and unreformed Republicans."

"That is all to the good, Simon, but nevertheless you have committed a major offense, and Evan suspects that at one time you planned a Spanish-supported uprising of your coreligionists. I will discuss it with you after the meal."

An hour later, the two men and Evan met in an antechamber of Llanandras. Luke came straight to the point. "Simon, you well know that the very act of importing arms is a capital offense. According to military law, I could take you outside and summarily execute you. However, just as you Papists find some solace in the government of the Protectorate, Cromwell would find good cheer in your support or at least neutrality in this time of potential instability. As you know, in addition to solving the murders, I have been sent here to uncover where the threat to the Protectorate lies. Despite your importation of arms, I am convinced it is not, at least for the moment, with the Papists."

Evan cut in, "Especially now that your vast arsenal has been confiscated. A tenth of it has been retained and divided into discrete parcels containing arms and ammunition considered sufficient to defend households against mob violence. My men will distribute these to the households you have named. I have already sent most of arms and ammunition to our own arsenal at Chepstow Castle."

After a considerable silenced, Luke quietly announced, "Simon, I will formally report to the government that we have impounded a large quantity of arms, but that the supply of a limited number of weapons to Catholic landowners is in the interests of national security. All landlords may need to defend themselves against a popular uprising, especially those in the name of the craziest of religious ideas. The Fifth Monarchy Men are an immediate threat with Vavasor Powell raising the peoples of northern and mid-Wales against the government. Thank goodness their leader in South Wales, Walter Cradoc, has come out in support of the Protector."

Simon commented, "Thank God the swing to extremism has been stopped. I am not surprised that many former Royalist peers are now offering their services to your government."

"Simon, you would improve your personal situation if you could help my investigation into the three murders and any threats to the government."

"How can I help?"

"Barris brought the wagons to the Pass where the cargoes were manhandled across the ridge to wagons provided by Merlyn Gwent. Merlyn hid the goods in the quarry while the cellars at West Field were being prepared. My problem is that Daffyd was killed at the very time and place where your operation was taking place. If I accept that, none of Gwent's team killed Daffyd. That leaves Black Barris and his gang."

"I do not know if Barris was involved, but it is highly unlikely. He is a ruthless criminal and would do anything to protect his smuggling network. He is a very wealthy man. He makes a fortune illegally importing Spanish fabrics and olives, and French wines for the aristocracy. Your authorities along the coast protect him. He had no reason to kill Daffyd. What will you do now?"

"Tomorrow I ride to the coast with the full company of dragoons. I will talk to Black Barris."

Simon changed the subject. "I hear you had an interesting time in Ludlow and that Ned Jenkins found his missing wife. That must be a great story?"

"You would not believe it, even if I were at liberty to tell it. One day Ned may reveal all, but I have a feeling that he is lost to this community for good."

"Is it true that his wife is Lady Penelope Abbott?"

"Yes."

"The missing heiress!"

"What do you mean?"

"Adrian, Baron Abbott, was a monster of a man. He abused his wife and only child, a daughter. After some legal battle, he and his wife reconciled, but the daughter was disinherited and disappeared. Recently, Baron Abbott was brutally killed, and his wife was charged with his murder. Penelope inherits the lot, which of course goes to her husband. Ned Jenkins will be a very powerful man. He won't need the piddling Jenkins's estates in mid-Wales. He will own half of Leicestershire."

Luke's dragoons were unhappy. Over recent weeks, they had camped outside of Rhayader, in one of Cadwallader's fields, and finally had been allocated excellent accommodation in the new cottages in the West Field. They had just settled in, and now they were ordered onto the road at sunrise.

The army cohort climbed up the Llanandras valley, across the ridge to the Pass, and down the other side, heading for Aberystwyth. The rain on the coastal slopes was intense. They took shelter in a large barn, while Luke negotiated feed for his horses.

Next morning under clear skies, they reached Aberystwyth, and Luke made his way to the nearest military authorities. He was surprised that the senior officer was not a soldier. The commandant of the harbor garrison was also captain of one of the frigates that lay at anchor. The naval commandant and two other senior naval officers were in turn surprised by the arrival of such a large military detachment.

"Colonel Tremayne, is this part of the new cavalry militia we have heard so much about?" asked the commandant.

"No, we are not militia. We are an elite unit of the national army based in Chepstow but currently on a mission to deal with subversion in mid-Wales."

"What brings you to Aberystwyth?"

"Black Barris."

The naval officers looked at each other awkwardly.

Luke spoke, "Don't be embarrassed, gentlemen. I heard that the authorities here protect Black Barris. You can let him know that I am not on any mission to close him down. I am making specific inquiries into a murder near the Pass some weeks ago."

One of the officers replied, "We have nothing for which to apologize. The Lord Protector should be grateful for men such as Black Barris. We let him trade his goods across the land in return for information regarding the movement of enemy ships in the Irish Sea. Black Barris is as much an agent of Oliver Cromwell as you and I."

A second officer spoke, "I shall get a message to him to meet you in the Green Mermaid at sunset. Go alone! Your men must remain within the harbor fortress at all times."

As the time for the meeting approached, Evan suggested that he and a few of the men follow Luke to the Green Mermaid.

Luke rejected the idea. "We are in Black Barris territory. Everybody is a lookout for him. Any stranger arouses suspicion. None of us can hide the fact in this close community that we are not only strangers but also English soldiers. I don't think we are very popular."

Luke had visited hundreds of taverns and alehouses during his military career. The Green Mermaid was no worse than many, and by the smell, most of the customers were fishermen.

Luke collected a ceramic mug of sweet ale and found a vacant spot on a crowded corner bench.

He was anxious. What if Black Barris did not speak English? He should have brought Evan or Bevan Stradling with him.

Suddenly, everybody who shared his bench jumped to their feet and disappeared. Coming toward him was a well-dressed olive-skinned man dressed as a gentleman with a bright red doublet and incredibly large lace collar and cuffs. Two burly bodyguards accompanied him. They immediately sat on either side of Luke.

"Colonel Tremayne, I am Brian Barris, known to most as Black Barris. You wish to speak to me."

Luke offered to buy Barris a drink, but before the offer had been completely articulated, a maid appeared with a flagon of ale and two bowls of soup.

"Colonel, it's cold outside. Fill up with this great fish and leek broth."

Luke willingly complied. Black Barris was more civilized than Luke had expected. After a refill of the broth, he began his questioning.

"Some weeks ago, your men took several wagon loads of weapons from here to the Pass, where they were transferred to local Papists. At the time and place of the exchange, a local magistrate, Sir Daffyd Morgan, was murdered, and several men disappeared. Do you know anything about it?"

"Yes, almost everything."

Luke could hardly believe his ears.

He had expected evasive denials.

"I was not involved in that particular trip. At the time, I was leading the navy to a stranded Spanish frigate. The transport of arms in the name of Lord Kimball was undertaken by my then deputy Sean Desmond."

"Did he kill Sir Daffyd?"

"No, he, his men, and the prisoners all proclaimed his innocence of such a deed."

"What do you mean *prisoners*?"

"Sean runs the side of the business dealing in the transport of people to work on the sugar plantations of the Americas. He found five or six people near the Pass in a state of shock. They said that one of their numbers had been shot dead. Sean had many armed men with him, including half a dozen Spaniards, and could not resist the temptation. He declared the people at the Pass vagrants and therefore legally fit subjects for transportation overseas. By the time I got back here, the vagrants were aboard a Bristol merchantman on their way to Spain or the Caribbean."

"Can I speak to Sean?"

"No."

'Why not?'

"He's dead. I shot him for absconding with several silver bars that were not his."

Luke was nonplussed.

"Colonel, is there anything else I can assist you with, apart from more soup?"

"Do you know where the weapons came from?"

"A Spanish ship of the line anchored off a local cove, the exact location of which I will not reveal."

"Was there anything out of the ordinary in this transfer?"

"Yes, a man who I have seen from time to time and who liaises with the Spaniards began a heated argument with the Spanish officer in charge of the unloading. I know a little Spanish. I come from Cornwall and spent my early life running blockades to take goods from England to Spain and back."

"What was the argument about?"

"The landlubber expected a large detachment of Spanish troops to accompany the weapons inland. The officer declared that orders had been changed, and in no circumstances would Spanish troops land in Wales other than the half dozen that were to accompany the weapons. If he had any argument with that decision, he should take it up with Lord Kimball. The uprising was cancelled."

Luke finished another bowl of his soup. He was entranced with the personality and candor of Black Barris.

21

"IT IS CLEAR THAT NEITHER Gwent's men nor your own killed Sir Daffyd. Who else was near the Pass at the same time? I heard that your men saw a lone horseman in the area. Did they see anybody else?"

"I don't know, but I will ask those that were on that trip and get an answer to you through my naval friends."

"Thank you for your cooperation."

"Delighted to help, but to be honest, it is in my own interests to get you out of here as soon as possible. The more nervous of my customers won't do any business if there are government agents in the region, especially when supported by armed troops."

"Rest assured, Barris. As soon as I receive your answer, we will return up the mountain."

The men shook hands, and Luke departed.

He was immediately apprehensive as he stepped out into a narrow alley. It was dark, and the street was alive with people. Couples huddled into doorways, and Luke was forced to step over bodies propped against the buildings. They were either too drunk to move or the victims of assaults rendered immobile or dead.

Several would-be pickpockets brushed against him. A woman emerged from one doorway and lifted her dress above her thighs, inviting Luke to take her home.

Luke quickened his pace.

His right hand had intuitively moved to his sword while his left now grasped his dagger, ready for use.

He then heard just behind him the thumping of heavy boots on the cobbles. He turned just in time to counter a tall figure about to strike him with a long cudgel. The blow hit him on the right shoulder and rendered his arm numb, forcing his sword from his hand.

His attacker now had the advantage of reach and raised his cudgel once more to deliver the coup de grace.

Suddenly, the attacker fell to the ground. He had been king hit from behind and rendered unconscious. A burly figure emerged from the darkness. He smiled at Luke and handed him back his sword. As the rescuer turned to leave, he twice stomped on the face of Luke's attacker.

Luke recognized the man who had saved him. It was one of Black Barris's bodyguards.

Luke took no chances. He ran to the gates of the naval garrison.

Next morning, a young naval lieutenant woke Luke from a deep sleep. There was a man at the gate who wanted to speak to him on behalf of Black Barris. The lieutenant suggested that he take Captain Williams with him as the man was Welsh and spoke no English.

Ten minutes later, Luke and Evan met the man on the pier beside an armed ship of the line, the Dragon. The informant sat on one of the bollards while Evan asked him a stream of questions, the answers to which were summarized for Luke's benefit. "This man took the wagons up the mountain. He says that whoever told you that a single rider passed them is a liar. They were passed, but only by a group of six or seven heavily armed horsemen. If their team had not had twice as many men, and even better armed than this group, he suspected they would have been attacked. He believes that they were highwaymen ready to rob any less protected traveler."

"Did he recognize any of these highwaymen?"

Luke was delighted with his answer. The man did not know their names, but two of them were regular members of the annual droves out of Rhyd. He had often taken coastal cattle to the Pass to take advantage of William Price's immediate payment scheme.

Back in Rhyd, Luke asked the community to gather that evening at the Red Kite to receive some good news. Evan informed the gathered throng in Welsh that their missing friends and relatives had been sold into service in the Caribbean. He admitted that to some this might appear worse than death, but at least now there was a possibility that one day they might return.

After the meeting, Luke, Evan, John, Edwyn, and Huw adjourned to an upstairs room to assess the situation. Following an outburst of self-congratulation in finding Ned Jenkins's wife and the probable survival of most of Sir Daffyd's party, Luke brought the group back to reality.

"No matter how satisfying these achievements might be, we still have three murders and an attempted murder to solve and local antigovernment subversives to uncover. We can rule out the smugglers, the household at Llanandras, and the wider Papist community on the murders and the subversion."

Evan was less sure. "I agree with most of what you say, Luke, but I am not completely convinced that the Papists are in the clear. They were importing weapons, colluding with our Spanish enemies, and are now better armed than most other civilians in the area. Why is Lord Kimball, a powerful, wealthy and influential Royalist peer, helping coreligionists in this isolated godforsaken part of the country? And what about the rumors that Spanish troops were to land in Wales and assist an insurrection? Their help may have been cancelled for the moment, but there is nothing to stop it being reactivated at a moment's notice."

"Up until recently, I would have agreed with you Evan," Luke replied. "Lord Kimball organized not only the importation of arms but also probably planned an invasion by Spanish troops to effect a Papist uprising in Wales. But since Cromwell took on the mantle of Lord Protector and brought an end to the reckless decline into democracy and radicalism, conservative property owners, including the Papists, accept the current government as better than any available options. The fact that the inquirer was told that Spanish troops and been ordered not to land in Wales directly reflected Kimball's change of heart."

Edwyn was positive. "We now have a possible explanation of both Daffyd's and Lawrence's murders, highwaymen. Groups of men were seen in the vicinity of both attacks. Our immediate aim should be to discover all we can about highwaymen operating in the area."

There was a loud knock on the door; and the Baptist preacher, Kendric Lloyd, entered, carrying a large bundle of papers.

He handed the bundle to Huw who quickly perused the pamphlets and explained, "Gentlemen, the pursuit of the highwaymen may have to wait. Kendric has brought us pamphlets, clearly of Fifth Monarchy origin, calling on an immediate insurrection in the name of the Lord Jesus against the Antichrist Oliver Cromwell. The Lord's military vanguards in this enterprise are to be the Saints of northern and mid-Wales. The document is signed by Vavasor Powell."

"That treacherous varlet. Why the Protector did not arrest him years ago baffles me. He has been behind every riot and affray against the government in north Wales for the last three years. Now he tries to spread his influence into this area," commented a bitter Evan.

Huw asked, "Where did you get these pamphlets, Kendric?"

"Every cottage, farm, and inn in Radnorshire, north into Montgomery and across the mountains to coast in Cardiganshire, knows their contents. Every quarryman, farmer, shepherd, herdsmen, and laborer in our uplands is affected by them."

"But they can hardly be influential in an illiterate community," pontificated Luke.

"The men who distributed them were Fifth Monarchy preachers who explained what was in the pamphlet to their local supporters. There are sufficient literate members to pass the message on to their ignorant neighbors," replied Kendric.

Luke asked, "This propaganda names no printer. We must find and close down the printer and discover who is financing the campaign."

Evan commented, "It will not be easy. Just before I joined this unit, I was attached to various castle garrisons in north Wales and spent much time closing down subversive printing presses. There are no printers openly working for the radical sects. They have all gone underground."

"This area seems to be the border between the Cromwell-hating north led by Powell and the southern part of the same sect led by Walter Cradoc who still see the Protector as the Lord Jesus's deputy. The movement has only split in the past year. I'll visit Cradoc for advice. He may even know where the printing presses are hidden and who is financing the northern subversives," said Luke.

"You visit Cradoc, and I will interrogate the local Fifth Monarchy sympathizers," suggested Evan.

"The Jenkins would certainly be in a position to fund an antigovernment uprising," he added.

Huw disagreed, "There is a big difference between a Fifth Monarchy coup conducted by the army, led by General Harrison, which the Jenkins would probably support, and a popular uprising of the gentry-hating lower orders inspired by Powell. Conway would be their first victim."

The soldiers returned to Llanandras where Luke had joined Evan, John, and his men in the new accommodation in the West Field cottages. It would be his base until the mission was complete.

Next morning, Luke had a change of plan. He would confront the locals before he rode south. He walked to the Priory and questioned James Jenkins regarding the pamphlet. "Have you seen this treasonable document before?" he asked.

"Yes, many times. This pamphlet is a translation into Welsh of one that was circulating in London before Cromwell proclaimed himself Protector. The Saints there had already lost faith in him when he sacked the assembly of religious persons. I am surprised it has taken so long to reach here."

"So this could have been printed in London or anywhere in England. It did not need a local press?

"We are not short of printers to spread our message, despite the attempts of the authorities to close them down. Our printing presses are still operating secretly all over England and Wales."

"Would you have any idea where this was printed?" continued Luke.

"It is not the best example of the printer's art. The letters are badly formed, and much of the printing is smudged. My guess is that it has been produced in difficult physical conditions, maybe in a cave or underground cellar."

"And how do you react to the sentiments it advocates?"

"These were sentiments that caused a division between my London parish and myself. At the time I preferred the approach of Cradoc and reaffirmed my faith in the Lord Protector. The government did not believe me, and on the basis of my parish's radicalism, the church was closed, and I came home."

"And do you still hold those progovernment views?"

"I would be a fool to admit to you that I now oppose the government you are sworn to defend. Seriously, I will certainly not encourage Mr. Derfel or Gwyn Jones to overthrow Cromwell in the name of a returning savior. Even if I supported an eventual uprising of the Saints against the government, I do not believe that the time is right, and there are too many government troops in the region. We have had enough of anarchy for the time being."

Luke left muttering to himself several opprobrious reflections on James Jenkins.

Evan joined him at the rectory gate and on hearing Luke's account of his meeting commented, "James Jenkins is both a hypocrite and fence sitter."

Luke was specifically critical. "He had no hesitation in hinting that Derfel and Jones were the potential rebels. He is devious and self-serving. It is a pity he was not the brother who was murdered."

Morgan Derfel met Luke and Evan at the rectory door. He led them into his library and asked, "You come about these pamphlets?"

A large pile of printed papers lay on his desk.

Luke was alarmed. "Burn them immediately! Your possession of them could have you jailed for sedition."

Evan asked, "Why have you so many?"

"Gwyn Jones brought them to me."

"So Jones is the organizer of our local insurgents!" announced a triumphant Luke.

22

"QUITE THE CONTRARY. AN ITINERANT Saint moved through the parish overnight and left this bundle for Gwyn to distribute to his local brethren. He realized their revolutionary potential and, given your presence in the area, came to me for advice."

"And what did you advise?" asked Evan.

"I have no liking for your Protector. He had the perfect opportunity to introduce God's kingdom, and he failed. If the army took up the mantle and called for Oliver Cromwell's overthrow, I would support such a call. However, this pamphlet wants a popular uprising in which we prepare for the Lord's coming by forcibly removing existing authority, abolishing tithes and taxes, releasing debtors from prisons, paying soldiers their exorbitant back pay, and wasting money on the undeserving poor. This appeals especially to the destitute and displaced. A dictatorship of the godless poor would soon engulf any angelic rule of the Saints."

"Did you tell this to Jones?" queried Luke.

"I am not a fool. Jones is one of the poor and displaced. He would be one to gain greatly from such a successful uprising. He has even told me which part of the Morgan estate he will appropriate for his own use. No, I raised with him the division within our ranks, suggesting that any uprising would fail if we were not unified.

"The virulent anti-Cromwell campaign preached throughout northern and mid-Wales by Vavasor Powell has been opposed by our southern Saints led by Walter Cradoc who still see Cromwell as the Lord's deputy. Unfortunately, we are in no man's land, both geographically and ideologically, between the opposing camps.

"I told Gwyn to talk to fellow Saints in both camps and then make up his mind. His considered position will then become that of mid-Wales. Such is his influence.

"I also mentioned that the timing of an immediate revolt was not good. The Protector has elite troops stationed throughout Wales, including your strong presence in our own parish."

"Has Gwyn left on this journey of enlightenment?" asked a sarcastic Evan.

"No. He travels north in the morning."

"Then I must see him before he leaves."

"You don't need to go far. He is preaching in the churchyard."

"You don't let him preach from the pulpit?" asked Evan with a sneering intonation in his voice.

"I would, but it would lead to my suspension by both local gentry and the Parliament.

Gentlemen, examine your own conscience! You cannot serve two masters. You too will have to decide whether it is the Lord Jesus or the Antichrist in Whitehall."

The soldiers ignored the subversive comment and made their way from the rectory to the churchyard.

Gwyn had just finished an arousing oration to his flock that by their clothing represented both the well-to-do farmer and the dregs of society. His self-confidence-boosting sermon emphasized that they alone would rule with the Lord on His return.

Gwyn approached the soldiers. "What do the agents of illegal authority want of a humble servant of the Lord?"

Luke produced the inflammatory pamphlet, which he had taken from Derfel's desk. "Are you behind this seditious document?"

Gwyn laughed. "Come, Colonel! If I were, would I confess to the government's instrument of oppression, the army? I agree with most of the complaints in this document. The poor are oppressed, especially through tithes and rents. The failure of the authorities to take care of the deserving poor is an insult to our Lord Jesus. Debt is destroying our people. On the other hand, I am not sure whether the overthrow of the Protector at this time would advance our cause. My own feeling at the moment is that we stay our hand until the Lord himself appears, or a number of leading army officers strike the first blow by removing Oliver Cromwell."

Evan asked, "Then why are you heading north into the land of the anti-Cromwellian Vavasor Powell?"

"Brother Powell has north Wales and much of mid-Wales convinced that an immediate insurrection against the government is God's will. I want to hear his views and perhaps influence him to a more cautious position."

"Gwyn, given the existence of this pamphlet, I would be in my rights as the representative of law and order to arrest you and your followers," Luke pronounced.

"But you won't. You will be hoping that I can persuade Powell to call off his campaign, and that mid and north Wales will follow Cradoc and rally around the Protector. After all, you have already uncovered a Papist plot and fear another, led by the person who paid for those stolen arms."

"What do you know about such a person?" asked an alert Evan.

"Nothing, but I need to. If Powell is to lead us into rebellion, we need to be armed. Who will supply these arms? Who will provide the money needed to sustain a revolt? As soon as I heard that your troops had recovered the stolen arms, I wondered whether they had not been intended for my more hawkish brethren."

"Do you know to whom they were intended?" queried Luke.

"No, but there are several wealthy hypocrites who might see some advantage in supporting the Saints."

"Gwyn, I will not be arresting you or any of your followers at this time, but I need to know the whereabouts of your people. Are any of your followers going north with you?"

"Only a young convert, Brother Rhun."

Luke smiled to himself. Trooper Rhun Talbot had excelled himself. Not only had he infiltrated the local Fifth Monarchy Men; he was now the trusted lieutenant of their leader.

The two officers returned to the West Field where they discussed the situation with John Martin.

John raised doubts concerning trooper Talbot. "Gwyn Jones is a charismatic leader and a persuasive preacher. Talbot may be a genuine convert to the Fifth Monarchy and will therefore be of little use to us."

"Time will tell," mused Luke who had not previously contemplated the possibility.

"We should take out some insurance. Let's follow Jones and Talbot. They may lead us to a nest of viperous traitors," suggested John.

"Agreed, but first the highwaymen need to be investigated. Let's start at the Red Kite."

Evan let it be known to the gathered drinkers that Luke and he suspected that the murderers of their beloved Sir Daffyd might have been the highwaymen who were known to be in the area at the time. Anybody who had any information should join Luke and himself in a small room off the drinking chamber. Unlimited ale was available at no cost to the informant.

Dai Herbert was the first to come forward.

He surprised the soldiers by defending the highwaymen.

"Don't attack the highwaymen. They are the one group to help us in times of trouble. They follow the legends of the past. They rob the rich and give to the poor. No one will believe they killed Sir Daffyd. What would be their motive?"

"So these highwaymen are well known to the local community and accepted by them. Who are they and where are they based?

"Silly question, sir. They always appear hooded, and their exploits range dozens of miles along the main road from Aberystwyth to Hereford. Their leader is known as Colonel Cwm, and locals know the group as the Cwm Brotherhood. They tend to attack wealthy traders following that highway. Occasionally, they kidnap rich locals for a reasonable ransom. Their victims are usually landlords who have raised rents too high or other oppressors of the people."

The next person to volunteer information was Kendric Lloyd, the Baptist preacher. "Before you arrived, the only armed forces that could protect the little people were the highwaymen led by Colonel Cwm. Several masters who had mistreated their servants had their barns and haystacks set alight. Many tenant farmers paid the highwaymen to protect them against enclosing landlords."

"Did Sir Daffyd have any contact with the highwaymen?"

"No, as Sir Daffyd was a generous landlord and master, the highwaymen never found a reason to attack the Morgans. As magistrate, Sir Daffyd was under pressure to arrest them, but he never did."

"Maybe he finally decided to act against them, confronted them near the Pass, and was killed. Is there anyone who could lead us to the highwaymen? If a small farmer is under threat from a wealthy landlord and needs the assistance of Colonel Cwm, how does he get in touch?"

"You inform that conniving dealer in the devilish arts and pagan rites, Goodwife Hedd."

"Is that true or simply part of your Christian detestation of powerful women?" asked Evan.

"Ask her! She is drinking in the next room."

Luke did.

Bronwyn who had taken a liking to Luke greeted him with a broad smile. She soon revealed her knowledge of English that enabled Luke to ask, "Did Colonel Cwm killed Sir Daffyd?"

"Up to a year ago, no way. The brotherhood admired Sir Daffyd."

"What changed?"

"There is no such person as Colonel Cwm. The leader of the brotherhood takes that name. I know of at least two changes in leadership in the last ten years. The current leader is relatively new and seems less interested in helping the poorthan himself."

"How do you contact them?"

"Just off the highway, halfway to the Pass, is a grotto dedicated to the heroes of the Welsh past. I conduct rituals there to maintain our contact with the land and our traditions. I leave a message in one of the receptacles left on the altar. Any member of the brotherhood who is passing checks for a message, although in recent months they have been very tardy in collecting the messages and even tardier in doing anything about the matters I have raised."

Luke whispered, "Cwm and his brotherhood are our major suspects in Daffyd's murder. Will you help us?"

"How can I?"

"Leave a message suggesting that the English soldiers are asking too many dangerous questions about them and that some action needs to be taken. We will hide in the grotto and follow whoever collects the message."

"Good. In that way, I will not be compromised and can continue to use them to my advantage.

"Colonel, you must visit me in the near future. You have certainly created a stir among the womenfolk of Rhyd. I could have made a fortune in creating love potions designed to cause you to fall in love with specific women. Unfortunately, I do not engage in such a dangerous game, but sadly at least two of my would-be clients have gone up the mountain and visited my evil sister to achieve these ends. Be careful of what you eat and drink in the presence of attractive women."

Evan was amused and chided Luke, "And I would not exclude Goody Hedd from the list of Welsh lasses who cannot resist the colonel's undoubted charms."

The next drinker to volunteer information was the tiny Baden Carew. Lawrence Jenkins had forced Baden off his land.

"I am glad you are onto that evil brotherhood. They carried out Jenkins's orders. I suspect it was the brotherhood that burnt my barn, killed my cattle, and left a message that I should leave the property immediately if I valued my life."

"This negative attitude toward the needy coincides with a change of leader?" asked Evan.

"That is the rumor."

"So the brotherhood under its new leader could have turned against Sir Daffyd, as it did against you and the oppressed?" surmised Evan.

"Probably."

Before leaving the Red Kite, Evan spoke to Kendric Lloyd and after some intense discussion Kendric left with the two soldiers. The three returned to the barracks in the West Field.

23

LUKE WAS HAPPY.

Evan with Kendric as guide would follow Gwyn Jones north, John would mount a watch at the grotto to entrap the highwaymen, and Luke with trooper Bevan Stradling as his Welsh interpreter would head south to talk to Walter Cradoc.

Later, Luke asked Evan, "How did you persuade Kendric Lloyd to help us?"

"Two very effective levers. I suggested that you suspected the Fifth Monarchy Men were a danger to the state and that keeping track of Gwyn Jones would help you prove it, and a silver shilling is a very welcome gift to any poverty-stricken cottager."

Next morning, later than anticipated, Luke with Stradling and another trooper left Rhyd intending to follow the Wye south, through Builth until the river, turned east toward Hay and Hereford. At that point, they would leave the Wye, cross the mountains, and enter the Usk valley. They would follow that river to their destination near the south coast.

The journey to Builth was uneventful. Given their late departure from Llanandras, Luke decided to stay overnight in that town. As they approached the Green Swan, a large inn with stables, they saw a crowd in the street jeering as four sturdy men forced the heads of two victims into a horse trough. Luke assumed they were local malefactors receiving their just desserts.

The three soldiers consumed a large meal of lamb stew and leeks, Stradling asked the serving maid why the two persons out the front of the inn were being so harshly treated.

"They are Quakers. They came in here and demanded that we cease serving ale to the drunkards and expel all the women who were not modestly dressed. They refused to acknowledge the authority of the constable who was drinking here when he asked them to leave.

Then a couple of the lads tried to provoke them into a fight and smashed their fists into the face of the younger man."

"Did it work?" continued Stradling.

"No, the man refused to retaliate and said in the name of the Lord Jesus he was willing to accept as many blows as his misguided attacker might offer. This infuriated many of the drinkers. They punched the two Quakers continually. When my master asked them all to leave, the lads dragged the Quakers to the horse trough."

At the end of the meal, the soldiers decided to walk about the town. A hundred yards down from the inn, they saw a crowd of twenty of more people cheering and jeering. They were hurling abuse at the two Quakers who were now shackled together and forced to pull a wagon by yokes placed around their necks. More and more people jumped on the wagon, and a drover applied his whip to the backs of the victims.

Luke and his men caught up with the mob. After some distance, there was a gasp of astonishment from the crowd. The constant whipping had shredded the shirts of the Quakers, revealing that the younger victim was a woman. The women in the crowd became almost hysterical in their intensified condemnation of this disgrace to their gender.

The procession stopped at a gap in an old wall that fronted the highway. The victims, bleeding profusely from mouth, nose, ears, and back, and now semiconscious, were placed in a sitting position in the wall. Luke was astounded at what happened next. Another wagon arrived, and men began to place large stones around the victims to which a builder applied mortar.

It suddenly dawned on Luke that the Quakers were about to be incarcerated alive within the wall. They would suffer the most hideous of deaths.

Luke ordered his men to run back to the inn. There they mounted their horses, primed their muskets, and charged down the street toward the mob. Instead of dispersing, it coalesced around the fast-filling gap in the wall. The jeering had ceased, and there was an unnerving silence.

Luke shouted, "In the name of the Lord Protector, I arrest these treacherous knaves. They will meet their just desserts at the hands of lawful authority."

Luke continued diplomatically, "Thank you, good people of Builth, for apprehending these villains!"

A middle-aged man stepped forward and introduced himself as the local constable. He ordered his men to place the two victims back on the cart. He asked Luke what he wanted done with them.

Luke replied, "Take them back to the Green Swan. I will have their wounds attended to and will take them south with me in the morning."

A serving girl at the inn sent word to a local woman skilled in herbs to dress the wounds. Her salves had an almost immediate effect on the weals that had covered the backs of the victims. She also gave them a potion that sent both of them into a deep sleep.

Luke, alarmed, turned on the woman, "Have you killed them? I did not rescue them from the mob for you to poison them."

"No. They will sleep for a day. It will give them time to recover from some of their injuries. Others will take a lot longer. They cannot travel for at least three days."

Stradling muttered, "Colonel, that is too long a delay if we are to reach Cradoc when you planned."

"We cannot leave them here," Luke quietly replied.

Stradling continued, "They may not be fit to ride with us, but they could be taken in a wagon."

"Only until we leave the Wye. We could not get a wagon across the mountains into the Usk valley," replied Luke.

"What do you intend to do with them?" asked the other trooper.

"Question and then release them, when we are well away from Builth. I have orders to arrest Quaker leaders, but not the rank and file."

Luke decided against the use of a wagon and was reconciled to losing two or three days. He would put the time to good use by interviewing some of the locals regarding rumors of an insurrection.

The constable was happy to be questioned. He was a wealthy yeoman who traded in cattle and horses.

Luke asked, "Have you heard rumors of an uprising against the government?"

The constable laughed. "I wondered why three government soldiers were in town. I hear rumors every day. The Papists are said to be ready to rise with Irish and Spanish help, Republicans and Parliamentarians in the bigger cities are plotting, and sectarians are active in the isolated regions of Wales plotting with the Lord's help to overthrow the Protector."

"I am most interested in these sectarians."

"The Quakers will destroy government and society by simply not recognizing any form of authority. If people followed their example, we would have anarchy. The Fifth Monarchy Men are much more realistic and popular, but at the moment are divided. I have seen a pamphlet calling on them to rise in the name of King Jesus and overthrow the Protector, but their popular leader in these parts, Walter Cradoc, continues to support the government as the best of bad alternatives."

"Such is not the case further up the Wye. We have strong indications that the Fifth Monarchists in the north are about to rise," confided Luke.

"They will need to be strong in that area because the closer you get to the English border and English garrison towns, people are less likely to risk their lives in a futile rebellion," suggested the pragmatic constable.

Luke changed the emphasis of his questioning. "What is the religious and political situation in Builth?"

"Our clergy were appointed by the Parliament and have not been disturbed by the Protector. They reflect a diversity of views. Most are moderate Puritans."

"And their congregations?"

"That is a different picture. Two of our local gentry are Papists, and they protect a considerable number of their coreligionists. I was alarmed a week or so ago when a high-ranking Catholic peer who was a leading Royalist during the wars visited the town."

"Lord Kimball?"

The constable laughed again. "Well, I am surprised. The government is more efficient than I thought. Yes, it was Lord Kimball."

"This town like most of Wales was Royalist?" asked Luke.

"To a man. But we were and are not Papists," replied the constable.

"Would it be fair to assume that this area would not join an isolated revolt by the northern Fifth Monarchy Men, but if an extensive uprising occurred throughout the country, Builth and its surrounding countryside would join the anti-Cromwellian cause?"

The constable smiled. "That does reflect the popular view. People want rid of Oliver Cromwell but are unwilling to risk life and fortune to achieve this end. Despite the religious rhetoric, the mob will only rise if they are guaranteed a profitable victory."

Midway through the following day, the two Quakers awoke and demanded to be allowed to leave.

Luke entered their room; and the man, espying his dress, shouted, "Be gone, agent of the Antichrist. Surrender yourself to the love of Christ and cast off the trappings of satanic authority and legalized violence."

The serving maid could not restrain herself. She strode across the room and struck the recovering Quaker man in the face. "You ungrateful wretch. This is the man who saved you from a horrible death by being walled up alive and has paid for your accommodation and nursing here."

Luke grabbed her hand as she prepared to deliver another slap. She turned toward Luke with a most inviting smile and suggested he buy her a drink when they were both free.

This potentially romantic interlude was rudely shattered.

The male Quaker shouted at the servant, "Rubbish wench! This soldier is the interfering busybody who stopped me from sacrificing myself in the name of Jesus. The more of us who are persecuted in His name, the more of us will reap our reward in heaven."

The Quaker girl intervened, "Father forgets that if we had died in the wall, our mission to spread God's word would have ended. I thank you, sir. What happens now?"

"I will question you on a matter that concerns the government, and you will accompany us south. At a convenient point, I will release you both."

The older man appeared a little calmer and asked, "What is this matter on which you wish to question us?"

"The government is ever alert to its enemies. As far as you Quakers are concerned, it keeps an eye on and occasionally arrests your leaders. It allows the populace for their own mixed reasons to deal with the rank and file."

"Then why did you free us?" asked the girl.

"The punishment did not fit the crime. The government is alert to but not alarmed by the Quakers. We are more concerned with rumors of an insurrection led by the Fifth Monarchy Men."

"Those devilish hypocrites. They claim to replace the tyranny of Oliver Cromwell with the benevolent rule of Jesus. In reality, they will exchange existing authority with the tyrannical dictatorship of a few misguided Saints. At least the Protector allows us to believe and preach. The Fifth Monarchy Men would not."

"In your travels, have you heard of any such insurrection?" persisted Luke.

"Yes, we can even give you details of their plans," said the Quaker girl.

24

LUKE COULD NOT BELIEVE HIS good fortune.

The girl continued in English, "But not here," as she looked apprehensively at the serving girl who had reentered the room some minutes earlier.

Stradling immediately whispered to Luke "She has a point. The servant visibly reacted to the Quaker wench's knowledge of the rebel plans."

Luke acted quickly.

He told the servant that her services as a nurse were no longer required. He thanked her for her defense of him earlier in the day and gave her a silver sixpence. He and his men would now assume complete responsibility for the care and detention of the Quakers.

The dismissed girl smiled seductively at Luke. "Drinks later, sir?"

After she had left the room, Luke confided to his men.

"If that girl reacted to the Quaker statement and the Quaker wench refuses to tell us anything here, her information must be detrimental to important locals.

"Stradling let it be known around the inn that we intend to leave Builth the day after next and that we will take the prisoners to Chepstow for interrogation.

"We must post a guard inside and outside this room until we leave."

Bevan Stradling mischievously suggested, "Perhaps, sir, you should take up the wench's offer. Not only is she an attractive girl, but you might also discover something about the Fifth Monarchist plot."

Luke ignored the suggestion and announced that he would take the first watch outside the Quaker's room.

Next morning before dawn, the soldiers secretly left for the south. The two troopers shared their long military saddles with the diminutive Quakers. Some miles south of Builth Luke's party stopped at a long but thin expanse of woodland that bordered the highway. It temporarily sheltered them from the icy winds sweeping up the valley.

Luke told the Quakers, "As soon as you mentioned the Fifth Monarchy plot, the serving maid was alarmed and probably passed the information on to others. That is why we mounted a guard in and outside your room all night. I half expected an attempt to silence you, and I expect we will be followed. Tell us what you know! Then you are free to go."

The Quaker girl replied. "Throughout the uplands of the Wye and its many tributaries, Fifth Monarchy preachers have been stoking up resentment and offering a solution to both current problems and eternal salvation in terms of an imminent uprising. Everywhere we went preaching God's true Word, the hypocrites had already been there. They had carefully explained in the most simple of terms the diabolical views contained in some pamphlet by their leader Vavasor Powell, so that even the most simple-minded received the message. Rise when we tell you, and all your troubles will be gone."

"Do these deluded people have a time and a place to gather?"

"Yes, the plot is carefully planned and well advanced. There are several places where these self-proclaimed Saints will gather. There is a cavern on the slopes of Snowdonia. There are the properties of sympathizers on the Upper Wye, and there is the estate of the parish constable in Builth. "That is why the girl at the inn became alarmed. Leading citizens of Builth are at the center of the planned coup. The constable and the innkeeper are just two of them.

"Many of the well-to-do supporters are former army officers whom Cromwell cashiered for their support of General Harrison or their opposition to him becoming the Protector. Their numbers have increased dramatically with rumors that Cromwell now wants to become king."

"When will the insurrection start?" asked a very interested Luke.

"No one knows the date. The people have been told that the leaders await the arrival of a military commander and sufficient arms and ammunition to ensure their victory."

"Have the followers been given any idea of what they will be asked to do?"

"One group from the north will march on Chester, and those from mid-Wales will march through Builth and on to Hereford. The capture of Chester and Hereford will coincide with a rebellion in London. These three victories will lead to the overthrow of the government throughout England and Wales. Army officers loyal to the Lord Jesus and not Oliver Cromwell will establish the rule of the Saints."

"What about the south of Wales?"

"The Fifth Monarchy Men in the south have remained members of the national church and loyal to Oliver Cromwell."

Stradling interrupted, "Sir, I can hear horses coming down the road from Builth."

"Not good news," replied Luke. "Take our horses further into the woods and let us lie low and hope they sweep past."

He turned to the Quakers. "Go quickly. Escape into the hills!"

The Quaker girl gave Luke a peck on the cheek and with her surly father disappeared through the woods.

From his vantage point up the largest tree in this small forest, Luke saw a posse of six horsemen galloping down the road. He recognized two of the men—the innkeeper and the constable. He held his breath as they approached. No one stopped. They were obviously anxious to overtake the soldiers and the Quakers, and to silence all five.

Luke climbed down from the tree. He commented to his men, "The Quaker wench has given us as much information as we could obtain from Cradoc. We must return immediately to Llanandras to inform the authorities. Let's go!"

"No, Colonel, we have a serious problem," said Stradling.

"While you were up the tree, I moved to the far side of the wood from where I could see the highway wind down into the next valley.

I did not see any horsemen. They have stopped not far beyond us. They probably suspect that we moved into this forest and are simply waiting for us to reenter the highway to provide them with an easy target."

"Let's make sure!" said Luke.

He instructed one trooper to stay hidden where he was and ordered Stradling to return to the far side of the forest and continue to monitor traffic further down the highway."

Luke crossed to the opposite side of the road and clambered over a high stone fence. He moved quietly along it. He heard voices only a hundred yards from where his group had taken temporary refuge. Six mounted men were receiving their orders.

The constable was clear. Two men were to continue down the highway and circle around the back of the woods. Two others were to return past the woods down the main road and block off any escape back toward Builth. The constable and another would blast their way into the sheltered woods from the road.

Each man carefully primed his muskets.

The constable gave the signal. The first two groups moved to their allotted positions. The constable waited for some time. Luke heard the imitated sound of a kite.

At that signal, the two remaining horsemen charged down the road and entered the wayside wood firing at random. All six horsemen now moved through the trees from three directions.

Luke ran back beside the stonewall, hoping to reach the woods to render assistance to his men.

He was too late. Still hidden behind the wall, he heard the constable announce, "Not very good, gentlemen! One dead trooper, but where are the other two soldiers and the two troublesome Quakers?"

The innkeeper responded, "They could not have gone far. We kept the forest in our sights at all times. Let's thoroughly search the area. Check the trees and ditches and the surrounding fields. Don't neglect the field opposite. There are several clumps of trees, and that high stone wall could conceal the troublesome four."

The constable commented, "I shall investigate that myself. He turned his horse around and was about to clear the stone fence exactly where Luke lay concealed.

One of his men shouted, "Stop! I hear drums."

Another ran through the woods to gain vision of the road further down the valley. He quickly returned to the group. "A full company of government infantry is marching up the road. Let's disappear!"

"No worry, I am the constable. I shall even ask those troops for assistance to apprehend two dangerous religious radicals."

"Too risky, with the colonel still alive! What if he suddenly appears and reveals all? We must not be associated with this place and especially not with the murder of a soldier. Let's return as fast as we can to Builth and overtly engage in our daily routine. We have never been here. You must not jeopardize the greater cause," advised the pragmatic innkeeper.

The constable reluctantly agreed, and they disappeared in the direction of Builth at the gallop, taking with them the troopers' three horses.

Luke searched the woods and eventually located the body of his trooper. He called quietly for Stradling who finally responded. Stradling had seen that the two horsemen circling round the back of the coppice had hidden in the furrows of the ploughed field. He thought his companion would have been safe high in the branches of a tree.

As they moved onto the highway, Luke stopped on the soft verge and swore, "God's blood! Look at the horseshoe prints of our attackers. They are ridged, as were those of the men who attacked young Kynon. Perhaps the murders in Rhyd have been executed by mercenaries from Builth."

The mounted infantry officer saw the two figures on the side of the road and trotted toward them. He vaguely recognized Luke as an officer attached to the garrison at Chepstow. "I am Captain Thomas Green. What are you doing here?"

Luke told his story. Captain Green had the body of the trooper placed on one of the many wagons that accompanied his unit. Luke was pleasantly surprised to see several small ships' cannons.

"Where are you headed?" Luke asked Green.

"To Llanandras. General Berry received an order from Secretary Thurloe to send reinforcements to mid-Wales to assist Colonel Tremayne. We will be under his command."

Luke replied, "Welcome to a difficult situation. I am Colonel Tremayne."

Luke gave Captain Green a run down on the situation at Rhyd and the surrounding region of the Upper Wye.

Green responded, "Then it looks as if our arrival is timely. Do you know who just attacked you?"

Luke replied, "Yes."

"Then let's distribute justice. They murdered one of the Protector's soldiers in cold blood. You should not be involved. You can hide under the canvas of one of the wagons until we complete our task."

"Not necessary. It was one of my men they killed. I want to see them squirm." Luke gave Green the details of the constable and innkeeper.

Green's task was made easier.

As the soldiers marched into town with drums beating, the two men whom Luke had named were the two men who welcomed Green outside of the inn.

A large crowd gathered.

Green, obviously a showman, remained mounted. He brought forth a large document from his saddlebag and pretended to read an indictment regarding the murder of a trooper and the disappearance of two civilians known as Quakers who had visited the town the day before.

His men surrounded the two murderers who had tried to disappear on seeing Luke.

Green stood in his stirrups and announced, "You, Mr. Constable and Mr. Innkeeper, are hereby charged with the murder of a soldier of the Protector. You are found guilty of murder by a military tribunal of one, myself, and are sentenced to immediate execution by firing squad."

The crowd was hushed.

Green hammered home his advantage. "We do not hold the town responsible for the sins of these men. Otherwise, I would give orders that it be razed to the ground. Nor am I inclined to provide you with a spectacle of a public execution. We will take these traitors out of town and execute them privately."

While Green spoke to the crowd, his men searched the inn and its surrounds. One of the soldiers appeared leading three horses.

"There, good people of Builth, is the proof. These are three cavalry horses stolen from the soldiers during the assault perpetrated by the two miscreants that cringe before me."

Green gave orders for the two prisoners to be tied to the tail of one of the wagons and ordered his troops to march north.

Just out of town, Luke spoke earnestly to Green. "Captain, these men are important cogs in the proposed insurrection. I need to question them before they are executed."

"I agree, Colonel. I had no intention of shooting them until the last drop of information is extracted from them. I believe, Colonel, you are an expert in that field."

As the soldiers marched north, they passed a peddler heading south. Captain Green accosted the traveler. "Sir, inform those at the Green Swan that the innkeeper and the local constable have received a temporary reprieve and will remain prisoners until a final decision is made regarding their fate."

25

LUKE WAS SITTING AT AN improvised desk of a large munitions crate in one of the new cottages in the West Field, discussing with Captain Green the accommodation of the recently arrived infantry

"Your infantry is very welcome, but they will have to live in their tents erected in the West Field and in the large newly built but unused barn. The local shepherds and herdsmen have returned to the cottages from which they had been evicted. My dragoons occupy the remainder of the buildings."

Luke looked at Thomas Green intently and then smiled. "Forgive me, Tom. I did not recognize you with all that facial hair and lined face. It's good to see you again after all these years. I thought you were still in Ireland."

"I wondered how long it would take you to recall that we served together in 1648, breaking the back of Irish resistance. Yes, until very recently, I remained there. Two months ago, my regiment was transferred from Cork to the Welsh Marches. Each of the four companies was sent to a different town, one each to Chester, Ludlow, Hereford, and Chepstow. We have been at Chepstow for only a few weeks. Three days ago, I received orders from General Berry to march up the Wye until I made contact with you. I was to give you these sealed orders."

Luke carefully read the letter and asked John to join them.

He then explained to the two officers. "Gentlemen, this bears out what I discovered in Builth. These are secret orders from Mr.

Thurloe, the Protector's head of intelligence. Thurloe has evidence of a planned Fifth Monarchy uprising in London led by Thomas Venner. Thurloe's spies report that Venner expects a simultaneous rising of the Saints in northern and mid-Wales. My orders are to prevent the disparate groups of Monarchy Men coalescing into a reasonable military force. That is why Tom is here, and the rest of his regiment is strengthening the garrisons at Chester, Ludlow, and Hereford."

Tom asked Luke, "Do you expect my men to march again in the next few days?"

"I'm not sure. Thurloe suggests that I scuttle the uprising by arresting its leaders and preventing the populace from receiving arms. Some of your men can watch a local grotto from where I hope we will be led to the head of a murderous gang of highwaymen."

Tom left to supervise his men. John commented, "You know Captain Green."

Luke replied, "After our initial victories in Ireland, the then Lieutenant Green led a small company of combined infantry and artillery to conquer and slate any remaining fortified castles and houses in Irish Royalist hands. He developed the use of small mobile cannons that could be moved across the country quickly. I am surprised to find him in an infantry regiment. He was a genius in the use of artillery. But he has brought several cannons with him. That will give us an immense advantage. Tell Tom to conceal them in the cellar of the barn! We should keep the advantage of surprise."

John was about to carry out his instructions when Lady Glynnis arrived unannounced. She ignored John. "Colonel, Llanandras has another problem. I hope it is not another murder!"

"What has happened?"

"Merlyn has disappeared. This really is not good enough, Luke! Our house is under military occupation, and yet our steward is abducted or worse."

"Who has been helping Merlyn since the death of his nephew?"

"Lady Alis. Before he left, Lord Kimball suggested that Edwyn Cadwallader be invited to assist her. Sir Daffyd would have loved that. However, Merlyn was so antagonistic that we either had to offer Edwyn Merlyn's position completely or forget the idea of his help.

"Then Arwin Arnold, our old rector, returned from Chester and offered to help. He had been a lawyer and had acted as a steward before the death of several of his siblings created a vacancy for him in the church."

"Merlyn was happy with that arrangement?"

"Yes, he and Arwin were longtime friends. Merlyn was nevertheless frustrated. He had hoped to use two herdsmen to replace Tudor as his personal assistants during the winter, the religious rivals, Kendric Lloyd and Gwyn Jones. But both of them are missing. Surely not more murders?"

"Don't worry, milady. Merlyn's choice is most intriguing. Both men are traveling the uplands of the shire carrying out their conflicting religious missions. As far as I know, no misfortune has befallen them.

"I will walk you back to the house and have a word with the Reverend Arnold."

As soon as they left the cottage, Glynnis turned her charms on Luke, "I thought you were avoiding me. My proposition still stands and has now become urgent. I am leaving for Hereford in three days. I will give you the details of my accommodation before I go."

She ushered Luke into Merlyn's office. Arnold was hunched over some documents on the desk. Luke introduced himself as the officer sent by the government to investigate the death of his former patron, Sir Daffyd Morgan. "Sir, since my arrival, there has been more deaths, Tudor Gwent and Lawrence Conway, and attempted murders of Kynon Hedd and a party led by myself, which led to the death of Darryn Lewis and the serious injury to Garyth Morris. Now Merlyn has disappeared. Was he troubled?"

"Most certainly! Merlyn was not the same man I knew nine months ago before I left Llanandras. Undoubtedly, the betrayal and then death of his nephew must have hurt him deeply. I also think that the failure of his plan to heavily arm his fellow Catholics was a major disappointment. He was the most fanatical of the local Papists."

"You've known him for a long time?"

"Most of our lives. When I came here nearly forty years ago as a young rector of St. Brioche, the Gwents were the largest landholders in the district. The heir to the family fortune was Merlyn, whom his father sent to Oxford and then to the Inns of Court. He was well trained to become lord of the manor, magistrate, and member of Parliament."

"What happened?"

"The war. The Gwents supported the king."

"So did the Morgans."

"Sir Daffyd committed himself to the Royalist war effort. He was a courageous officer, but he did not risk his estates. The Gwents on the other hand donated an immense amount of gold and silver to the king and mortgaged their properties to raise even more funds for his son Charles Stuart. After the war, the little they had left was confiscated by the victorious Parliament. Debts were called in, and the Gwent land fell into the hands of the Morgans, the Jenkins, the Cadwalladers, and newcomers such as William Price.

"Merlyn's father, unable to cope with the loss of status, committed suicide.

"A sympathetic and perhaps guilt-ridden Sir Daffyd found Merlyn employment as his steward."

"No wonder Merlyn was not happy to receive me when I arrived at Llanandras. Did he see action during the wars?"

"Yes, he belonged to the most ill-disciplined but most loyal of the king's cavalry. He joined Lord Goring's notorious regiment, meting out summary punishment to the king's enemies."

"So Merlyn, the efficient steward of Llanandras, has cause to hate almost every landowner in the area, including his employers, the Morgans?"

"Yes."

"When did you see him last?"

"Two days ago."

"So why are Lady Glynnis and yourself convinced that something has happened to him?"

"Come with me!"

Arwin led Luke to a series of rooms that had been occupied by the steward. "Colonel, you will not notice the difference as you have not been in these rooms previously. Some of Merlyn's clothes have gone, and nearly all the little personal items that he treasured are missing. More serious is that his heavy cavalry saber, which he kept on the wall of his bedchamber, has disappeared."

"This implies that Merlyn has left of his own free will. He has not been killed or abducted as Lady Glynnis assumed. Should his disappearance therefore be a worry?"

"Yes, I do not think Merlyn is himself. Cranog has not been very reassuring about his future, and the suggestion that Edwyn Cadwallader be invited to Llanandras may have been the last straw. It may have turned his mind.

"He may now feel that he owes the Morgans little and is out to turn back history. From a few incoherent comments he made, I fear he has something specific and martial in mind. His old military saddle, packsack, and carbines that were kept in the stables are also missing. Merlyn is about to reignite the war."

"But on whose side?" muttered an alarmed Luke.

Luke returned to the West Field to be greeted by an embarrassed Tom Green.

"Colonel, I have blundered. I sent my men to the grotto as you ordered, and through a misunderstanding, your troopers thought they were relieved of their duty. They returned here."

"So what exactly went wrong?"

"Not long after your troopers left, a horseman arrived and collected the document you had left there to entrap the highwaymen."

"Yes?"

"He simply pocketed the document and rode off. My men followed him as far as they could on foot, but they could not keep up."

"Damn! It was my fault, Tom. We'll question the locals about whom they saw on the road near the grotto as well as any sightings of a missing steward."

Luke and John later introduced Tom to the Red Kite. As they approached the door of the inn, a horseman riding from the direction of the Priory accosted them. "Can another soldier join this group?"

"Welcome, Ned. You know Lieutenant Martin. The newcomer is Captain Tom Green, who has just marched a company of infantry up from Chepstow. This is Captain Ned Jenkins, formerly of the garrison at Hereford."

"I know of Tom. Another company of his regiment has been added to the garrison at Ludlow where I have just reenlisted."

The four soldiers found their way into a backroom of the inn. Luke asked bluntly, "Ned, why are you here? All garrisons in the Marches have been put on alert for an expected Welsh uprising.

"If you have reenlisted, you should be at your new post."

"I urgently had to consult Father and Edwyn Cadwallader.

"Legal action has been taken in the courts by unnamed creditors to reclaim the property that Lawrence gave to my wife. I was astonished to find that Father has received similar writs to reclaim property that it is claimed Lawrence mortgaged in return for capital to buy more estates. This included much of the traditional land of the Jenkins and not simply properties that Lawrence had procured in his own name.

"The major plaintiff is well known to us all, our former family friend, William Price."

"Can we help?" asked Luke.

"Yes, I need Edwyn to represent the family in court, and I hope he can unravel whether Price and others have any genuine claim to the properties listed. If Price succeeds, the Jenkins will be ruined, and Lady Penelope will have to return to being an army officer's penurious wife."

"Quite the opposite, Ned. Your wife is a wealthy heiress and only needs to prove her identity to claim her inheritance. But on a matter just to hand. Did you pass any horsemen riding from the direction of the Pass heading downriver in your ride from the Priory?"

"The only person that passed me on horseback was Huw Cadwallader. I ascertained from him that Edwyn was not at home, so I will have to wait until tomorrow to approach him with my proposition."

26

Rhyd, Two Days Earlier

EVAN AND KENDRIC HAD TO quickly change their plans. Evan had assumed that Gwyn Jones accompanied by his new acolyte Rhun Talbot would walk north in search of advice.

They rode.

The soldiers had to return quickly to the stables at Llanandras and collect horses. The road north to Rhayader was fairly busy. Evan and Kendric soon came in sight of their quarry but remained inconspicuous, obscured behind two other groups of travelers.

South of Rhayader, Gwyn turned off the highway to the east. A mile from the junction, this broad well-used track subdivided into five separate paths. The Fifth Monarchy Men took the one that continued due east. It wound through an extensive forest and emerged onto sloping fields, which rose behind a large and long farmhouse and enormous barn, supplemented by several other new outbuildings.

From their hiding place on the edge of the forest, Evan and Kendric watched their quarry enter the house. The watchers waited for over an hour Evan finally concluded, "They will spend the night there. We should push on to Rhayader and obtain a room for ourselves."

They had just reentered the main road to Rhayader when a convoy of four wagons passed them heading south.

Evan took little notice until Kendric, looking behind himself, noted, "Those wagons have turned into the track we have just left."

Evan signaled for Kendric to turn back. Both men became excited when the wagons continued on to the same farmhouse visited by Gwyn and Rhun.

The wagon master ignored the house and led his convoy directly through the open doors of the barn. Within minutes, the wagons had disappeared and the door closed.

Evan suggested, "Let's find rooms in town and return later tonight and see what those wagons contain."

They were about to leave when a small door into the barn opened, and five men emerged. One of them was known to Evan. "God's blood! I met the smaller man with the limp in Aberystwyth. He is one of Black Barris's deputies."

After finding accommodation at the White Dragon, Evan entered its small drinking chamber. He approached two local tipplers who were well into their cups. "Lads, a silver sixpence in return for information?"

"Make that a shilling," slurred the taller of the two.

Evan described the location of the farmhouse that he and Kendric had under surveillance. "Who owns that property and how does he make a living?"

"That's Olwyn Price. He is a cattle dealer and transporter of goods. In season, he acts for his brother, William Price, the dominant drover in the business. Olwyn has a gigantic barn, which stores goods brought from the coast or the north awaiting shipment south or east, or the reverse. I just saw a convoy of wagons heading his way an hour ago as I came here."

"More likely three or four hours ago," muttered Evan to himself. "Is Olwyn a troublemaker?" he probed.

The shorter drunk eyed him warily. "Why would that interest you?"

His companion intervened, "How would we know? We are a couple of laborers. We do not socialize with the likes of Olwyn Price. You would never find him in an alehouse."

"So he is one of those religious radical who tries to reform your morals and mine?" said Evan, attempting to find common cause with the two drunks.

"Know nothing about religion. That befuddled tub of lard sitting against the wall is the local sexton. He can tell you all about the hypocritical churchgoers," suggested the shorter man.

Evan paid both men a sixpence and wandered over to the obese drinker who was far more sober than the couple he had just left.

"Good man, I inquire about Olwyn Price."

"Do I look stupid? No one talks to strangers about their own people."

Luke pressed a shilling into his hand and asked, "Is Olwyn a regular churchgoer?"

"Olwyn never misses a service."

"He is a very religious man then?"

The sexton laughed. "Not likely. He carries out most of his business after church. It is the time when people pay their debts and make deals for the transportation of their goods."

"Does Olwyn support the radical sectarians that seem strong in this area?"

"Olwyn would support any group if it increased his business. He would deal with the Devil himself if the rewards were good."

"Are his deals illegal?"

The sexton laughed again. "What's illegal? Matters that in London and England may be technically against the law according to the changing governments of last ten years are simply ignored here. Trade in all sorts of items continues unabated, whether it be legal or not."

While Evan had been talking, Kendric entered the room and soon was engaged in conversation with a group at the far end of the room.

Evan thanked the sexton and moved toward Kendric who introduced him to the group as a military officer on the trail of the troublesome Fifth Monarchy Men. These drinkers were local Baptists who were delighted to have their charismatic leader, Kendric, among them. They confirmed that Olwyn was not a religious fanatic but an unscrupulous businessman whose only god was profit.

Many hours later, Evan and Kendric tied their horses to a tree in the forest adjacent to Olwyn's barn. There was no moon. It was very cold. Frozen puddles cracked with a disturbingly loud noise as Evan tried to make his way quietly to the barn.

The main door was too big to open quietly, and they tried the small door to its left. It was locked, and they heard voices within. Olwyn had placed guards in his barn overnight.

The two men circumnavigated the building. They found no means of entry. Evan admitted defeat, and they returned to the edge of the forest.

"What do we do now?" asked a shivering Kendric.

"Wait until daylight, and I will talk to the wagoner whom I met in Aberystwyth, pretending to be acting for the excise. I will demand that he open the barn and reveal the newly arrived cargo on the wagons."

True to his word, just after sunrise, Evan rode into the courtyard of the farmhouse and approached the wagoners as they were preparing their carts for the day's journey. The wagoner that Evan knew was surprised to see him.

Evan asked, "Remove the coverings of the four wagons that arrived last night! I am on the trail of illegal goods."

"No, sir, these are now the goods of Mr. Olwyn Price on whose land you stand. I would need his permission."

"Then go and get it!"

The wagoner returned sometime later with a gentleman whom Evan assumed was Price, despite his appearance. Olwyn could never be mistaken for his brother. Olwyn was twice his brother's size, a giant of a man with closely cropped black hair, whose clothing did not reflect the opulence revealed by his house and outbuildings.

Olwyn was not happy.

"What is the meaning of this intrusion? You are trespassing."

Evan did not back off. "These wagons may contain illegal goods, and I am entitled as a government official to see what is in your barn and in the newly arrived wagons. If you refuse me permission, I will return with a troop of horse and forcibly inspect your premises."

The wagoner intervened, "Mr. Price, I know this officer. He has interviewed my master, Mr. Barris, and does have a very large body of troops at his call. We have nothing to hide. Let him search!"

Olwyn nodded his head in approval and as he left said, "Captain, when you have finished here, will you do me the courtesy of visiting me at the house?"

Evan inspected the four wagons. He found nothing suspicious. There were containers of flour, biscuits, oatmeal, dried fish, peas, and beans. There was a large cask of Spanish wine. In one box, he found six muskets with powder and shot, hardly sufficient to mount a rebellion. Another wagon was filled with fine slate and wood.

An hour later, Evan was shown into the hall of the farmhouse and was quickly joined by Olwyn.

"Are all the four wagons moving on?" Evan inquired.

"Two are headed for Builth, the third with the building material is going to Llanandras in Rhyd, and the fourth remains here. After its goods are unloaded, it will take some cheese and salted meat back to the coast for the use of your navy. I trust, Captain, that your inspection found everything in order?"

"Yes, sir. I am sorry to have troubled you. We have had problems with convoys from the coast organized by Black Barris. I suspected that your latest arrivals might have been part of a similar illegal scheme."

"I deal daily with Black Barris. He is a showman who pretends he is a dangerous smuggler. He is simply a brilliant merchant who has a monopoly of goods leaving the coast. You deal with Barris or no one. Please join me for breakfast!"

Evan and Olwyn had a pleasant meal of bacon dipped in melted cheese and smoked fish that had just arrived from the coast.

Evan asked, "Another of my duties is to track a dangerous religious preacher. I had reports that he came here yesterday afternoon."

"Not to see me, Captain. I have no time for religious fanatics, unless they pay well. Unfortunately, I cannot say the same for some of my servants who are completely taken in by these cults."

He spoke to the servant serving the meal. The man left the room and returned with a tall well-built man in his forties whose face seemed frozen in a permanent scowl.

Olwyn spoke bluntly, "Jeremiah, did you organize a religious meeting yesterday? I have warned you several times. Maybe it's time to dismiss you."

"No, master, I have not organized a meeting since you forbade it."

Evan intervened, "But you did receive a leading troublemaker, Gwyn Jones of Rhyd, yesterday afternoon."

The servant was slightly shaken. "Yes, sir, but it was not for a meeting."

"What was it for then?" asked Olwyn.

"Brother Jones wanted advice."

"Did you provide it?" asked Evan.

"Yes. He wanted directions, which I gave him."

"Where is he now?" asked Olwyn.

"He and his young companion left at dawn, taking a short cut over the fields to avoid Rhayader."

"Where were they going?" continued Olwyn.

"North."

"Not to the Pass and onto the coast or east toward England?" probed Evan.

"He did not say."

Evan was direct. "Are you a follower of Vavasor Powell?"

"I am a follower of the Lord Jesus who will soon reign over us."

"How soon will that be?" Evan riposted.

The servant could not resist the provocation. "Sooner than the world expects. I trust *you* are prepared for the great day."

This religious rant was too much for Olwyn who sent his servant Jeremiah from the room.

He then turned to Evan. "I trust the army will deal with these fanatics. *Lord Jesus* is not good for business."

"And *Lord Jesus* is not good for the Protector either at this time," remarked Evan.

"I heard that dragoons and now a company of infantry have moved into Rhyd. The government must be very worried," Olwyn commented.

"Do they have cause?"

"Unlike my brother, I keep out of politics. The Protector has provided the security, which was missing for over a decade, in which trade flourishes. People may yearn for the return of the king, but those with possessions will not risk the upheaval that an attempt to restore the monarch would bring. If there is an uprising against Cromwell, it will come from his former supporters among the Puritan radicals and the army."

"The Fifth Monarchy Men?"

"Only some of them. Those in the south remain devoted to Cromwell, but those to the north are restless and simply waiting for a trigger."

"What do you mean *a trigger?*"

"These Saints are ready to rise. The preaching of Powell and his acolytes has been very effective in Radnor and Montgomery, but less so in Brecon. They simply await a military leader and, above all, weapons."

27

"THEY LACK WEAPONS?" EVAN REPEATED.

"Yes. I should know. I have received orders from dozens of individuals and groups for muskets and ammunition, which I have had trouble filling."

"Why is that?"

"I deal through Black Barris for military equipment. He imports weapons and ammunition from Ireland and Europe. The government frigates at Aberystwyth have successfully intercepted the last few shipments, and the government seems to have closed down the Irish sources. The last load, which got through, was not one I was involved in. The Morgans of Llanandras imported it direct from Spain through Barris. I gather you prevented it being stolen by an unknown party and then confiscated most of it for your own use."

"Have you heard any names mentioned as potential military leaders of a Fifth Monarchy uprising?"

"You would have a better idea than I. Cromwell expelled dozens of experienced officers from the army for holding such views, including his one-time deputy, General Thomas Harrison. Many of them seek revenge for the termination of their military careers. To lead an uprising against the man responsible for their unfair dismissal would be a great temptation. When the time comes, the Fifth Monarchy Men will not lack experienced military leaders."

"Would such an uprising obtain the help of Royalists and Catholics?"

"If I was involved, it would. The old adage that a common enemy makes you allies would be paramount in my thinking, but these religious extremists don't think logically. They hate the Protector as a betrayer of the truth, but they hate the king and the pope even more deeply. If the Papists rose in rebellion tomorrow, the Fifth Monarchy Men would assist the Protector in subduing them and then rise against him themselves the very next day."

Evan changed the subject, "What about your brother? Does he have strong views on the issues of the day?"

"Although I am his agent for the annual droves, he and I are only brothers by birth. We have nothing in common except the desire to improve our worldly goods. I do not know Billie's views on anything. He is a very private person who is obsessed with the accumulation of land. He told me five years ago that in a decade's time, Sir Daffyd and Sir Conway would be taking their hats off in his presence."

"Did he fight in the Civil War?"

"Yes. He lived in England from the time that he was a small boy. I did not see him for twenty-five years. At the outbreak of the Civil War, he joined the forces of Parliament and was a quartermaster for over a decade. When he returned to Wales as a wealthy cattle dealer and drover, he mentioned that he had only recently left the army. No doubt he began his accumulation of wealth by purloining much of the army's property over a long period of time."

"Could your brother be the military leader the Saints are awaiting?"

"Not likely. Have you met my brother? Leader of men, he is definitely not. He may advise them or more likely arm them, but Billie's aims and those of the Saints do not coincide."

It was midmorning by the time Evan returned to Kendric who had been waiting in the chilly atmosphere for several hours. Kendric was direct. "I am starving. I suppose Price gave you with breakfast?"

"Yes, and also some very useful information. Come, I will get you some food in Rhayader, where we can decide what to do next."

Evan and Kendric had almost reached the conjunction of the several tracks at the other end of the forest when two ruffians jumped from the overhanging branches and knocked both men from their horses.

More cutthroats appeared from behind the trees. Swinging their cudgels with great effect, they initially knocked both Evan and Kendric to the ground.

Evan managed to get to his feet and draw his sword.

Kendric was unarmed except for a dagger. Nevertheless, he managed to wrestle a cudgel from one of his attackers.

Back to back, the two men held off the attackers, despite receiving several blows to their bodies.

Evan knew they could not hold out much longer.

Just as all hope had gone, he heard one of the ruffians shout, and the group disappeared as suddenly as they had come.

Galloping down the road ahead of a large wagon filled with several of his men was Olwyn Price. Had he come to witness the successful assault of a nosey officer?

"Thank goodness I got here in time. Lift these men onto the wagon and take them back to the house!" ordered Olwyn.

They were carried into a large bedchamber. Hot water was brought, and the victims' cuts and bruises were cleaned and examined by a man Olwyn proclaimed as a wizard with sick animals.

Kendric received his long overdue breakfast.

A suspicious Evan commented, "You knew we were about to be attacked."

"And you are lucky that I did, or you would be dead."

"How did you know?"

"Just after you left, a servant alerted me to an unauthorized meeting of the religious fanatics in my barn led by Jeremiah. It finished about five minutes before you left.

"The effrontery of the man! After denying he had organized a meeting, he left our presence and immediately conducted a service.

"The servant also reported that those Saints not of my employ disappeared quickly into the forest.

"I guessed that they might have been ordered to deal with you. Clearly, they only expected to attack one victim. The presence of this other fellow probably saved your life. It delayed them long enough for me to come to the rescue."

"But why attack me?" muttered Evan.

"Don't be naive! Your questions concerning the Saints suggest you know of a planned uprising. If that uprising is imminent, as I suspect, it was prudent to silence you.

"Or it could simply be that you are a soldier loyal to Oliver Cromwell. You are openly proclaiming yourself as a government military officer, in the eyes of these people, an agent of Satan.

"You are lucky that I am not an enemy. I could have kidnapped both of you, and have Barris sell you into slavery in the Americas, at a good profit."

"Why didn't you?" asked a shaken Evan.

"I have nothing to hide, and given the large concentration of soldiers in Rhyd, it would have been a foolish enterprise."

Kendric interrupted as he continued to fill his mouth with bread and cheese, "Captain, we have lost our quarry. They are now several hours ahead of us."

"Your man is right. Your original quarry has long gone. You will never catch them."

"Damnation! The colonel will not be pleased," remarked Evan.

Olwyn was all smiles. "Don't despair, Captain. Following the unauthorized use of my barn, I dismissed Jeremiah. He immediately headed out across the field. You can still see him from here, climbing the upland track to the left. He will be going to the same place as your original quarry. *The Saints*, the term these Fifth Monarchy Men use of themselves, are gathering in those hills."

"Our horses ran off when we were attacked. Can I borrow two of yours?" asked Evan.

"No need. The path is not suitable to horses. It leads up and down hillsides across several valleys and eventually reaches the main road between Llanidloes and Newtown, a road that goes eventually to Ludlow or Shrewsbury."

"Both are English garrison towns protecting the Welsh Marches," exclaimed Evan.

"A gathering of Saints in our area would put them in a good position to strike against either of those English towns," observed Olwyn.

Evan and Kendric declared themselves fit and set out after Brother Jeremiah.

After several hours of walking, Evan and Kendric were frustrated. Evan was too cautious.

If Jeremiah looked back and saw two men following him, he would take diversionary action. They must not be seen. Consequently, Evan waited until the bends in the track or the occasional forested areas concealed their presence and enabled them to make upground.

After each period of delay, they could never be sure that Jeremiah was still ahead of them. If he was at all suspicious, he could easily disappear when night fell.

The following morning, as mist covered the uplands, Evan and Kendric resumed their trek. Visibility was low.

Kendric was unhappy. "This is a waste of time, Captain. Jeremiah could be anywhere. If he has seen us, he could be waiting in ambush, especially as you think he organized the previous attack. Where did our attackers go? They may have also headed in this direction."

"Some of my people live in the next valley. Let's rest there until the weather clears. They may know something of the Fifth Monarchy movements."

"A splendid idea," said a wet and frustrated Evan.

Kendric received a warm welcome from his fellow Baptists who saw few people during the winter months. They knew nothing of Fifth Monarchy plans but did remark on the increased activity on the track he had just come up.

Evan and Kendric sat in front of a warm fire, dried their clothes, and partook of a potage of oatmeal, lamb, and leek. The head of the household advised against their desire to return down the track in the near future. The bad weather had set in. They must stay until conditions improved.

Evan dozed, while Kendric led a service of prayer and Bible readings. Toward nightfall, a loud knocking on the door woke Evan and broke the calm and serenity of a period of silent prayers.

The head of the house opened the door, with Evan, sword drawn, close behind him.

The body of a wounded man slumped across the threshold. "Heaven preserve us! I know this man. It is Rhun Talbot," said Evan.

The lad had passed out. He was carried onto the only bench in the house, and the women present began to tend his wounds, which Evan assessed as two or three musket shots. The victim had lost a lot of blood, which Evan considered the major concern. While the patient remained unconscious, Evan took his dagger and, pricking around in the wounds, located most of the shot, which luckily had remained largely intact. He removed all of the offending musket balls.

It was late the next day when Rhun recovered consciousness and was fed the warming and sustaining potage by the women of the house. As he regained his senses, he recognized Evan.

"Captain Williams, what are you doing here?"

"Following you and Gwyn."

"Then it was you who had him killed. Why did you do it? Why did you follow us?"

Kendric intervened, "How did Brother Gwyn die? Who shot at you?"

"Last night, we arrived at a wooded area in which there was a large cave inhabited by five or six men who knew Gwyn. Gwyn discussed his problems with them well into the night. I fell asleep.

"Next morning, Gwyn continued his debate with the cave dwellers who confessed that they were an advance party of a major gathering of Saints from all over mid-Wales. Just before midday, a group of people arrived, who on seeing Gwyn and I went into a huddle with the cave dwellers. Half an hour later, Brother Jeremiah, whom we had met in Mr. Price's farm, arrived. He was very angry. He ordered those around him to detain Gwyn. I slid away."

"Why was Jeremiah unhappy with Gwyn? They were fellow local leaders of the Fifth Monarchy," asked Evan.

"Jeremiah accused Gwyn of being a traitor to the Lord Jesus in that he led the enemies of Christ, the military agents of Satan, first to him and the base of the Rhayader saints within Mr. Price's household and now to their secret meeting place in the hills.

"With that accusation, he plunged his dagger into Gwyn. His supporters took turns to stab him many times."

"What did you do?"

"I ran from my hiding place near the cave's entrance and hurtled down the track.

"Jeremiah ordered his men to shoot.

"I was hit several times, but I stumbled on through the mist. At one point, I lost my footing, fell off the track, and rolled down a steep embankment. This probably saved my life. In the thick fog, I could not be seen.

"Sometime later during a brief moment of clear weather, I saw the smoke of this chimney and made my way here."

28

WHEN THE WEATHER IMPROVED, KENDRIC decided to stay in the valley and minister to the even most distant of his flock.

Evan started toward Rhyd with Rhun, even though the wounded trooper had not fully recovered. They obtained horses from Olwyn Price on the agreement that the army units based at Llanandras would obtain their supplies from him.

As they trotted south, Evan suggested that Rhun should give up his covert role as a Fifth Monarchy Man and, when well, return to full-time duty as a trooper.

Rhun's reply astounded him.

"I will never again be a trooper in Satan's army. Your plotting and conniving led to the death of a good person. Gwyn will be avenged. The Lord Jesus will guide me. The Saints will not forgive the army when I explain why our leader was killed. Gwyn and I inadvertently betrayed the cause. I must seek redemption by dedicating myself completely to the service of the Lord."

"Rhun, you are wrong. It was not Gwyn and yourself that led us to the Saints. You evaded us.

"It was Jeremiah whom we followed.

"Your anger should be directed against him."

Rhun did not listen.

As soon as they crossed the Wye near the Red Kite, Rhun dismounted, handed the lead of his horse to Evan, and walked off.

Evan, somewhat disconcerted, ambled on to the barracks in the West Field.

Next morning, Luke convened a council of war with Evan, Tom Green, and John Martin.

He brought all parties up to date with each other's adventures, his near fatal encounters near Builth, Evan's experience east of Rhayader, and Merlyn Gwent's mysterious disappearance.

Luke then summarized the state of their investigation.

"Our mission here was to uncover any subversive activity, solve the murder of Sir Daffyd, and make recommendations regarding the local government of the area.

"Under the first heading, we have clear proof that the Fifth Monarchy Men are about to rise. The government is alert to the situation and has sent Tom here, and reinforced our garrisons in Chester, Ludlow, and Hereford. Our immediate aim is to stop the Saints gathering in sufficient numbers to cause trouble, cut off any possible supply of weapons and ammunition, and arrest any leaders we can isolate."

Evan commented, "We have done much of that already. We have identified leaders in Builth and Rhayader, prevented arms reaching them, and have a good relationship with the men who may be employed to deliver them their weapons, Black Barris and Olwyn Price. Serious interrogation of the Builth leaders may give us more information, and Kendric Lloyd may have more to tell us when he returns. Religious radicals inhabit the isolated cottages in the narrow valleys. If they are not Fifth Monarchy Men, they are Baptists. Kendric's Baptist flock will be our first line of information, if not defense."

After a considerable discussion as to priorities and execution, Luke finally enunciated a consensus. "Two immediate actions, interrogate the Builth leaders and arrest Jeremiah."

Luke continued, "Under our second remit, solving the murder of Sir Daffyd, we still have a long way to go. We only know who did not kill him. The men used by Gwent and Black Barris are cleared. We do have a new suspect, Colonel Cwm and his highwaymen. Unfortunately, our initial steps to entrap them failed. In addition, the attempts to murder young Kynon Hedd, the attack on us that killed Darryn Lewis, the murder of Tudor Gwent, and the killing of Lawrence Jenkins all require explanation. The horse prints of the Builth leaders at the grove where they killed our trooper, and those of men who attacked Kynon Hedd are similar, if not identical. Because of this, let's assume that all of these deaths are related. To pursue five separate murder investigations is beyond our resources and probably outside our remit."

John asked, "Do we have enough men to waste on any murder inquiries? All our resources should be devoted to containing the imminent uprising."

Luke replied firmly, "As we have isolated the main aspects of this uprising, our special unit can leave the operations required to contain the troublemakers to Tom and his infantry and the troops waiting in the garrisons at Chester, Shrewsbury, Ludlow, and Hereford. We will concentrate on the highwaymen."

John squirmed.

Luke continued, "Pertinent to our third responsibility of making recommendations regarding the governance of this difficult area, I doubt if either gentry family is in a position to do the job. Cranog wants to resign from everything, and there is no appropriate heir, while Conway will be bankrupt if Price is successful in his legal activities."

Luke issued his orders of the day. He and Evan would interrogate the Builth Saints, and Tom would take a half company of men into the hills east of Rhayader and track down Jeremiah.

Later, Luke would talk to William Price. John would increase the number of patrols of dragoons throughout the Rhyd area to isolate and deal with any overt trouble.

The innkeeper and constable from Builth provided no information. They refused to answer any questions, proclaiming that whatever they did, they acted under the command of Lord Jesus who would soon rule over all of Wales. The army of the Antichrist had no authority over them.

Luke persisted, "Did the Lord order you to kill Kynon Hedd? Did the Lord order you to kill us as we climbed toward the ridge near the Pass? Did the Lord order you to kill my trooper south of Builth?"

The Fifth Monarchy Men remained mute.

Luke's response was immediate. "You have already been found guilty of murder by Captain Green. I sentence you to death by hanging. It shall take place as soon as a scaffold is erected."

After the men were taking way to await their fate, Evan muttered, "Why bother? A pistol shot behind the ear will suffice. I am sure there are comrades of the murdered trooper, especially Stradling, who would relish the task." Luke nodded agreement.

Within ten minutes, two shots were heard, and later two bodies were tossed into a hastily dug pit and covered with lime.

Luke rode to the farm of William Price. He was out of luck. A servant informed him that Mr. Price was away on business.

Luke moved on to the neighbors, Anthony Griffith and Emlyn Vaughan.

It was a bad day for Luke's investigation. Both farmers were away.

Vaughan's valet thought they could have gone together to Builth or Rhayader.

"Could I ask you a few questions instead of your master?" asked the opportunistic Luke.

"As a servant who needs employment since I was demobilized by the Protector, I will not comment unfavorably on my master."

"You fought for Parliament?"

"For twelve years. I was at Marston Moor and Naseby and later at Worcester. For the last three years of my service, I was a sergeant in the Hereford garrison."

"You would have known Captain Jenkins then?"

"Very well. He recruited me. There are not many supporters of Parliament in this part of Wales. Most are Royalist. Later, it was he who obtained this position for me with Mr. Vaughan when the defense of Hereford was reorganized, leaving both of us without a position."

"I am helping Captain Jenkins and his family. I am not primarily prying into the life of your master, but did Mr. Price, Mr. Griffith, and Mr. Lawrence Jenkins go away together at regular intervals?"

"I have never thought about it before, but there has been a history of initiating joint activity, although no regular pattern of timing."

"What do you mean?"

"Mr. Price often summons Mr. Griffith and my master. They gather at Mr. Price's and move off together. Mr. Lawrence Jenkins may have joined them later, but I have no knowledge of that."

"Where do they go?"

"I have no idea, but the ostler tells me the master's horse is often distressed, as if it has been ridden hard and far."

"More than a business trip to Rhayader or Builth?"

"As an infantryman, I know nothing of horses, but the stable hands all agreed that the horse had been over exerted. Once I overheard the ostler ask the master what he had been up to get his horse in such a state. Mr. Vaughan initially verbally abused him for impertinence but quickly calmed down and explained he and other farmers had been chasing hares in the uplands, which probably accounted for the horse's condition."

"You say these joint adventures do not conform to a regular pattern, but are they frequent?"

"One to three times a month."

"From here you can see down the road to Mr. Price's drive. Did you see the group ride off from there this morning?"

"Yes, I did and there were four men, not the usual three."

"Maybe Mr. Price has a guest?"

"He has, a heavily armed horseman. I thought it was one of your men."

Luke replied that it was not, but he had a very good idea who it was. Merlyn Gwent.

"Have you heard whispers regarding a planned insurrection focused on Rhyd?" he asked.

"Colonel, I have seen you in the Red Kite. Every night there are new rumors of rebellions, infidelities, and murders. Everything is rumor. All I know is that you foiled a Papist plot and have tried to weaken the sectarians by killing Gwyn Jones.

"Unfortunately, this will have the opposite effect. The local radicals of all persuasions are now convinced that the government is an agent of evil and must be destroyed.

"In the absence of Kendric Lloyd, who according to that young firebrand, Rhun Talbot, you also killed, the progovernment Baptists are changing sides. An insurrection against the government could start here in Rhyd at any moment."

"All lies! A fellow Saint killed Jones because he refused to commit to the uprising. Kendric is alive and well, trying to stiffen the Baptists of Rhayader in their support for the Protector."

"Then Rhun Talbot is a dangerous man, much more extreme than Jones. Strange, when he first appeared on the scene, the gossip at the Red Kite was that he was one of your spies."

"Whatever he was, he must be detained. Thank you for your help. If an insurrection does occur, join the infantry company in the barracks at Llanandras. They are short of experienced sergeants. On the other hand, Captain Jenkins has reenlisted in the garrison at Ludlow. You may wish to return there with him."

"Thank you, Colonel. For the moment, I am happy here. My war ended a long time ago. I will sit out any local confrontation."

Luke was not unhappy. Price, Griffith, and Vaughan often rode away together and probably overexerted their horses. They either rode hard or far or both.

And Merlyn Gwent was hiding on Mr. Price's farm and had joined the others on their mysterious rides.

The immediate task was to silence Rhun Talbot permanently.

29

LUKE DROPPED INTO THE RED Kite to test whether Vaughan's servant had correctly assessed the sentiment of local sectarians.

The inn was almost empty, but the few men present oozed resentment. Luke was pleased to see the convalescing Garyth Morris.

"Good to see you out and about Garyth. What's the problem here?"

"You, Colonel! Your men have murdered both Lloyd and Jones. You have turned the whole community against you."

"We killed neither. Jones was murdered by his own people, and Lloyd is preaching in the uplands to the east of Rhayader."

"Unfortunately, the people will believe their new hero, the young Welsh firebrand Rhun Talbot, rather than an English colonel. You are a brave man coming here alone. I am in no condition to assist you if those three in the corner suddenly turn on you. Just speaking English may be enough to trigger their fury into action."

"I will leave immediately, but where is everybody? I half expected a large rebellious crowd ready to descend on the army barracks."

"Young Talbot has led them north to recover the body of Jones and to unite with others of their faith to inaugurate the government of the Lord Jesus. Many Baptists have joined them in disgust at your alleged assassination of Kendric. And I would not be surprised if a few Papists, disappointed at the cancellation of their insurrection, did not take advantage of the situation to add to the antigovernment sentiment."

Luke left rapidly by a side door.

At the barracks, he immediately convened a meeting with Evan, John, and Tom's deputy.

"What's the urgency?" asked Evan.

"Tom is in trouble. How many men did he take?"

"About twenty-five," replied the deputy.

"Not enough! Hundreds of Saints are converging on the area, all fed with lies that the army murdered both Jones and Lloyd. Jeremiah and Rhun are preparing a massacre. We must mobilize every man in the barracks. "Evan, have our entire company of dragoons ready to ride in ten minutes!

"Lieutenant, have all your remaining infantry on the road at the same time! Let's hope we can reach Tom before the fanatics overrun him."

"But, Evan, you were warned against taking horses on the track we must use to reach Tom," stated an apprehensive John.

"That is what Olwyn Price, a cautious businessman said, but my experience suggests that experienced horsemen such as our men can make it," Evan riposted.

A full company of dragoons galloped north.

Meanwhile, East of Rhayader

Tom was worried. His men had climbed to the first of the ridges that allowed travelers to see the valleys below them. Coming up the vale from the direction of Rhyd were hundreds of men. They would reach the track to the fanatics' cave well ahead of his unit. From his distance, he could not see if the mob was armed.

Suddenly, a man appeared around the bend on the track. Kendric Lloyd greeted Tom warmly, "What are you doing here, Captain?"

"I come to arrest Brother Jeremiah for murder and to confiscate any arms in the hands of the fanatics."

"You are too late. Look down the dale. The uprising of the Fifth Monarchy Men has begun. If similar numbers come from the north and east, Colonel Tremayne is in serious trouble. You must return to Rhyd and consider redeployment in the light of enhanced rebel numbers."

"We are well-armed and experienced soldiers not long removed from the bloody suppression of the Papist Irish. This is an equally poorly armed and inexperienced enemy. One of my men is worth ten of that rabble. Do you ride, Brother Kendric?"

"Yes."

"I will press on, but can you return to Olwyn Price, borrow a horse in the name of the army, and ride back to Rhyd to raise the alarm? Inform Luke of what is happening."

Kendric nodded and continued down the track.

Sometime later, Tom reached the vicinity of the cavern where Gwyn Jones had been murdered. He heard noise just ahead of him up the path. He acted quickly. He placed twelve of his men, two rows of six above the path to the left and up a steep incline and twelve in the middle of the track in three rows of four.

Another hour passed as Tom waited for the Saints to attack.

Tom was pleased with his defensive formation. Every so often, a Saint appeared around the bend, tempting the soldiers to pursue him. Tom would not break ranks.

Eventually, with much noise, the mob rounded the bend, waving staves and cudgels.

Tom shouted a warning, "Retreat or die!"

The first of the Welsh Saints, probably not understanding the warning delivered in English, ran fanatically toward the musketeers on the track.

The first row fired, and two of assailants fell. The second row fired, and another three crashed to the ground. Those remaining turned and crashed into those behind them. The musket fire from the soldiers on the upper slope wounded many more of the retreating Saints.

Two more saintly sorties occurred with the same result.

A third was mounted, but this time, the Saints were armed with muskets and moved down the track deployed in rows. They were eventually repelled, but Tom lost five of his men on the track.

Tom's confidence remained high until he was totally surprised and wrong-footed by the next move of his opponents.

Without warning, six or seven horseman crashed down the slope of the hill, overrunning the musketeers on the incline and seriously disconcerting those on the track as they were hit them from behind and from the side. At the same time, hordes of cudgel waving men came up the slopes from below.

Tom was eventually reduced to six active men who presented a forlorn square of defiance on the track, now surrounded on all sides. They waited for the volley that would end their lives.

Instead the powerful voice of a preacher rang out, applauding the Lord Jesus for providing this the first of many victories against the army of the Antichrist. These men should not be killed yet, but paraded before the entire world as a symbol of the Lord's invincibility. He emerged from behind his followers.

Tom gave his last order. "Direct all your fire at that madman!"

They did.

Brother Jeremiah fell to the ground, fatally wounded.

Stepping over the fallen body, Rhun Talbot shouted, "Brethren, look what the army of the Antichrist has done to our leader. These men do not deserve to live. Kill them now!"

Before the Saints could act, thundering up the track and up the slopes from below, rodethe dragoons. They immediately dismounted and with sustained musket fire moved progressively up the track.

The death toll was enormous, as the Saints appeared to have few weapons.

The sight of Kendric Lloyd who rode with the cavalry led many of the rebels to surrender. They had joined the crusade to avenge the death of a man who was not only alive but also riding with the government troops.

Luke pushed on and soon reached the cavern where Gwyn had been murdered and where he hoped to find a cache of arms.

Luke's dragoons moved up and down the track and followed some of the rebels into the two nearest valleys.

Eventually, the infantry arrived, and Tom was delighted to see the rest of his company. He had lost half of his initial group killed and another quarter seriously injured.

The rebels, due almost entirely to Luke's dragoons, lost thirty dead and another ten seriously wounded. Luke ordered the immediate execution of the latter.

The officers assessed the situation. Luke felt that two issues remained unresolved.

"Rhun is still free. He is a greater danger than Gwyn or Jeremiah. "And who were the horsemen that turned the tide of battle? If the insurgents have cavalry, our task is much more difficult, and it also suggests that the rebels have the support of people with money. Tom, did you recognize any of them?"

"No, but I heard one of rebels cry out when they appeared *God be praised! It is Cwm.*"

"I thought as much," exclaimed Luke smugly.

"Have we any prisoners?" asked Tom.

"No, I allowed the rank and file to escape. Many were Baptists who were tricked into this fatal mission."

"I have prisoners. Two fanatics were determined to die for the cause and failed to retreat. My men captured them before they could do any harm," replied Tom's deputy.

"Unfortunately, from an interrogators point of view, the two men were determined to exhibit their total commitment to the cause and their absolute faith in the ultimate victory of the Saints. They saw their task was to goad the soldiers. Their expected death as a consequence of the army's reaction would make them martyrs.

"Their tirade was in Welsh, which none of the officers other than Evan could understand. He interpreted for his colleagues. "They tell us that this is a hollow victory, and there are thousands of them ready to rise all over England and Wales. They will be well armed and supported by leading officers in the army itself. And that of today, the Lord Jesus has a leader to stand beside the Archangel Michael in the implementation of the Fifth Monarchy, the direct rule of Christ on earth, Brother Rhun."

"Do they know where he is?" asked Luke.

"Given his godlike status, they would rather die than reveal his location."

As they spoke, another prisoner was brought to the officers. He had been knocked out but was not badly wounded. His face lit up when he saw Kendric. The two men embraced each other. Kendric explained that this was one of his deputies from Rhyd who had been intensely loyal to the Protector until Rhun Talbot misled him into believing that the army had murdered his leader.

Luke asked, "Kendric, question him about Cwm's role in this little battle."

Kendric obliged, "Where did Colonel Cwm come from? Was he expected by the Fifth Monarchy Men?"

"When Cwm and his horsemen seemed to have brought us victory, I asked one of the Saints whether such help was expected. He said that Colonel Cwm in the last few months had expressed support for the movement. He had promised to arm them, and although the army had thwarted the plan, he still managed to provide a few weapons. Colonel Cwm could not personally provide military leadership for the group, but he would soon present them with the experienced military figure they needed," explained Kendric's deputy.

Evan asked if there was anything else the prisoner thought the soldiers should know.

The man replied. "Rhun does not trust Cwm. Rhun claims that the Saints must win without such tainted assistance. They did not need the help of evil men."

30

THE DEFEAT OF THE SMALL group of Saints by Luke's men east of Rhayader reverberated across the hills and valleys of mid-Wales. If Luke had thought that his actions would stifle the incipient uprising, he was mistaken. A cry had gone out that a battle had been lost, but a war was about to be won.

Luke had two immediate tasks, to capture Rhun Talbot and to anticipate the next move of his followers. Kendric Lloyd would help with the latter. His Baptist flock, after being completely misled by Talbot, was anxious to avenge the death of so many of their brethren.

Luke and the Baptists had an advantage. It was difficult for religious minorities to get their message across vast areas of land and at the same time maintain secrecy. As many herdsmen, shepherds, and small land users were not sure whom and what they believed and often changed allegiances, Fifth Monarchy secrets could not be contained.

Kendric remained in the region of the skirmish to help many of his flock that had suffered losses because of the lies of Rhun and Jeremiah. He could monitor the Fifth Monarchy activity and get information of importance back to Luke.

Four days later, the officers were eating together back at their barracks at Llanandras, when an orderly announced that there was an infantry captain wishing to speak to them.

The man entered the room. Tom jumped to his feet and hugged the newcomer. "Stephen, what are you doing here?"

"Come to help you out, you old rogue."

The new arrival turned to Luke.

"Sir, I am Captain Stephen Strutt of the same Irish regiment as Tom, placing myself, as ordered, under your command. Tom's men went to Chepstow, mine initially to Ludlow. My full company is about an hour behind me."

A surprised Luke asked, "What exact orders did you receive?"

"Following the skirmish east of Rhayader, I was to march immediately to Rhyd and reinforce the troops already there."

"London must anticipate a serious revolt in this area. They have acted very quickly," mused Evan.

Luke was uneasy. "Who issued your orders?"

"The acting governor of Ludlow Castle, Major Ned Jenkins. He had just taken up the position. He said he was here in Rhyd only days ago and understood the seriousness of the situation."

"That is true, Stephen. Only a few days ago, he was sitting where you are now. He didn't mention any possibility of his new position at that time," said Tom.

"He would not have known. While he was here, the governor was taken ill, and the Major General Berry's adjutant went through the establishment of the garrison and discovered that the newly reenlisted Captain Jenkins, now promoted to major, was the most experienced," answered Strutt.

"Did Jenkins issue the order to march here on his own authority, or did it come down from on high?" asked the concerned Luke.

"It came from Jenkins, but he did spend a lot of time with the adjutant before I received the order."

Luke was troubled. "We face a major crisis. I am gravely worried on two fronts.

"First, either the high command or Ned Jenkins knows more about an intended insurrection in this area than we do. A company of dragoons and three quarters of an infantry company is more than we need here given our assessment of the situation.

"Second, the decision reflects an abysmal failure of strategy. The Protector would be better served if Strutt's company had remained at Ludlow. It is a major risk to denude Ludlow Castle of loyal troops. Who is my nearest senior officer?"

"The regional major general, James Berry. He has responsibility for all of Wales and the border counties of Shropshire, Worcester, and Hereford," advised Evan.

"Captain Strutt, did Major Jenkins raise with you the issue of weakening the Ludlow garrison by your removal?" asked an increasingly anxious Luke.

"No, but I did. The major said that he had received orders and the money to reenlist over a hundred former veterans to fill the gap we would leave," answered Strutt.

"Tom, have your men ready to march at a moment's notice. Stephen, your company will not be stopping here. I am going to Hereford to speak with General Berry. There is something seriously amiss."

Evan was hesitant. "Luke, this visit to Berry might be tricky."

"What do you mean?"

"Of the major generals, Berry has the most extreme religious views. In the past, he has been very close to Vavasor Powell and is known to encourage Quakers within the army. When he was called south from Scotland to suppress the Royalist's revolt in the West Country, General Monk, his commander in Scotland, breathed a sigh of relief."

"I know James Berry. We fought together in Scotland before Monk was transferred to command our army in that sad country. Are you suggesting that Berry himself may be fostering the rebellion?"

"We all know that this Fifth Monarchy insurrection will not succeed without the support of the senior military. Many other officers with Berry's views have been cashiered. Maybe he is a sleeping agent waiting to lead a major revolt out of Wales. He may have ordered Stephen's men out of Ludlow to reinforce it with potential insurgents."

"Berry outranks me, but I still carry my special authorization in the Protector's name. It would probably carry no weight with a man about to throw off the Protector's authority. Even if I took our whole company of dragoons and the two companies of infantry with me, we would not be able to coerce the garrison at Hereford without a major confrontation."

"Can you get help from more conservative major generals?" asked Tom.

"Tobias Bridge is a possibility from Cheshire. Edward Whalley has responsibility for Warwickshire but is based on the east coast in Lincoln. The only practical source of reinforcements from a major general absolutely loyal to the Protector is from Desborough, who is in Bristol.

"But, gentlemen, we must not risk a major confrontation between units of the army. United we stand, divided we fall. I will confront James Berry man to man. If I am not back within ten days, inform John Thurloe of developments."

"What do the rest of us do while we wait?"

"Evan, keep the dragoons on patrol and respond to any information from Kendric. Tom and Stephen, in two days, I want you to march both companies of infantry to Hay-on-Wye where you will be in position to move to the defense of Hereford or Ludlow as the need arises. Wait at Hay for further orders from myself or General Berry!"

Hereford

Luke was well received by the senior officers at Hereford. James Berry was away for a day or two in Worcester; but Berry's deputy, the garrison commandant, had received orders to consider seriously any intelligence from Luke Tremayne and his special unit. Oliver Cromwell himself had signed the orders.

Luke smiled inwardly. Despite the civilian veneer of intelligence work under Thurloe, the Protector still relied on the military, on Luke Tremayne.

During a sumptuous meal with a dozen officers, Luke asked, "Are you aware of an imminent uprising by religious radicals in mid-Wales, whose immediate objective might be the capture of this town?"

The colonel commandant who had been presiding over the dinner responded, "General Berry has received warnings from London and the details of your brush with the rebels near Rhayader. The general consensus was that if you, with one company of dragoons and one of infantry, had no trouble in routing these fanatics, this county and city with its large number of troops and within easy reach of reinforcements should have no problems. Frankly, we were hoping that your actions would prevent any further trouble."

"I would agree if it is a rising of the poorly armed inferior classes. My information is that this insurrection will be led by experienced military men in key positions, and it will rely on officers across the country joining the revolt."

"Is that why you are here? Do you have the names of potential traitors?" asked the commandant. "Are there any in this room?"

"It is more serious than that. I know your commanding officer and major general for the area. James Berry is a radical. He supported those troublesome agitators a decade ago. He is friend of the man whose inflammatory writing is behind the imminent insurrection, Vavasor Powell. There are many officers who hold views similar to Berry whom the Protector has already axed. Will he take strong enough action against people who have similar views to his own?"

"Yes, he will," boomed a voice from the door of the chamber. In strode James Berry. The officers rose as Berry took his place at the head of the table. "Continue your discourse, Luke. I have orders to listen to your advice."

"It's great to see you, James, but as you overheard, we have a potential uprising not only from civilian Saints but also from well-placed men in the military, men whom the Protector failed to cashier. How can I be sure that you and all of your officers here with radical religious views will stand against your friends?"

"Luke, despite my sympathies with the radicals among whom I do have many friends, like you, I have had one overriding loyalty since the early forties, loyalty to Oliver Cromwell. Many people who have similar religious views to myself remain loyal to Cromwell. As you know, even the extremist Fifth Monarchy people are split. My friend Vavasor Powell has not been able to convince the Saints in South

Wales and throughout England other than in parts of London that the Protector has betrayed God and should be overthrown. If your men arrested Powell, I would endorse it. Let's discuss this sensitive matter in my room after supper."

Later in his chamber, Berry offered Luke some Irish whiskey; and the two men sat in front of a smoking fire, which his orderlies, not expecting his return, were struggling to light.

Berry was direct. "Why have you left your post in mid-Wales in the current situation to come here?"

"I fear rebellion at Ludlow. What can you tell me about Major Ned Jenkins's appointment as governor of Ludlow castle."

"Nothing. I will send for the garrison commandant."

The garrison commander entered the room, and Luke asked him what he knew about Ned Jenkins, past and present.

The officer smiled. "Well, the highlight of his service was that he misplaced his wife. She just disappeared."

"I am aware of that. Did he give any reason why he retired when he did?"

"Ned Jenkins did not retire. I cashiered him. I may have been unfair, but his brother James, a cleric, was such an extreme sectarian that I could not risk Ned's continued presence in this sensitive garrison. I reported him to London as a potential subversive."

"If he is such a subversive, why has he been allowed to reenlist, promoted to major, and appointed as acting governor of the garrison at Ludlow? Ludlow could be critical in the imminent uprising."

"I know nothing of this," replied the Hereford commander.

Luke turned to James Berry. "Your adjutant ordered the appointment and gave Jenkins special instructions that may endanger us all."

"Not true, Luke. My adjutant has either been with me in Worcester or here in the next room for weeks. All officers of this garrison and that at Worcester have been confined to barracks because of the imminent threat. The man who appointed Jenkins is an imposter."

Luke sighed. "Then it's even worse than I first thought. Jenkins ordered the company of Irish infantry that had been sent to reinforce the garrison there to march off into mid-Wales."

31

"To what end?" asked Berry.

"My guess is that he is ridding Ludlow of troops sympathetic to the Protector and replacing them with resentful veterans, cashiered by Cromwell. These new troops at Ludlow will strengthen the backbone of the Fifth Monarchy insurgents, who without them would cause us little trouble."

"Where will the mob meet the rebel troops?"

"The Welsh rebels cannot come down the Wye. Two companies of my infantry block their path at Hay. The coastal rebels will come across the Pass near Llangurig and be joined by their Brecon and Radnor allies who will then move north. They would follow the valley of the Severn through Newtown and then cut across to the Teme through Knighton onto Ludlow. Others may come from Llandrindod across country, north of the Radnor Forest, and join the main group at Knighton."

Berry summoned his senior officers to join Luke and himself and asked an orderly to bring a map. He informed them of what he and Luke had just discussed and outlined his response to the crisis.

"Gentlemen, the two companies of infantry that Luke has ordered to Hay will stay there until we have a clear idea of the rebel movements. If they march south, one of those companies will move across country and come in behind the rebels, blocking any retreat to Ludlow. I will immediately ask General Desborough to send two regiments of infantry and one of cavalry to assist us. The newly created cavalry militia will also be mobilized.

"Luke, return to Rhyd and have your dragoons harass the Welsh insurgents as they move toward Ludlow. You may be able to dissuade many of them from proceeding."

An officer asked, "What if they ignore Hereford? Worcester is a much more worthwhile target and is not as well defended as here. It would be a much easier route from Ludlow down the Teme and then along the Severn."

A number of those present mumbled agreement.

Berry responded, "A good point. Desborough can send his troops directly to Worcester. From there they can reach here, if the need arises."

Luke left the meeting satisfied. Berry had the situation in hand.

He was well aware that Lady Glynnis Morgan was in town, and she had given him her address.

He ambled slowly along the streets of Hereford toward a large manor house on the edge of town.

He was in two minds.

He liked Glynnis as a person and even more so as a seductive woman who aroused more than his interest.

On the other hand, he was uneasy about playing a major role in any attempt to illegally influence the Morgan succession. He must talk to Glynnis and reiterate his position.

Admitted to the house by a liveried servant, he waited quietly in the hall. His mind returned to the military matters that were of immediate concern. His passion for the likeable gentlewoman subsided as he thought of the conflict ahead.

That was just as well. Glynnis eventually entered the room with Rhoslyn.

Glynnis was all smiles. "This is a very pleasant surprise, Luke."

Luke, for the benefit of Rhoslyn, explained that he had dropped in to see if Glynnis needed an escort home.

Glynnis replied, "That is very kind of you, Luke. Unbeknown to me, Rhoslyn is taking up residence here, awaiting the visit of a special friend."

"Luke knows of my association with Edwyn," confessed a blushing Rhoslyn.

Luke teased, "Lady Glynnis, are you curtailing the time the young lovers have alone together?"

"Not at all. Rhoslyn is just about to go riding with Edwyn. Will you stay for refreshments, even though I will be the only person left in the house?" said Glynnis with a knowing smile that she concealed from Rhoslyn.

Luke returned to Rhyd in good spirits.

No one could anticipate in advance the behavior of senior officers, but Luke was intuitively convinced that they would remain loyal to the Protector.

Evan and John were happy to see him. The dragoon patrols had uncovered movements of small groups of men along most of the roads, but they did not reveal their destination nor were they excessively armed.

Kendric sent one urgent message, and it was shattering. The rebel Saints now had a military leader, and arms and ammunition were headed their way.

As the officers discussed this development, a soldier rushed into the room. "Colonel, four wagons have arrived in our barracks. The lead wagoner gave me this letter addressed to Sir Evan Williams."

"What is in the wagons, soldier?"

"Hundreds of muskets, sir."

The officers ran from the room and were soon rolling back the covers of the wagons. They were indeed full of weapons and ammunition.

Evan read the letter aloud, "*I was paid in advance to ship these weapons to Ludlow Castle. Black Barris had unexpectedly received a large shipment from Spain. He had so many orders that he has used other carriers than myself. I believe just as many weapons as I have redirected to you will be heading east at this moment. You may be able to stop them before they reach their destination. One of my wagoners learnt from Barris's man that their overnight stop was Newtown. I trust the army will remember its loyal servant, Olwyn Price."*

Luke did not hesitate. "We must hunt down these wagons."

Just then, Kendric ran across the courtyard and addressed Evan in Welsh. Luke picked up the word Leominster. Evan translated immediately. "Kendric tells me that the instruction has gone out across the hills and valleys of Wales. The faithful are to move immediately to Leominster where they will be armed and joined by their military allies."

"Were the faithful told of their ultimate destination?" Evan asked Kendric.

Kendric shook his head in the negative.

Luke suddenly exploded. "This is very significant. If they gather at Leominster and are joined by troops from Ludlow, they have an open route down the Teme and the Severn to Worcester. Hereford is not the target.

"I will send a courier to Tom and Stephen. Tom's company should move immediately across country to be within striking distance of Leominster, with the intention of following the rebels to Worcester and blocking their retreat. Stephen is to proceed to Hereford and place himself under the command of the garrison commander. The courier will then report all this to General Berry."

In the attempt to find the ammunition wagons, Luke divided his company. He would lead half of it along the main east-west route from the Pass into England, while Evan with a quarter of the men scouted the many valleys east of Rhayader, known haunts of the Saints. John remained at the barracks, maintaining daily patrols around Rhyd.

Evan was the first to encounter evidence of rebel activity. He trotted past the cavern where Gwyn had been murdered and in the vicinity of the battle with the local insurgents. The cavern had been used since the skirmish. There were several smashed wooden crates that were identical with those that Olwyn had redirected to Rhyd. Some locals would now be well armed as they set out for Leominster.

Evan was confused and worried when he saw on one of the broken fragments of wood a hastily painted *PRI*. He searched frantically for the missing pieces and finally found *CE*. Evan was furious. Olwyn was a double agent.

He had sent some weapons to the army to win their support, but he had still delivered others to the rebels. Could his comments about the wagons heading to Newtown be taken seriously? It could have been a clever move to get the dragoons out of the way.

Foolishly, Luke had taken half the unit with him—fifty men on a wild goose chase! Evan's own twenty-five troopers could be confronted by hundreds of armed rebels. He would send one of his men north to inform Luke of the possible trickery. He would stay put while another rider went back to Rhyd, with orders for John Martin's men to join him at the cavern.

One of his men who seemed to enjoy the exercise was piecing together the rest of box, interested to see what the carriers had painted on it. It confirmed Evan's worst fears. Below the name were the letters *RH*, Price Rhayader.

Evan walked away from the jigsaw fanatic and was instructing two of his troopers regarding the messages they were to give to Luke and John when the diligent trooper ran across to him. "Captain, I have completed one side of the box. It does not read *Price Rhayader*. It reads *Price Rhyd*."

Evan was even more confused. He muttered aloud, "I can understand a property owner such as William Price with an extensive carrying trade importing arms, although strictly illegal. These are troubled times. But why would he then distribute them to the dangerous dispossessed?"

One of his troopers answered, "Perhaps, sir, Mr. William Price was not involved. These may have been stolen from a wagon heading in his direction. After all, the theft of weapons is common practice in this part of the world."

"I have another worry. How did they get the crates up to here? The track is not wide enough for wagons, and they are too heavy and bulky to be carried on horseback," asked Evan.

Another trooper offered an explanation, "Sir, I noticed from time to time on the softer parts of the track there are light wheel tracks. One or two men hauled the crates up here manually, perhaps only one to a small two-wheeled cart. There are no recent hoof prints except for our own animals."

Before Evan could comprehend this avalanche of advice from his men, a trooper he had sent ahead of the party as a scout reported back. "Captain, although I did not notice a lot of horse activity leading up to the cavern, further up the track, it is a very different matter. I think six to eight horsemen rode across country and joined up with the rebel sectarians just north of here."

Evan ordered his men to remount. He would not deplete his numbers by sending couriers to Luke or John. When the unit reached the ridge of the mountain, they had a clear view of the valley below and the next range of uplands. Evan could clearly see fifty to sixty men climbing the opposite slope with several horsemen accompanying them.

Evan ordered his men to quicken their pace. "They will have seen us. We must catch up to them before they join up with other groups."

For the rest of the day, Evan's dragoons slowly gained on the rebels who were spared confrontation by the descent of night. There was no moonlight, and any attempt to move further up the track could be disastrous. They had neither provisions nor tents. They would go hungry and sleep on their blankets. They bunched together in a cozy group under weather-protecting trees. Their horses were tied to branches further down the slope. Two unfortunate dragoons mounted guard on the animals. Another was posted several yards up the track to warn of anyone coming down the mountain.

The sole advance guard was tired. And he was wet. He sought the shelter of the forest. Given the conditions, there was no way he could prime his musket. His sword was his only defense and his cornet the instrument to deliver a warning. He had orders to blast a note on it at any hint of trouble.

He fell asleep.

He was awakened by a series of small but accurate blasts. Someone was lobbing grenades at the sleeping dragoons. He ran back full of guilt, hoping that not many of his comrades had been killed.

He was appalled. There was smoldering wood and blankets. Small shrubs had been shredded. He tripped over a small crater created by one of the grenades. Then it struck him. There were no bodies. Had the fanatical enemies taken the bodies away to desecrate them? Surely someone would have survived.

He sat on a log, totally confused and disoriented.

Then he froze. A hand grabbed his shoulder from behind, and a dagger was placed across his throat.

"I should slice it. Did you desert your post? There was no cornet blast."

It was Evan.

The dragoon whispered, "Did many die?"

"No, but no thanks to you. All of us live."

Evan explained, "Sometime during the night, one of your comrades guarding the horses moved further into the forest to urinate. He saw in the distance a small light. He investigated and discovered a group of six men with grenades. The light had been a trial attempt to light the wick. He assessed the situation. He ran back here, aroused his comrades, and we all hid away from the camp. We then circled around behind the amateur grenadiers, and after they had dispatched their missiles, we cut their throats, although the man on horseback escaped."

"I missed all the excitement," announced the relieved advance guard.

His comrades booed.

32

LUKE HAD LED HIS DRAGOONS much further north and turned northeast at Llangurig to follow the main east-west road toward Ludlow. The large number of small groups all heading east immediately alerted him. It was not market day, nor were any fairs scheduled in any of the towns along the way.

One of the travelers was asked his destination. The answer sent a further shiver of apprehension through the soldiers. "We are on a mission for God. He will lead us wherever He wills."

Luke was in a dilemma. If he rounded up the hundreds of travelers dispersed over several miles and forced them to retreat into the west and ensured that they did not double back, he would seriously delay his pursuit of the wagons loaded with arms.

Stradling pointed out that the travelers were unarmed apart from staves and daggers. He had only seen one musket. He suggested, "There are several north-south crossroads ahead. We should overtake the wagons well before these roads. We can seize the arms and then come back and divert the travelers away from Leominster and Ludlow."

An hour later, Luke smiled. Ahead of him, making heavy weather of a slight slope, were four wagons. Within minutes, the wagons were completely surrounded. Luke inspected the cargo. The wagons were loaded with weapons and ammunition, including grenades and mortars. Hastily painted on the side of each case was *Ludlow Castle*.

Luke broke open several of the containers.

He was appalled.

He turned to Stradling and denounced Black Barris. "He is a murdering monster. Look at this shot! It is the wrong size. Use these balls in those muskets, and the gun will explode in your face."

He turned toward the head wagoner. "Your master is a scoundrel. Where did he obtain this cargo?"

"From many sources. A Spanish frigate provided the muskets mainly stolen from your army in Ireland, and a French privateer had captured loads of ammunition from an Ottoman galley and was selling it very cheaply."

"We know why. The muskets and shot are incompatible."

A small detachment of his men immediately escorted the wagons north toward the nearest government arsenal at Chester, where the faulty ammunition would be melted down.

The rest of Luke's horse now proceeded to the nearest crossroad. They camped in the middle of the road and began turning back all travelers, declaring that the road east to Ludlow was closed. The disappointed travelers were then escorted many miles out of their way. Luke felt that even the slightest delay in their trek east would aid the government's situation.

Luke's men had been in position for a day and a half when a troop of cavalry thundered up the road from Ludlow. Luke had his dragoons dismounted and formed into a defensive square. He rode out to meet the leader of the advancing troops.

It was Ned Jenkins.

He greeted Luke effusively, "What are you doing here?"

Luke was cautious. He would not reveal what he knew or what he suspected. "I am ordered by General Berry to block the passage out of Wales of any possible insurgents and to seize all arms and ammunition. I have already confiscated four wagons of weapons and I am now diverting potential rebels away from Ludlow and Leominster."

Ned retained his jovial friendly demeanor. "Luke, the weapons you have confiscated were meant for my garrison at Ludlow. Could you return them?"

"You were tricked, Ned. The muskets were all right, but the ammunition was useless."

Luke explained the problem and then probed, "Why did you buy your arms from Barris, instead of the army's regular supplier?"

"I heard that Ludlow could be the focus of rebel attention, and the normal supplier was unable to fill the order for months. I had to protect my town. What does Berry plan to do to curtail the rumored insurrection?"

Luke lied. "No idea, except that reinforcements are heading in this direction from all over England. If the rebellion starts today, the rebels may have some initial success, but eventually, the weight of numbers will ensure victory for the government."

"Not if those very reinforcements join the rebels," commented Ned ominously, as he bid his farewell.

Luke was troubled. Ned's parting remark worried him. Could any of the local garrisons be trusted to support the Protector? The success of the Fifth Monarchy insurgency depended on the desertion of government troops. The most loyal troops to the Protector within marching distance of Ludlow were in the West County under General Desborough. Could they reach the trouble spots before the rebels achieved victory?

With nightfall, Luke's men made camp in a small wood a few yards east of the crossroads. They lay close together for warmth without benefit of tent or blanket. Food, which each dragoon carried in his knapsack, consisted of dry bread and hard cheese. They drank from a crystal clear stream that ran through the wood.

Luke had just dozed off when he was awakened by one of the sentries who was accompanied by a buxom wench whose bodice had been ripped and face badly bruised.

She explained, "Kind sir, my daughters and I were set upon by a band of brigands just before dusk. They have assaulted us. I managed to escape. Please rescue my daughters."

"How long have you been walking since you escaped?"

"Only a few minutes. The rogues are camped like you just off the highway, about half a mile nearer Ludlow."

"How did you manage to escape?"

"They have been drinking heavily, having stolen a wagon load of beer. The monster that was tormenting me finally fell asleep. His companions were too busy molesting my daughters to notice my escape. By now they will all be asleep. It should be easy for you to capture them."

"How many are there?"

"Five."

Luke woke ten of his dragoons and led by the distraught woman walked silently up the highway.

The outline of the camp was visible, as the rogues had not extinguished their campfire. Luke could clearly make out the bodies of five men and three women, all apparently fast asleep.

Luke fired his carbine to awaken the sleeping group.

The men rose slowly to their feet. Luke was astonished. One of them was Ned Jenkins.

Luke was at his moralizing best. "Have you no shame? How can you bring such dishonor to your family?"

Luke was suddenly apprehensive. The women, instead of thanking Luke or running off, clung to the gang members in the most amorous manner.

He nevertheless continued, "I have no option but to disarm you and take you to the nearest town for incarceration."

The men and the women laughed.

Ned responded, "On what grounds? A few of my men decided not to return to Ludlow with the main troop. Instead, they enjoy the company of their womenfolk before they go into battle."

Luke was uneasy. Ned put him out of his misery. "Enough chatter. Luke, if you look around, you will see that this coppice is surrounded by a hundred of my men. I am surprised you fell so easily into my trap. You are my prisoner."

Luke assessed the situation. He was hopelessly outnumbered. He asked, "What next?"

"You and I will with ride immediately to Ludlow Castle. After we are well gone, your men will be released. Any who wish to join me at Ludlow Castle will be welcomed."

"What is all this about, Ned?"

"Simple, in an insurrection against the Protector, a valuable card in our hand is the capture of one of his leading officers. You are a major bargaining chip in what lies ahead. Consider yourself the first casualty in the campaign."

The next morning in the confines of Ludlow Castle, Ned resumed his conversation with Luke. "Now tell me the truth about the government's plans to forestall and contain the rebellion."

"I told you all I know. Reinforcements are pouring in from across the country. In the meantime, I was to harass potential rebels as they moved out of Wales and to confiscate all weapons and ammunition I came across.

"Ned, why are you doing this? You were a loyal and efficient officer for Cromwell for more than a decade."

"Exactly so. And what did I get in return? I was cashiered without pay or pension as a designated traitor to the government. And what was my offense? I continued to believe in the imminent return of the Lord Jesus and the need to prepare the way for Him. This was a view expressed by General Harrison and the Parliament of Saints. Cromwell sacked Harrison and that godly Parliament and took upon himself, in all but name, the role of king. He placed himself above the Lord."

"So despite what you told me weeks ago about your religious views, you are one with your brothers, and possibly Father, in adherence to a hard-line Fifth Monarchy position. Have you no time for the views of your one time leader Walter Cradoc, who still sees Cromwell as the mouthpiece of the Lord?"

"Cradoc is blind to the betrayal by Cromwell of everything we stand for. "Can't you see it, Luke?"

His government is increasingly made up of former Royalists or the most rigid of Presbyterians.

"It was our faith that enabled my family to stand up for the cause of Parliament in that most Royalist of regions, Rhyd. My father was disgusted that on the death of Sir Daffyd, his Royalist ineffectual son was appointed magistrate by this government, and Father's decade of loyal support and service continued to be ignored."

Luke changed the subject. "Now that you have revealed your true colors, were you behind any of the crimes that have affected Rhyd in the last few months, the murder of Sir Daffyd, the attempts on myself and Kynon Hedd, and the shooting of Tudor Gwent?"

"No. I am a soldier, not a murderer. After all, one of the major crimes in Rhyd was the murder of my own brother."

"I assume that you are gathering together veterans who had a similar experience to yourself to lead an insurgency, which will be swelled by the thousands of Saints coming out of Wales. You will lose. Have you thought of the effect of that loss on your wife and child?"

Luke noticed that Ned's hand began to shake and his first words were barely audible. "That she-devil. Cohabitation with my wife has been horrendous. She has continued to openly take many lovers. Then a week or so ago, she admitted that the child was neither Lawrence's nor mine. The next day, a lawyer told her officially that she was now a wealthy woman in her own right. On the receipt of that news, she told me to leave Barton Oak and never return."

Luke felt deeply sorry for the man. He had been present when Ned and his wife were reunited. The reunion had promised so much.

Luke noticed increased activity in the courtyard of the castle and the constant stream of officers that brought information to or asked questions of Ned.

"Looks as if you are ready to move south!" Luke noted.

"Yes, the Saints, despite your efforts, are gathering en masse at Leominster, and wagonloads of weapons have arrived from North Wales through Shrewsbury. It will not be sufficient, but the Lord will see us through. I expect that officers at both Hereford and Worcester will come over to us with their considerable arsenals.

"Why don't you join us, Luke?"

Luke did not respond but asked, "What are your immediate objectives?"

"As you will be deep in the dungeon of this castle until I need to use you, such critical information I can safely reveal. Hundreds of the most poorly armed Saints will be thrown at Hereford as a diversion, but the main thrust of my experienced troops will be to Worcester, as a gateway Gloucester. By then, the rest of England will have joined us."

An orderly entered the room and whispered to Ned. He turned to Luke, "Most annoying! There is a further enforced delay."

"In that case, for old time's sake, can I ask you a few questions regarding Rhyd?"

33

"What do you know about Colonel Cwm, the whereabouts of Merlyn Gwent, and the activities of William Price?"

"I know nothing about Merlyn Gwent. Colonel Cwm is the name taken by the leader of a brotherhood of alleged highwaymen. These men are well-to-do landowners and their servants who enforced law and order in the neighborhood of Rhyd. The previous leader was very close to Sir Daffyd Morgan who relied on him to enforce unpopular decisions. I always suspected it was Rowland Parry. Some months before Sir Daffyd's death, a new leader took over and moved the emphasis of the brotherhood away from providing justice for the poor to criminal activities enriching themselves."

"Who are the members?"

"William Price and his partners."

"Does Cwm and/or Price support your insurrection?"

"The Saints have reported that the Cwm Brotherhood has appeared twice to save them from your men. Price pretends to be sympathetic and has assisted in small ways, but his heart is not with the Lord. Our victory would greatly diminish his power and position."

"What role then has Price played?"

"He has obtained arms and ammunition, but always at a distance. If things went awry, he could not be held accountable. He negotiated with the religious leaders of the Fifth Monarchy and myself to take over military leadership of the movement in this area."

"Are you friends?"

"The opposite. If I do not survive, and you do, track William Price down and destroy him."

"A strange attitude toward an ally?"

"He is a blackmailer and, given your information regarding the oversized musket balls, a potential mass murderer. It was Price who supplied that deadly ammunition, not Black Barris."

"A blackmailer?"

"He felt the need to blackmail me into taking over the role as military leader. I would have done it without any incentives, but Price suggested that if I accepted the offer, he would stop all legal action against my family. Father would keep all of our estates, but all those obtained by Lawrence, except for one given to my wife, would be his."

An orderly informed Ned that the wagonloads of munitions were now ready to move.

"Enough of this pleasant chat! The army of God must march to Leominster where I will organize and arm its thousands of recruits into an effective force. While I see some advantages in taking you with me, it is more practical to confine you to the dungeon. Unfortunately, because I need every able-bodied man, your warders are the older Saints whose faith exceeds their physical abilities. Consequently, I cannot risk your escape by allowing you the normal freedoms a prisoner of your status would expect."

The cell in which Luke was confined provided no opportunity to escape. It was a hole in the ground with thick stonewalls and a slate floor. The ceiling included a metal grille through which, when opened, the prisoner was lowered by ropes to the floor, twelve feet below.

No food was provided on the first night, and it was not until the midday following that a warder opened the grille and lowered a container of food. No words were spoken.

At night, it was pitch black, and the rats did not hesitate to crawl over him and indulge in the occasional bite. Luke tried desperately to stay awake for fear that these hungry rodents might attack him as he slept. He used his food container to sweep them aside. He was so worried that he ate only a few mouthfuls of food and gave the rest to his ravenous companions.

On the third morning of his imprisonment, he heard the warder shuffle over the grille. Suddenly, he crashed onto the grille making the sound of a low-pitched bell. He had been rendered unconscious by another figure.

The grille was opened, and instead of the food being lowered, the newcomer lowered a thick-knotted rope and whispered, "Colonel, can you climb up the rope, or do I need to find a ladder?"

"Is that you, Stradling?"

"Yes, sir. Please hurry."

Luke managed the swinging rope with some difficulty.

Stradling then led him up a set of stairs, along a corridor, and into a dilapidated part of the castle. They entered a small room.

"We can hide here the whole day. Nobody enters this part of the castle. There is a token guard around the perimeter, but only during the day. The warders are elderly or partially disabled veterans. Most of the activity concerns a hospital. Apparently, several of the travelers were hurt or fell sick while traveling. They have been sent here to recover. They may also be preparing to receive the wounded once fighting begins. You were the only prisoner."

"How did you get here?"

"After you were abducted, Major Jenkins's men led us back toward Newtown for several miles. They then let us go. I ordered the men to set up a roadblock to stop further recruits or weapons reaching Ludlow, while I came in search of you. I arrived just in time to see the rebel army move out. I rode in as another late recruit. As most of those left at the castle were newcomers, few knew each other. I was never challenged and I spent yesterday discreetly discovering where you were and how to reach you without being seen."

That night, the two soldiers had little trouble in escaping the castle.

As soon as they left Ludlow, Luke gave Stradling his orders.

"Ride to Hereford. Inform Berry or the commandant of the castle that the insurgent army is about to march on Worcester! Jenkins will send decoy troops in the direction of Hereford to mislead him.

"Take the byways! You will avoid passing through enemy lines. The enemy are probably still at Leominster so if you give that town a wide berth, you should not encounter any of them."

Luke eventually found his men on the outskirts of Newtown and was delighted to find that Evan's detachment had come across country and rejoined the unit. Evan was in the process of planning an assault on Ludlow to rescue the colonel.

The two officers agreed to ignore the veterans at Ludlow and proceed with all haste toward Leominster and move in behind the insurgent army, harassing its rear and cutting off its retreat.

The Saints had moved more quickly than expected. Luke's advance scouts on reaching Leominster found it deserted. The rebels had left town. Luke's desire to participate in the ensuing battle was also immediately thwarted. Just after they arrived in Leominster, a cavalry regiment sent by Desborough arrived to take over the role of cutting off the retreat of the hopefully defeated enemy.

In addition, troops of the new cavalry militia were to harass the rear of the enemy army, executing on the spot any stragglers that they encountered.

Luke was ordered back to Ludlow Castle.

The main battle did not last long. Berry had assembled such an overwhelming force of well-armed experienced troops that when the hoped-for mutiny of government troops did not occur, the insurgents were dispersed within an hour.

Berry issued orders that the fleeing Saints, once disarmed, should be allowed to fade away; but former army officers who had taken up arms against the Protector were to be executed on the spot. Those that had fled were to be hunted down and shot.

Ned Jenkins was spared this ignominy. In the first charge, he was killed by a burst of concentrated musket fire. Luke felt that this was an end Ned had deliberately courted.

At a meeting convened by General Berry two days later, Luke heard that the only serious resistance the government troops faced was from a unit of Welsh infantry who marched at their opponents singing psalms, as Puritan troops did in the early days of the Civil

War. A horseman who had aroused his men to a fever pitch of passion and enthusiasm led the charge.

They advanced in the face of overwhelming and accurate fire. Almost to a man they died, except the body of their leader, whom Luke assumed was Rhun Talbot, was not found.

Later that day, Berry summoned Luke to a private meeting.

"John Thurloe has sent you new orders. Return to Rhyd immediately and hunt down all Fifth Monarchy leaders maintaining an antigovernment stance, continue your investigations into the murders that have engulfed the Rhyd region, and within three months make recommendations to Secretary Thurloe of persons fit to serve on the bench in both the counties of Radnor and Brecon."

"General, before I do that, I will visit Ned Jenkins's widow. Despite his treachery, he was a man of principle who believed in his cause. The Protector should try to reconcile men such as he before it is too late."

"Dangerous talk, Tremayne! As soldiers, we carry out orders, not influence government policy."

Luke arrived at Ned's estate. Lady Penelope's valet indicated that she was otherwise engaged and he should return at another time. As they spoke, Luke noticed a gentleman's hat and gloves on the hall table. His friendship for Ned overcame his manners. He pushed past the valet and moved toward a chamber from which he heard giggles and laughter.

He pushed on the door. It was barred from the inside. He demanded entry, or he would demolish it.

There was no response.

He demolished it.

He was confronted by a rapidly dressing Penelope Abbott. The window was open, and a smallish man ran away across the manicured lawn of the estate into the neighboring wood.

Luke was at his moralizing best. "A deplorable way for a newly widowed woman to act!"

Penelope laughed and stopped dressing. She turned toward Luke, revealing her bare breasts and rigid nipples. "Don't be a hypocrite, Colonel! Given the same opportunity, you would readily replace my runaway lover."

She moved toward Luke. He could not deny lust was raising its ugly head. He grabbed Penelope by the shoulders and uttered, "My lady, you are an attractive and beautiful woman, and if circumstances were different, I could not resist your charms. But your late husband was a friend, and within days of his death, such activity is unforgivable."

"You are more concerned for reputation than Ned ever was."

"My lady, finish dressing and let me ask you a few questions."

Half an hour later, an appropriately dressed Lady Penelope and Luke were in the hall, eating a delightful midday meal.

Penelope spoke, "Colonel, I do not apologize for my behavior, and given how I have been treated by men, especially the Jenkins, I had to fend for myself. For years I had one weapon, my seductive charm."

"And now with that and your newfound wealth, you will be unstoppable. What went wrong with your renewed cohabitation with Ned?"

"When Ned and you arrived, I played the part of a delighted wife restored to her connubial state. For a while our renewed acquaintance was pleasant and fulfilling, but Ned quickly reverted to his religious and military obsessions. My needs are simple, Colonel."

She leaned across the table and squeezed Luke's hand and whispered, "You could readily satisfy them."

Luke warmed to this sensual woman. Whether as a response to his growing lust or as a legitimate part of his inquiries, he asked, "Who is the man who just escaped across the lawn?"

"Come, Luke, a lady never reveals such secrets."

Luke made his farewells that included a lingering sensual kiss.

As he went through the hall, he noticed the hat and gloves of the scarpering lover were still on the small table. He took them. They may aid his investigation. He had added a personal quest to those set down by Thurloe.

34

BACK AT LLANANDRAS, CRANOG INVITED Luke to dine with the household. They wanted an update on the fate of Ned and Morgan.

Luke reported the bare outline of Ned's courageous death, leading a suicidal charge against an elite company of musketeers.

Cranog intimated that he would visit Conway and convey his sympathies.

On Merlyn, Luke had nothing to report.

A servant interrupted the meal, informing Luke that a naval officer waited without and needed to see him as a matter of urgency. Luke left the supper and met the officer in the hall.

"Colonel, we met at Aberystwyth. I am the deputy commander of the naval base. My superior officer has sent me here on a delicate and urgent matter that affects the members of this household."

"What is so urgent that a senior naval officer acts as courier? Surely one of your ratings could have carried the message?"

"This is too delicate to entrust to anyone junior."

"Well, what is it?"

"A man confined on one of our frigates claims to be Sir Daffyd Morgan."

Luke drew in a deep breath and responded firmly, "That cannot be. His body lies in the crypt of the chapel a few yards from where we stand."

"He is not alone. There are five or six men with him who swear that he is lord of the manor of Llanandras and magistrate in their community of Rhyd."

"How can I help?"

"One of the household must return with me to Aberystwyth to identity the claimant. I thought you might introduce me to the family so that I can explain the situation."

"No, too insensitive! We must not raise the hopes of the family or shock them into some traumatic state until we are sure. I will return with you. As I have never met Sir Daffyd, I will bring with me his best friend. It is dark now, and traveling to and over the Pass at night is not desirable. Stay in our barracks overnight! In the morning, the three of us will leave for Aberystwyth."

Luke returned to the dining hall and made his excuses. He had received urgent orders that required him to go to the coast first thing in the morning and that there were matters that he had to rearrange before then.

Luke rode to Cadwalladers. Huw opened the door and remarked, "This is an ungodly hour for a social visit."

"I agree, Huw, but the information I bring warrants the intrusion."

Luke informed Huw of the naval officer's news.

Huw visibly paled, dropped the jug he had been carrying, and then fell forward in a complete faint.

A servant fetched Edwyn who was at the far end of the house.

Luke asked, "Does your father often suffer from fainting fits?"

"No, but I have known him to feel faint when he receives bad news. What did you tell him before he collapsed?"

"I told him that Sir Daffyd might be alive."

Luke explained the situation.

"Pray God that it is Sir Daffyd and not some conniving imposter."

"If it is Sir Daffyd then whose body lies in the crypt?"

"Who knows? Only the clothes and the general build and complexion of the body identified the corpse. The face had been blown away," commented an intrigued Edwyn.

After a few minutes, Huw recovered. Luke asked if he would join him in a trip to Aberystwyth to identify the man claiming to be Sir Daffyd. Luke was surprised by the reply.

"No, Colonel. I will not make the trip and then discover he is an imposter. Edwyn will go in my place."

The commandant warmly welcomed Luke and Edwyn.

Luke then suggested, "Your deputy said that you have several men who were Daffyd's companions. We should see them first. Edwyn would recognize most inhabitants of Rhyd."

"Easily done, Colonel. They are working on the docks. If you look through this window, Mr. Cadwallader, you can see them on the nearest wharf."

Edwyn moved to the window and immediately let out a cry of exultation. "I know them all. They are the men who disappeared with Daffyd and were believed to have been sold into slavery by Black Barris."

Luke asked, "Commandant, how did these men come into your custody?"

"Ships of the line patrolling the seas between the Americas and Europe captured several Spanish transports, many of them carrying slaves. Admiral Blake ordered his captains to sell the rescued African and Irish slaves in the Caribbean. Any English, Scottish, or Welsh slaves were freed and put upon a partially disabled English frigate that Blake ordered home for repairs. It was blown off course before it reached its homeport of Plymouth. It sheltered here until the storms abated. The Welshmen aboard sought permission to disembark."

Edwyn was clearly nervous as he and Luke were ferried out to the frigate on the commandant's barge.

Everybody jumped to attention as the commandant came aboard. Luke and Edwyn were led to a cabin, outside of which stood a burly sailor armed with a Turkish-type scimitar.

The commandant spoke through the closed door. "Sir, I bring with me the son of Sir Daffyd Morgan's best friend. He will solve your identity once and for all."

Edwyn entered the cabin and immediately hugged its occupant and affirmed, "This is Sir Daffyd."

Luke and the commandant withdrew and allowed Daffyd and Edwyn to renew their relationship in private.

Half an hour later, Luke reentered the cabin, and Edwyn introduced him as the man sent by Oliver Cromwell himself to solve Daffyd's murder.

Luke explained that he still has a number of questions to ask. "Sir Daffyd, could you detail your activities over the last nine months, starting with the night of your alleged murder?"

"For the last nine months, I have been sailing around the ocean or working as a slave.

The smugglers captured us at the Pass then put us aboard a small Dutch merchant ship, which sailed to Cadiz. There, we Rhyd men were sold as one lot to a Castilian nobleman.

Months later, we were sold again to his son who had a sugar plantation in the Caribbean. We were sailing to that destination when the Spanish ship was attacked by Admiral Blake."

"Who lies buried in the crypt of your chapel?"

"A rather unsavory local by the name of Tecwyn Hedd."

"How did the locals mistake him for you?"

"In my younger days, I sired several illegitimate children. Tecwyn was one of them. In later life, he developed the same body shape, complexion, and reddish hair as myself."

"But that does not explain how he came to be wearing your clothes and the family ring. What exactly happened on that night?"

The commandant arrived with a flagon of Spanish wine, and the four men began to imbibe on a steady basis.

Daffyd began his explanation. "On the night in question, I received an urgent request from an organization with which I had had many dealings to meet just below the Pass at midnight and to come alone. I was surprised and suspicious. Although I had dealt with the organization previously, it now had a new leader of whom I knew little. The very request to meet at night, in such a lonely place and at midnight, alerted me to possible danger. I took with me my valet, Tadd Bowen, and a group of men from the Red Kite. Not far from the Pass, Tecwyn Hedd came running down the track. Tadd grabbed him.

"I threatened to have him put into the stocks for harassing his sister-in-law. The sniveling worm pleaded with me to be merciful. He wouldn't dare say he should be treated better because he was my son, but the implication was there in his tone."

"What happened next?" asked a captivated Luke.

"It suddenly dawned on me how I could take further precautions against an unexpected attack. I ordered Tecwyn to remove his clothes, all of them, and I did likewise. We exchanged clothes, and I placed my family ring on his finger. Tecwyn was then placed on my horse, and I walked beside him with Tadd on the other side.

"We had almost reached the Pass when two almost simultaneous shots were heard, and Tecwyn fell from the horse, his face obliterated. The assailants were excellent shots. The rest of us dived for cover and stayed down for some time. One of the men claimed he heard a horse gallop off down the main highway.

"We then foolishly relaxed and were about to bury Tecwyn where he fell, when out of the darkness a large band of heavily armed men surrounded us. They declared we were vagrants who would be shipped abroad as slaves."

Luke smiled, "Thank you, Sir Daffyd. You have solved two of my five murders. You did not die, and Tecwyn was shot by unknown assailants who thought he was you."

Edwyn then outlined some of the events that had occurred in Rhyd during Daffyd's absence.

"Surely Rhyd could not produce so many murders in such a short time?" spluttered a surprised Daffyd.

Eventually, he asked, "How is Cranog coping? At least he has Merlyn to help him."

"Cranog is unhappy and planning to renounce his lordship of the manor and headship of the Morgan family. He wishes to become a bard. Your return will make him doubly happy. He is no longer lord of the manor, and you can take steps, as you promised, to legitimize one of your bastards as the eventual successor to yourself," reported Edwyn.

"And he does not have Merlyn. After the murder of his nephew, Gwent went peculiar. He has now disappeared," added Luke.

Daffyd asked, "Are all these developments related?"

"I believe so. The same man or group is behind the attempt on Kynon Hedd, on your life and on mine, and in the murders of Tudor Gwent and Lawrence Jenkins," pontificated Luke.

The next day, Luke and Daffyd left Aberystwyth for Rhyd. Edwyn would return the following day with the rest of the men. Luke would prepare the household at Llanandras and the community of Rhyd for the good but emotional news.

On arrival at Llanandras, Luke spoke to Cranog who summoned the whole household. Glynnis was as feisty as ever. "This is appalling. Why are we summoned here on the say-so of a soldier?"

"Sir Cranog and your ladyships, I bring great news. The news is so overwhelming that I have come ahead to prepare you for it. Lady Alis, would you be so kind as to move into the hall?"

Luke spoke to her quietly before she did so. As a result, Lady Alis ran from the room.

Luke waited a few minutes and continued, "By now, Lady Alis is reunited with her husband. Sir Daffyd is alive and awaits you all in the hall."

Luke was almost knocked over as the women raced for the door. Cranog was all smiles. "This is the best news ever."

Luke moved on to the Red Kite. He sent messages to all those with returning family to come to the inn immediately. It was a matter of life and death. As the unruly crowd gathered, some indicating their discontent of having been summoned on an inclement afternoon, to hear a government soldier whom many still believed had seriously disrupted the local community.

Luke quietly explained that missing sons and husbands had been rescued and that the younger Mr. Cadwallader would arrive with them the next day. There was wild cheering. Luke was overwhelmed with flagons of beer. His part in the suppression of the local Fifth Monarchy Men was forgiven.

35

LUKE HAD A CONFIDENTIAL MEETING with Daffyd two days later. He explained that the three aspects of his mission, despite Daffyd's return, remained—solving the successful and attempted murders; the unearthing and suppression of antigovernment activity, especially the capture of Rhun; and advising on the future governance of the area.

Daffyd was very sensitive to the last aspect. "Surely the government will restore me to my traditional role as magistrate for both Radnor and Brecon?"

"It is not cut and dried. Unfortunately, your estate and your people were involved in creating a large arsenal that could have been used against the government. On the other hand, your rivals also are rapidly losing ground. Sir Conway must explain the role of his family in the recent uprising, and the aspiring yeomen, Price, Vaughan, and Griffith, have done little to convince me of their loyalty to the government. Your friend Huw Cadwallader stands well above the rest, but I doubt that he would offer himself as a magistrate against yourself."

"May I ask you a few questions regarding the first part of my mission, the murders and attempted murders?"

Daffyd nodded his agreement.

"What is your connection with the Cwm Brotherhood?"

Daffyd was uneasy. "Do I have a connection with those brigands?"

"Come, Sir Daffyd. You colluded with these highwaymen on numerous occasions in the past, activity if reported to the authorities would undoubtedly prevent your reappointment to the bench of magistrates."

"I sense an element of blackmail in those comments, Colonel."

"Be that as it may, what exactly was your relationship with this group?"

"They are hardly your normal brotherhood of highwaymen. They were a group of respectable property owners who given the absence of law enforcement agencies in this area enabled me to execute government policy and maintain law and order. The guise of highwaymen prevented any awkward questions being asked and freed me from any formal connection with some of their necessary but ruthless activity. Men I could not convict in the courts were dealt with and punished through their actions."

"Do you know the membership of this group?"

"Not in detail, but most of the landowners of the area were members from time to time. Emlyn Vaughan coordinates their activities. Every few years, they elect a new leader who takes the name of Colonel Cwm. This is a small community that knows that in their time, Parry, Vaughan, Griffith, Price, Lawrence Jenkins, and even Huw Cadwallader are or were members."

"So what happened twelve months ago?"

"The group had a change of leader who dramatically altered the objectives of the Cwm Brotherhood. It began to act as a criminal organization. Innocent travelers were attacked, and it used its physical power to coerce people into accepting new tenurial conditions or even to force people off the land. It became a weapon of the wealthy classes against those of inferior status. That is why I sent a message through Vaughan that I wished to meet Colonel Cwm to discuss the situation. The reply was to meet near the Pass on that eventful night."

"How did you receive Cwm's reply suggesting that rendezvous?"

"I received it earlier that day. It was fortuitous that I could keep that appointment and thwart the illicit drive at the same time."

"Who delivered Cwm's reply?"

"Vaughan."

"Who is the current Cwm and why would he wish to kill you?"

"I spent countless hours during my captivity pondering both those questions. Your second question is easy to answer. I am the most powerful person in Rhyd. Despite my support of the Royalist cause during the Civil Wars, I have obviously convinced parliamentarian and protectoral governments that I am loyal to them. The obvious motive is to weaken my power and influence.

"But who would contemplate my murder to achieve it? That is a more difficult question. The Jenkins would head the list followed by all the aspiring landowners in the area, excluding my friend Huw Cadwallader."

"Yet your death would leave the Morgan lands intact, and your steward Merlyn Gwent has proved a most able defender of the family's position."

"The person behind the attempt on my life may have counted on the inability and lack of interest by my heir Cranog. He would be easily manipulated.

"I would not be surprised if Merlyn's disappearance is part of the same plot. Without Merlyn, Cranog would be an easy victim to the predatory landowners of the area. That is why just before my abduction I proposed to legitimize one of my illegitimate children and make him my heir. Cranog was in full agreement with this plan."

"Will you proceed with this now?"

"Yes, as a matter of urgency. This issue lies at the bottom of the attempt on young Kynon Hedd. My would-be murderer wanted to wipe out any potential heirs who might have ability. The community believes that Kynon is the youngest of my bastard children. When rumors spread through Rhyd regarding to my intention to raise one of these children to be the Morgan heir, many thought that it would be Kynon.

"It won't be."

"Who will it be?"

"I have yet to finally decide, as I must consider developments during my absence."

"Tell me about Merlyn Gwent!"

"Up to the Civil War fifteen years ago, the Gwents had been the most powerful family in Rhyd for centuries. Merlyn's ancestors provided the magistrates and members of Parliament for the region for over two hundred years. Merlyn's grandfather began to sell off some of his properties that brought the Jenkins into the area. His father, in order to provide men and money for Charles I, mortgaged all his remaining properties. He lost everything and committed suicide.

"His eldest son, Merlyn, was training as a lawyer when the war began. He was appointed, perhaps due to his father's generosity, as a captain in Lord Goring's notorious cavalry. They terrorized the West Country, kneecapping the main supporters of parliament. Merlyn eventually headed a special unit of mounted grenadiers."

"That explains one small mystery," muttered Luke inaudibly to himself. Daffyd continued, "He returned here on the death of his father but had no future in the region. I had always been friendly with the Gwents and held similar political views, although in religion we differed strongly. The Gwents were Papists. At the time, I had just married my second wife Alis who was also a Papist. She persuaded me that Merlyn would be an ideal steward for our properties, although he had not completed his law studies due to the outbreak of war."

"Who currently holds most of the former Gwent land?"

"It was divided between Jenkins, Vaughan, Cadwallader, Griffith, Price, and myself."

"Did Merlyn express anger or antagonism toward those that held his family's traditional possessions?"

"No, but from the beginning of his stewardship, he was determined to accumulate property and eventually regain the family holdings. A steward is well rewarded, and Merlyn purchased several smallholdings up the river. Once he accumulates enough land to live off, he will resign his position here. That is why I do not believe he has disappeared of his own free will."

"You never thought Merlyn might be Colonel Cwm?"

"To what end?"

"His experiences with Goring would have made him an ideal member, especially in the last twelve months where coercion and brutality seem to have become their hallmark."

"No, the evidence is that this behavior benefitted the very people that one would have thought were Merlyn's enemies. Why would he assist those who dispossessed his family to dispossess others?"

"My deputy suspects that members of the Cwm Brotherhood who on two occasions assisted the rebels had among their number experienced cavalry men. Your statement about grenadiers almost proves that one of them was Merlyn. My men were subject to a grenade attack."

A servant interrupted the confidential meeting and spoke quietly to Daffyd. Daffyd nodded to the servant and then turned toward Luke, "Colonel, you may soon have an answer to all those questions."

The servant left the room and immediately returned, with Merlyn Gwent.

Daffyd was delighted. "Thank God you are alive! Colonel Tremayne is very interested in your recent adventures."

"I prefer to speak to you alone. Some of what I wish to reveal could lead to my immediate arrest by the colonel."

"Given everything that has happened, complete disclosure will be in the best interests of all, and the colonel will not be swayed by technicalities of law breaking," said Daffyd.

"I will judge that after I have heard Mr. Gwent's story. What have you done since you disappeared?"

"When I left here a week or so ago, I had no intention of ever returning. Your death, Cranog's incompetence, the failure of my work for Lord Kimball in rearming the Catholic gentry, and finally the murder of my nephew temporarily unhinged me.

"I sought revenge by joining the only armed organization in the area. I knew that Mr. Vaughan was the contact for the Cwm Brotherhood."

"You were the horseman who assisted the rebels against my men on two occasions, once with an effective barrage of grenades."

"The brotherhood had orders to assist the rebels to reach Leominster and to ensure that they were adequately armed. We were not to join the actual insurrection itself, but I could not stand by and see you murder many innocent and poorly armed poor people who were simply trying to improve their position in life."

"Why join Cwm, especially as of late it seems to be made up of your traditional enemies, and the very people who were dispossessing the small landholders and reducing the wages of the lowliest worker?"

"That is the very reason I joined, to destroy the new brotherhood. I joined because I disagreed with most of their recent actions. I was determined to destroy their current leadership.

"Cwm was responsible for my nephew's death. Before he was murdered, Tudor told he had sold the stolen arms to the brotherhood. These people murdered Tudor so that the destination would never be revealed. They were not aware that he had revealed this me when I brought him food minutes before his departure and death."

"Did you discover who currently leads the group and who murdered your nephew?"

"I am almost certain. Members wear masks and collect a new horse from Vaughan's stables before every mission, to conceal their identity. But there are some things you can't conceal. I was determined to unearth his identity and kill him.

"But then I heard that you, Sir Daffyd, had returned. This put an entirely different perspective on the problem I confronted. My depression lifted, and I believe that with your assistance I can bring Cwm to justice legally. I would like to resume my position as steward."

"Delighted to have you back. I am sure Colonel Tremayne will see your membership of Cwm as an undercover activity to assist him in discovering the murderer of your nephew. He might even agree that you were a government spy working within that organization whose subversive deeds you have just revealed."

Daffyd winked at Luke, assuming his total compliance with the face-saving interpretation of Gwent's role.

Luke did not respond to Daffyd's suggestion.

He inexplicably changed the direction of the discussion.

"Sir Daffyd, the person that tried to kill you will now probably try again. I must station several of my men in the house, and one will accompany you at all times. Merlyn, ensure that none of our potential suspects, that is all the landowners of Rhyd, visit Sir Daffyd without your presence. You cannot trust anybody. I will try to reduce the list of suspects as quickly as I can. Who would top of your list, Merlyn?"

"William Price," he answered solemnly.

"Why?" Luke asked.

"You might wear a hood and ride strange horses to hide your identity, but you can't change your voice. For a man, Price has a high-pitched voice. During my time with the brotherhood, a man with a high-pitched voice gave the orders. William Price is probably Colonel Cwm."

"But would he gain from Sir Daffyd's death?"

"Yes, if the Morgans remained strong, they could thwart his ambitions to be the largest and most powerful man in Rhyd. Specifically, Sir Daffyd singlehandedly denies Price one-half of his potential droving clientele by supporting his rival."

36

DAFFYD INTERJECTED, "IF PRICE IS Cwm, then I don't think he tried to kill me to increase his power and wealth. He is already the wealthiest man in the community, and with his general support of more radical Puritanism, he could expect new favors from the Lord Protector. As I represent the defeated Royalist connection in Rhyd, in current circumstances, killing me would not have been necessary. You will possibly recommend him as the next magistrate."

"So you don't think it was Price?"

"I am not saying that, but if it was him, his attempt was for a specific reason. I had made clear that I would no longer cooperate with the brotherhood as they had departed from their traditional role of imposing law and order. They had slipped into out-and-out criminal activities and used their power to force unwilling farmers to give up their land to the likes of Jenkins, Price, Vaughan, and Griffith. This change probably occurred when Price took over as Colonel Cwm."

"Sir, I have always assumed that whoever tried to kill you was also responsible for the deaths of Tudor Gwent and Lawrence Jenkins and the attempts on Kynon Hedd. The first two are explicable. Tudor was sending the stolen weapons to Price, and Lawrence may have discovered business practices of his partner that Price would not have liked being made public, but why would he try to kill Kynon?"

"I have no idea," Daffyd answered.

Merlyn interjected, "Sir, in the month before your disappearance, it was widely rumored that you were about to disinherit Cranog and name Kynon Hedd as your successor. Price wanted the Morgan household to remain weak. Kynon as your named heir is a lad with ability and promise. Price has always thought well ahead."

Daffyd shook his head in disbelief. "I don't know how these rumors start. I am fond of Kynon, and his mother remains one of my dearest friends. Following the unfortunate death of her husband, I have been perhaps overgenerous in both time and money to aid the Hedd household, which may have created the popular opinion, although Huw Cadwallader has been more generous than I."

"Who will you name?" persisted Luke.

Daffyd smiled again. "My choice will be announced soon."

"Does anybody know who it will be?"

"On the night of my capture, I did tell someone."

"Who?"

"Come, Colonel, concentrate on the essentials! Start investigating William Price."

Luke agreed. He arrived at Price's farm and was ushered into the hall by a servant. While he waited, he noticed on the hall table several hats. He had seen one similar before, at the house of Lady Penelope Abbott.

Sometime later, another man appeared who introduced himself as Price's newly appointed steward. He announced that his master was away for the week doing business in Hereford, Leominster, Ludlow, and Rhayader.

Luke was certain that most of it was being spent near Ludlow.

It was a fine day. Luke decided to walk the short distance to the adjacent farm owned by Emlyn Vaughan. He left his horse tied to Price's hitching rail.

As he walked up the short drive, a big man with a mass of unkempt black hair accosted him. Luke introduced himself and indicated that he had a few questions to ask concerning the brotherhood. The Welshman replied in English, indicating that he was Emlyn Vaughan and that they had met weeks before at the Priory.

He invited Luke into his house, and the two settled down in a small room off the entrance hall.

Luke was direct. "Emlyn, who are the current members of the brotherhood?"

"I don't know, and even if I did, I could not tell you."

"I do not believe you. In this small community, you must know the people you ride with."

"I no longer ride. Most of the older property owners have retired. I recognize one or two of the current activists, but others remain a mystery."

"How does the brotherhood maintain its secrecy?"

"Not very effectively. Most of its activity and procedures are hardly secret. Everybody knows that Bronwyn Hedd will get messages to us, and that I am its public face. When Cwm wants action, he alters a broken weather vane on a partly demolished building to point in the opposite direction. Active members know to meet at a certain place and time."

"So you do not organize these missions?"

"My role for a decade or more has been simple. I am a horse breeder, and every time I see the weather vane in the altered direction, I take six of my almost identical horses to a particular place. The brotherhood leases these for the duration of their rides. I collect the horses on the day following such activity and turn the weathervane back to its original position."

"Emlyn, my concern with the brotherhood is to uncover its role in the attempted murder of Sir Daffyd, in other murders, and in the recent insurrection. I know that the brotherhood rode to the assistance of the rebels on at least two separate occasions. As you admit your role in assisting them by providing their horses, I could have you arrested for treason."

"Colonel, I have no say in or knowledge of any mission since I retired as an active member. All I know is that the new Colonel Cwm is William Price. I am not revealing secrets. Anybody who has been held up in the last few months has reported that Colonel Cwm made demands in a high-pitched voice. No one else in Rhyd has such a voice."

"Could Cwm use some of the brotherhood's procedures to organize raids and rides of his own with hooded men who were not members of the brotherhood?"

"Cwm could do what he liked."

"So Price could use his own men, put on hoods, and indulge in activity that the brotherhood would never contemplate?"

"Anybody could put a group of ruffians together, wear hoods, and create trouble."

"Do you have a view as who tried to murder Sir Daffyd?"

"No, but I would not concentrate solely on the brotherhood. Daffyd as a lad had his way with the married women and virgins of the village. At the time, this created much jealousy and hatred of the then predatory heir to the Morgan fortune."

"Would such people wait so long to exact vengeance?"

"Maybe they have only recently become aware of the truth. It could be a bastard son born to one of these women who never revealed the fact until the lad or wench matured. They may be so distraught to discover they are not their nominal father's child that they become slightly unhinged and seek to destroy Daffyd."

"Wouldn't it be more likely that they would seek to benefit from their newly discovered relationship to exact some reward? Do you have anybody in mind who would fit into this revenge category?" probed Luke.

"I would look into the extended Bithel family. In their youth, the sisters Dilys and Bronwyn slept around, and both were embarrassingly fertile. Dilys passed her offspring onto couples who were childless and always concealed the father's name. Bronwyn was less discreet, and she mothered at least two of Daffyd's children."

"The circumstances free Bronwyn from suspicion. The rumors were that Daffyd was about to legitimize one of his bastards, and the popular consensus was that it would be Kynon. She was the last person to want Daffyd dead, until he had formally recognized her son."

"True, but it ignores Dilys. She is a vicious evil witch who hates her sister. Daffyd seduced her years before he found solace in Bronwyn. Dilys believed it was her sister who had destroyed the spell she had woven around Daffyd to keep him as her lover and benefactor. Daffyd was the father of at least one of her children. God knows who and where he is now. She could have poisoned this person's mind against Daffyd to provoke the attempt on his life."

"Thanks, Emlyn. In your eyes, half the Rhyd community should be my suspects," joked Luke.

"You need also to consider the Llanandras household. Gwent can never forget his ancestry and must resent the patronizing assistance given to him by Sir Daffyd. And then there is Lady Glynnis. Would you stand by and allow your father-in-law to destroy your future as lady of the manor? She must hate the thought that Daffyd would legitimize one of his bastards before she could secure an heir with a child by Cranog."

"Are you suggesting that the main motive for the attempt on Sir Daffyd will be found in his history of reproduction and succession?"

"Yes, that will provide more fruitful leads than concentrating on the Cwm Brotherhood."

Suddenly without warning, the door was thrust open, and Huw Cadwallader strode into the room. He appeared angry and distraught and was swinging his constable's cudgel. He advanced on Emlyn, and then seeing Luke, he uttered a cry and fell to the floor unconscious.

Emlyn and Luke looked at each other in amazement.

"That was an unusual and dramatic entry," said a stunned Luke.

"Completely out of character. Huw did not wait for my servants to introduce him, nor did he knock on the door. Most discourteous! It must have been a matter of life and death for him to behave in such a manner," concluded an equally astonished Emlyn.

Luke reported, "Huw is very unwell. This is the second or third time he has collapsed in recent weeks."

Huw eventually recovered and apologized for his behavior. He had no memory of bursting into the room unannounced and had no recollection of why he had come.

Huw asked, "Why are you here, Luke?"

"At least I can remember," said Luke, trying to be funny. "I am questioning Emlyn as to the role of the brotherhood in recent events."

"With great success, I trust?"

"No, not really. This community offers up a host of additional suspects."

Huw left, but Emlyn insisted that one his servants accompany the constable home.

Emlyn remained disturbed. "Maybe in your hardly-secret advice regarding the governance of this area, you could suggest that Huw is no longer capable of holding his position. If he is collapsing without warning, he could be a danger to himself and others."

"Why would Huw want to see you so urgently?"

"No idea. Our paths rarely cross. I am friendly with Price, Griffith, and the Jenkins, while he moves within the orbit of the Morgans."

"Does this mean that the brotherhood largely represents the former group?"

"Not at all. Traditionally, it has assisted the magistrate of the area who for centuries has been either a Gwent or a Morgan."

"Was Sir Daffyd a member in his youth when his father was magistrate?"

"Ask him!"

"Emlyn, are the horses you make available to the brotherhood in your stables at the moment?"

"No, they are in the home field. Do you want to inspect them?"

Luke nodded his head and was led across the courtyard and through a small gate into the nearest field. Five or six horses were grazing happily on lush grass, and two others were skittishly galloping around the enclosure. Luke moved to inspect that part of the field that the galloping horses had just covered. They had left deep impressions where they had halted and changed course. The ground revealed hoof prints that were ridged. The brotherhood horses could have been used in both the attempt on Kynon and himself. Perhaps he had too readily assumed that the would-be killers had come from Builth.

Luke walked back to the Price's to collect his horse.

He must see William Price as a matter of urgency.

37

Two DAYS AFTER HIS VISIT to Vaughan, a servant arrived at the barracks with a note from William Price, suggesting an urgent meeting at the Red Kite.

Luke accepted and decided on a show of strength. His dragoons surrounded the inn and disarmed anyone entering the establishment.

Price was allowed through the cordon, and after a curt introduction, Luke came directly to the point.

"Why should I not arrest you, William Price, for several murders and with treason in that you aided the recent insurrection?"

"Because even if I was distantly involved in any of the matters you raised, I acted in the interests of the Protector's government. Arms and ammunition are very profitable commodities. Every businessman in the area accepted orders for such from the government and the insurgent groups alike. It did not reflect a political position.

"And I ensured that the weapons supplied to the Fifth Monarchy extremists could not harm the government. The shot I provided could not be used safely in the muskets that I supplied."

"And the Saints would blow their own heads off without knowing what they were doing," commented a disgusted Luke.

"Don't be a hypocrite, Colonel! Those fanatics took up arms against the government you serve. I did you a service. A few hundred less religious madmen, the better it is for the government. Your superiors will not think badly of me for such a contribution. I could almost claim that I was operating under cover for Oliver Cromwell. Nothing I did harmed the Protectorate."

"Even if I accept you as a loyal Cromwellian, despite the evidence of Ned Jenkins, how do I persuade myself not to arrest you for murder?"

"You can't take evidence from a dead man. And whom am I accused of murdering?"

"Tudor Gwent and Lawrence Jenkins, and then there are the attempted murders of Sir Daffyd, Kynon Hedd, and myself."

"Absolute rubbish! You cannot associate me with any of those atrocities. Tudor worked for me, and Lawrence was my business partner."

"I am not saying that you carried out the murders yourself, but that you ordered them."

"What's my motive? Why would I risk my expanding empire on such useless ploys?"

"The Morgans and the Jenkins had the status and power you craved. With a strong Morgan out of the way, your rise to the top would be much easier. The same applies to the Jenkins. While pretending to be their friend, you entrapped Lawrence into deals and decisions, which he ultimately decided were immoral or illegal, and threatened to reveal all. That would have been the end of you."

"Lawrence was my business partner. We had disagreements, and Lawrence frankly made many errors. That is why on his death I had to claim more than appeared to be fair from the Jenkins to compensate me for Lawrence's stupidity. But you cannot prove that I murdered him.

"The same applies to Tudor Gwent. He got himself into a mess, promising arms to an eager buyer and not delivering. Someone in the armament business taught him a lesson. Murder was maybe a step too far, but a man who goes back on his word needs an unforgettable reprimand. A good thrashing would have been my preferred approach. Someone overreacted. And why would I have it in for that Hedd brat? His father was a good drover who died because of the stupidity of his brother."

Luke was frustrated. He realized that to get William Price into court in the first place and have him convicted in the second would be nigh impossible. He had no direct evidence of Price's involvement. It was all circumstantial.

Price had the money to buy witnesses in his favor and the power to silence those against him.

Luke lowered the tension by asking, "If you are innocent, who is behind the spate of murders in Rhyd?"

"I don't have names, but I know why Jenkins and Gwent were killed."

"Tell me!

"Lawrence was killed by one of the dispossessed tenant farmers. Tudor made a deal with some evil munitions merchants, failed to deliver, and paid the ultimate price."

Luke gave up and struck below the belt. "And how is the seductive Lady Penelope Abbott?"

"Fine. I wondered whether you had recognized me when I had to leave her presence in such a hurry."

"I had my suspicions that were confirmed the other day when I visited your farm and saw a hat identical with the one I had seen at her manor house."

"A most admirable arrangement. I visited Lady Penelope to sort out the mess that Lawrence and Ned had created regarding her property. One thing led to another. You know the rest. If you have no further questions, I must leave."

Luke threw his hands in the air and exclaimed, "You are right, Mr. Price. At present, a court of law or even a military tribunal may find my evidence wanting. However, some heavy interrogation of your men may change that.

"In the meantime, I will arrest you and hold you in our barracks at Llanandras until my inquiries are completed. Drink and eat up. Neither of us is in a hurry."

"How dare you! You have no authority to arrest me."

"As an officer in time of rebellion, I am placing you under the protective custody of the army."

Suddenly, the door was thrust open, and a man entered. He tossed back his cloak and shouted at Price, "You murdering hypocrite! We trusted you, and you betrayed us. I deliver the judgment of God on your withered soul."

With that, Rhun Talbot hurled a shortened pike through Price's chest with such force that it pinned the now-dying man to the wall. Price was coughing up blood.

Luke struck at Rhun with his sword, which left a sizable slash under the killer's chest. Luke's men rushed to his aid and apprehended Rhun who offered no resistance.

Luke ordered the dragoons to incarcerate Rhun in the cellar in the West Field and to double the guard on this makeshift prison.

Luke knew he could do little for Price. He was aware from battlefield experience that to remove the pike hastened death.

Price signaled for him to come close. Luke half expected him to unleash his dagger and attempt to kill him.

"There is no time for a clergyman to ease my progress to the next world."

He stopped talking as he coughed up mouthfuls of blood to add to those being pumped out of his shattered chest.

Luke whispered, "Confess to the murders of which you are accused?" Price readily complied, "I ordered the death of those you mentioned. Lawrence threatened to report me to the authorities for a series of illegal acts and for coercing several people off their land. Young Kynon worried me. Cranog did not concern me. But a revitalized Morgan household led by a mature Kynon might cause me problems down the line, especially if the Royalists returned to favor. Your inquiries were also a worry so I tried to take you out as you climbed toward the Pass."

"You misused the brotherhood to achieve these dastardly deeds?"

"No, I mobilized the brotherhood to help the insurgents on two occasions, but the coercion of unwilling land users was done by my own men wearing masks in the manner of the brotherhood. We used brotherhood horses from Emlyn Vaughan to conceal this fact."

"That was a mistake. Vaughan's horses were shod in a particular way. The shoes were ridged. And the attempt on Sir Daffyd?"

"Of that I am entirely innocent. On the night of his abduction, I was to meet him near the Pass, but when I saw he was not alone, I departed. I did not attempt to kill him, but I know who did."

William Price coughed again and expired.

Luke sought to question Rhun Talbot and ordered that he be brought back to the inn.

There was a long delay. Eventually, Evan appeared and announced, "Talbot has escaped."

Luke was livid. "How can that be? He left here under a heavy guard of our men. And this is the second major blunder. How did Talbot get through our cordon, especially armed with an overtly visible half pike?"

"Apparently, Talbot was in the Red Kite before we encircled it, probably hiding in an upper room. His followers engineered his escape. When our men took Rhun outside, a number of drinkers joined in ostensibly to assist. Somehow in the bundling along of countless bodies, one of Talbot's adherents replaced Rhun. When our men were left alone by the mob of willing assistants, they realized that the man they had in custody was not Rhun Talbot. Even more humiliating, the short pike that one of the dragoons had confiscated was wrested from him in a lighthearted gambol."

"Rhun is free and armed with his lethal half pike," Luke repeated in disbelief at the incompetence that the situation reflected.

"Yes, but he is wounded and losing blood," reported Evan, trying to be positive.

Luke sent patrols in every direction and was soon rewarded with the news he wanted to hear. A Baptist whose father had died as a result of Rhun's lies reported the escapee heading toward the Pass up one of the minor valleys. He was bleeding badly and leaving a traceable trail.

Luke called off the patrols and with Evan and a troop of dragoons quickly found the trail of blood.

Evan was bemused.

"Where is he heading?"

"His followers live up this valley. The people treat him as a god. To think he was once one of us," mused Luke.

"By the amount of blood he is losing, he must find help soon, or we will only be required to pick up his body," stated Evan.

As they made their way up the narrow valley, they soon entered dense woodland where it was convenient to dismount. It was difficult to follow in file. The soldiers spread out and leading their horses made their way individually through the thick undergrowth.

After some time, Luke realized he had lost contact with his men. Almost simultaneously, he smelt food and entering a clearing saw a woman stirring a large pot.

"Good woman, I mean you no harm. Have you seen a wounded man in the last half hour?"

"Colonel Tremayne, how nice of you to visit me. Your reputation precedes you."

"I am sorry. Who are you?"

"I am Dilys Bithel. Undoubtedly, my saintly sister has lied about me. Has that hypocrite Daffyd Morgan sent you to finally silence me?"

"Focus on my question, witch, and I will soon be on my way. Have you seen a wounded man?"

"Don't be so cross, Luke. This is not the picture I get of you from several women who have come to me secretly to receive potions so that they can win your love. Have any of them succeeded? You should thank me for delivering such beauties into your arms.

"My magic keeps Rhyd in turmoil. The death of that saintly Mabon Hedd can be blamed on me. His brother Tecwyn obtained syrup from me to dull his sibling's senses so that he could seduce my sister. Mabon unknowingly took a swig of it during the drove and was too slow in getting out of the path of rampaging cattle that Tecwyn had deliberately stampeded.

"And as for the innocent Elizabeth Jenkins behaving in an inappropriate manner at your first meeting, I take all the credit. Her maids came here seeking love potions for their own use. I suggested as a joke they could lace their mistress's drink with it and watch its effects. Did you take advantage of her?"

The witch giggled.

Luke was in a hurry.

"I have no time for idle chatter. Answer my question!"

"Yes, the madman who has inflamed the hills and valleys of the Wye with a fanaticism that would destroy us all did stagger into my cave less than an hour ago. I was tempted to give him a potion that would ease his pain permanently, but he threatened me with his half pike and demanded I staunch the flow of blood from his chest. After I achieved that, he fed himself from my pot. I have just replaced what he stole with fresh rabbits, which take hours to soften."

"You dislike him?"

"You are very astute, Colonel," Dilys remarked sarcastically.

"He and his ilk would execute me for witchcraft the minute he gained power. The very presence of such fanatics in these hills and valleys has seriously reduced my clientele. Thank you for ridding me of so many of those pests."

"Where is the wounded man now?"

38

"HE CONTINUED UP THE VALLEY, but he will not get far. He has lost too much blood."

"Have you seen anybody else in the area today?"

"A couple of pesky Quakers who were hopelessly lost."

"You helped them?"

The witch laughed. "You might say that. I gave them false directions and fed them a healthy meal of rabbit, laced with drugs. They will be seeing more than their Holy Spirit by now."

She laughed again.

"Would you like a drink?" she asked with a mischievous look on her face.

"Not after what you have just told me," Luke replied with conviction.

The witch smiled, turned her back, and entered into her cave.

Although there was no longer a trail of blood to follow, Luke continued to climb. His experience in the American wilderness was of great assistance. He followed the freshly broken twigs and trampled undergrowth.

From time to time, Luke shouted, hoping to reconnect with his men; but his delay at the witch's cave had given them time to move well beyond him.

Darkness fell, and the light misty rain regressed into a thick fog. Luke found a dry patch under a thick bush and settled down for the night.

At daybreak, he continued up the valley. The early morning fog and rain gave way to a bright blue sky. Slowly Luke became aware of strange singing and chanting.

Had Rhun met his followers? Were they now conducting a religious meeting?

Luke crept cautiously toward the noise.

A deranged woman was running in circles, shouting and screaming. Lying near her was an elderly man.

Luke recognized both. They were the Quakers he had rescued at Builth. Dilys's cruel joke had worked too well. The girl was temporarily demented, and her father was in a coma or worse.

Luke made the girl aware of his presence gradually. He retraced his steps by a few hundred yards and began singing an old army ballad. It was the only song he could recall.

As he rounded the bend in the path where he expected to find the Quakers, the girl was gone. Her father had not moved. Luke cautiously, approached the prone body, half fearing that Dilys had added a fatal ingredient to her potion. He was relieved to find the man breathing slowly but otherwise sleeping peacefully.

As he turned away from the father, the terrified girl confronted him. From her rantings as she cowered before him, Luke deduced that she thought he was a fire-breathing dragon.

The girl was clearly in a disturbed state and a danger to herself. Luke had no experience of dealing with such a condition. His only recourse was to empty the girl's stomach. She was a fragile child, and Luke had no trouble in sticking his fingers down her throat and provoking her to vomit. She then drank from his water bottle. He calmed her, cradling her in his arms.

Her father stirred. He became very apprehensive when he saw his daughter in Luke's arms.

He ran at Luke in an effort to free his daughter.

Luke restrained him and with some difficulty explained the situation. The father had not imbibed as much of the potion as his daughter and had virtually slept off its effects. He took his daughter from Luke and placed her on some soft moss.

Luke resumed his trek up the valley.

He was increasingly cautious. He had not sighted Rhun, yet his quarry knew he was there. Rhun's lethal ability with the half pike worried him. As a former cavalry officer, he still carried a sword, a concealed dagger, and a carbine, which in the misty Welsh uplands was difficult to prime. He sorely needed the massed musket power of his dragoons.

Should he wait for his men or take on Rhun alone?

Luke soon left the undergrowth and trees behind. He was now on the open grasslands on which there were no places to hide.

Yet Rhun was nowhere to be seen. He was not ahead. There was no one on the upper slopes. He had doubled back, and Luke's men had not yet reached beyond the tree line.

Luke hoped that Rhun would run into the dragoons who were somewhere on the slope below.

Luke had no option but to descend, but not along the path he had just climbed. He moved as slowly and as quietly as he could for fear of alerting a fanatical pike-hurling Rhun.

His composure was ruffled when he heard something crashing through the undergrowth in his direction. He was relieved when a deer bounded past him but immediately concerned by the possibility that Rhun might have frightened it.

Then he heard voices.

The Quakers were pleased to see him, and the girl had almost recovered her senses.

She asked, "And what are you doing here, Colonel?"

"I am tracking down a vicious killer."

"Isn't that dangerous by yourself?"

"I am not alone. Several of my dragoons are somewhere on this hill."

"Father says the old woman in the cave gave me something to make me insane."

"Yes, some sort of herb that made you see monsters that were not there."

"I am hungry. Have you any food?" she asked.

"No, I have no food. You would be very hungry. I made you vomit to rid you of the poison. Let's return to the witch. She will give us a hearty meal."

It took some time to reach the witch's cave. Luke was alert. It was too quiet. The pot was still cooking away, and the smell suggested venison had replaced rabbit.

Luke called out, "Dilys, it is Luke Tremayne returning. Where are you?"

There was no response.

He turned to the Quakers. "You two stay here. Do not move until I call you. If something happens to me, find my men and tell them what occurred."

Luke moved into the open clearing from which he could see into the entrance of the cave.

The witch was lying on the ground in a pool of blood. Her frail body had several large puncture marks. She had been stabbed several times with a pike.

Luke arose from inspecting the body to feel a pike pushing into his back. Rhun made him kneel and tied his ankles together. Then he tied his hands together behind his back.

"Waste no time on the evil sorceress! The Lord Jesus has told us we must not suffer a witch to live. I have obeyed His orders."

"Rhun, you have had an amazing few months since I innocently assigned you to infiltrate the Fifth Monarchy Men of Rhyd."

"For that blessing, I thank you, Colonel. I came to know the Lord and have been enabled to do His will very effectively. Unfortunately, the forces of Satan, with you at the forefront, temporarily defeated us. For those sins against the Lord Jesus, you must die."

Luke played for time with the fanciful thought that Rhun would suddenly be mown down by concentrated musket fire.

"What will you do after you kill me?"

"Our people will survive and will march again for the Lord. I will take refuge in Snowdonia until the time is right to emerge and destroy the agents of the Antichrist, the minions of the Protector."

It may have been the imminence of death, but Luke now thought he heard a noise in the undergrowth. Rhun heard it too.

"Your men are coming. I sentence you to everlasting damnation," shouted a triumphant Rhun

With that he hurled his pike at the defenseless Luke who was still on his knees, with his hands and feet tied.

Luke shut his eyes and intuitively rolled to one side. He heard a tremendous thump, a gurgling sound, and a scream. He opened his eyes to see lying at his feet the body of the Quaker girl. The pike had gone right through her and had embedded itself many inches into the ground, just missing his leg. Her body had diverted the direction of the pike sufficiently so that it missed Luke.

The girl's father ran to the scene and cried openly over the body of his daughter.

A shocked Luke asked pathetically, "What happened?"

"She believed you reflected the inner Spirit of the Lord. She had crept as close as she could to you with some hope that with the Lord's help, she could free you, and when that man hurled his pike, she threw herself into its path."

At that moment, the dragoons rode into the clearing.

"My god, what has happened here?" asked Evan.

"Two more murders committed by Rhun. The old witch at the door of the cave probably deserved all she got, but we should return her body to relatives in Rhyd. The girl lying in front of me gave her life for mine. She and her grieving father are the two Quakers I rescued at Builth."

"Where is Rhun?"

"He escaped back up the hill, but he has no pike. Let's get him, and we take no prisoners," ordered an avenging Luke.

The soldiers acknowledged the directive.

When the dragoons reached the tree line, Rhun was visible on the open grassland not far ahead. His loss of blood was taking its effect, and he moved very slowly.

The soldiers advanced in a single rank with muskets primed. As Rhun staggered on toward the summit, Luke ordered his men to fire. At least five bullets hit the charismatic rebel.

Luke alone approached the body and discharged his carbine into the man's head. "That is for the wench you just killed."

He then turned toward his men. "There will be no Christian burial for this animal. Roll his body over the cliff to our right. Let the red kite that soars above pick his bones."

Early next morning, Luke received a message from one of his patrols. There had been a major fire at Vaughan's farm. Emlyn was near death.

Luke cursed his own ineptitude. If Price told the truth in his dying minutes, the would-be murderer was still out there in the community, and Vaughan with his connection to the brotherhood probably knew something that the murderer wanted concealed.

Luke inspected the site. This was no accident. It was arson and attempted murder. Emlyn had entered the barn and had been coshed severely. As he lay unconscious and bleeding, the barn was torched. By sheer chance, Emlyn had fallen into bales of wet silage that did not burn. His servants noticed the smoke, entered the building, and pulled him out.

Bronwyn Hedd had given him a potion to relieve the pain and to induce sleep. He could not be questioned for some time.

Luke called a meeting of his officers. "Gentlemen, just when our task here appeared almost completed, we face another. We have answers for all the issues that were raised except for the attempt on Sir Daffyd and now Emlyn Vaughan. This latest attempt suggests that William Price was telling the truth in denying any involvement in trying to kill Daffyd. I am certain that Daffyd's would-be killer and the person who has attempted to silence Emlyn is one and the same. We must be getting close."

"Perhaps we have been looking in entirely the wrong direction," announced Evan.

"What do you mean?" Luke responded.

"We should be looking closer to home. What about his wife?"

"What motive?"

"Lady Alis is a strong Papist. She and Gwent were determined to ship arms for the Papist gentry. Perhaps Daffyd got in the way," replied Evan.

"Maybe it was personal. Perhaps Alis and Merlyn were lovers, or at least looking to unite two old families," contributed John.

"Or more likely Alis and your old friend Kimball," added Evan.

Luke admitted that Alis and Kimball did appear close, but they were relatives.

The three officers were quiet for some minutes when Luke pronounced, "We cannot trust anyone. Our perpetrator could be a member of the family or a close friend. In the broader community, it could be a jealous husband who has suddenly discovered he is not the father of his wife's child. It could be anyone who was dissatisfied with Daffyd as a magistrate."

"We will never find the potential killer," grizzled a dispirited John.

"That is why we must give him or her every opportunity to kill Daffyd or Emlyn, while at the same time reexamining all of possible suspects," declared Luke.

"I will start with Lady Glynnis," he added eagerly.

39

LUKE MET LADY GLYNNIS PRIVATELY. Both chose not to mention their Hereford experience, but their body language oozed affection and intimacy. Luke went straight to his concern, "Your ladyship, I do not wish to alarm you, but whoever failed to kill Sir Daffyd may try again. Consequently, who within the family or among his close friends might harbor a deep-seated but concealed hatred of him?"

"Did you have anybody in mind?"

"I suspect everybody, even you."

"What impertinence, Colonel!"

"You took to being mistress of Llanandras with a verve and confidence that reflected a strong and decisive character. Were you not unhappy that Daffyd planned to remove Cranog and yourself from inheriting the house and title and bestow it upon one of his many bastards?"

"You read my reactions correctly, Colonel. The weakness in your argument is that my husband made clear before our marriage and ever since of his intention to forego his rights to succession. Just before Daffyd's return, despite my pleading, he was about to disinherit himself and pass the manor on to one of Daffyd's illegitimate sons. Yes, I would love to be mistress of Llanandras again, but it can never happen."

Luke admired the feisty lady yet felt sorry for her. How would she cope as the wife of a melancholy bard?

He next spoke to Merlyn. "I am glad that Daffyd has accepted you back into the fold. Wrack your brains regarding the events preceding his abduction! Did anything occur that would have provoked an attempt to kill him?"

"As magistrate, he crossed many of the lower orders, but he had not held a petty sessions for months and was absent from the most recent general sessions. Anyhow, the inferior classes would more likely burn his barn or steal his cattle."

"What about the household?"

"I do not know what you mean?"

"Were his relationships with his wife, son, daughter-in-law, and yourself harmonious?"

"Extremely so. There had been some irritation with Lady Alis and myself regarding the import of weapons for the Catholic gentry, but he reconciled himself to that activity when Lord Kimball pointed out that in these dangerous times, the Catholic gentry would be a bulwark of law and order against the seditious sectarian Protestants who were making converts across the Upper Wye."

"There was nothing out of the ordinary?"

"My nephew reported that the customers in the Red Kite were all agog on hearing that Sir Daffyd was about to disinherit Cranog and legitimize one of his many bastard sons as his heir apparent."

"Can Daffyd do this legally?"

"It's a gray area. It is much more likely if Cranog renounced his position, and the new heir was a blood relation."

"He could not leave it to a stranger, for example, to yourself or his friend, Huw Cadwallader?"

"Very difficult! The key legal issue for a successor who is not the eldest surviving son is being a blood relation."

Luke would probe Daffyd further on this point, but first he would see Bronwyn Hedd.

He took Stradling with him as interpreter, only to discover that Bronwyn had a good command of English, which she had deliberately played down in earlier discussions.

Bronwyn was in her cottage, preparing food to take to her son at Cadwalladers. She clearly welcomed Luke's visit. She oozed sexuality, and her deep brown eyes began to disconcert him.

He forced himself to become serious very quickly.

"Bronwyn, I may have been looking in the wrong places in my attempt to uncover the person who tried to kill Sir Daffyd. I have concentrated on questions of power and property. Emlyn Vaughan suggests that it was more likely related to personal relations within the wider community and specifically connected with Sir Daffyd's clutch of illegitimate children."

"No, I don't think so! Daffyd has been generous to all his children by supporting for a very long time their mothers and the families into which they were placed. I cannot see any of Daffyd's partners wishing him dead."

"But most of these children do not know their real heredity?"

"True, but in this community, people are aware of Daffyd's past indiscretions and of his present immense wealth and power. Every young adult hopes he is the child of Sir Daffyd. It is a positive factor."

"Surely this situation would infuriate the nominal fathers of these children?"

"Not often a problem. In most cases, the pregnant girl was married to their current husbands when their pregnancy was well advanced. The prospective bridegroom knew he was not the father of the child his new wife carried."

"This picture of harmony between Daffyd, the women he seduced, and the offspring of the liaisons was not universal. Your sister did not accept her fate."

Bronwyn shivered. "The very thought of Dilys, even though she is dead, fills me with dread. She used all the arts that mother taught us to destroy and divide this community. She created deadly potions for women to be rid of their husbands or discarded lovers. For years, most of my work was to provide antidotes to such poisons and counter magic to lift her curses."

"Would she have directed much of her evil against Sir Daffyd?"

"Yes, and without my help, he would have succumbed to her power. Given the rising level of complaints, he banished her from Rhyd and forbade any members of the community to consult her."

"Although not with much success."

"True. Many of those who were refused harmful potions by me went to Dilys."

"Could she have been behind the attempts on Daffyd's life?"

"If Daffyd died of poisoning or was ill with some unknown disease and faded away slowly, I would suspect witchcraft. But the attempt on Daffyd was by musket. That is not the way of a witch."

"Where is your sister's body? She cannot be buried in holy ground."

"Daffyd has secretly buried her on his estate."

"Would she have tried to kill Daffyd to prevent him from making Kynon his heir? In that way, she would punish Daffyd and destroy your chances of seeing Kynon as heir to the Morgan fortune."

"Don't listen to parish gossip. Daffyd never intended to make Kynon his heir. He made that clear to me years ago."

Luke suddenly paused. "How did that make you feel?"

"Relieved. Kynon adored my husband Mabon. I would not want to destroy his memory of his father."

"Surely he heard rumors of his elevated ancestry?"

"Yes, but it is a joke among the young that they are or are not descended from the lord of the manor of Llanandras. He does not take it seriously, and I am not about to disabuse him."

"Did Daffyd give you a reason why he will not make Kynon his heir? The community thought your lad was a certainty, as did William Price in his aborted attempt to kill him."

"No, but I did. Although Daffyd and I were sleeping together at the time, he was not my only partner. I told him a year or so ago that Kynon might not have been his son. After all, the boy reveals none of Daffyd's unfortunate physical features."

"How did Daffyd react to that piece of news?"

"He was quite relaxed about it as he was well aware of my reputation and behavior. He was intrigued to know who the father might be, if it was not him."

"And who might it be?"

"Colonel, I did not tell Daffyd, and I will not tell you."

"Bronwyn, you must realize that Daffyd's would-be murderer is still out there, waiting for another opportunity to strike. If you have even the slightest hint who might be responsible, tell me before it is too late. At the moment, I have men protecting Sir Daffyd, but I expect orders to withdraw my men in a few weeks. He would then be defenseless."

"Except for my magic," pouted Bronwyn.

"Is there nothing you can tell me?"

Bronwyn remained silent for some time and then without warning began to cry. Luke comforted her. She was a warm and sensual woman who seemed to melt into his arms. Eventually, she explained, "Forgive my tears, Colonel. I am very frightened for Kynon."

"Why Kynon? The man who organized the attempt on his life is dead."

"On the night of Sir Daffyd's abduction, Kynon defied me and disappeared into the night and followed Tecwyn. He claims he was near the Pass and saw the man who shot Daffyd."

"Did he tell you whom?"

"No, he said I would not believe him."

"I will see him, now. Let's hope the would-be murderer didn't see him that night."

"I'll come with you. Just wait until these cakes are ready! I take Kynon extra food each morning and something for Mr. Cadwallader who is not very well."

"Yes, Huw has not been himself since the return of Daffyd. The shock seems to have been too much for him. He has fainted several times."

An hour later, Luke and Bronwyn arrived at the Cadwallader Farm to be met by Kynon who was carrying a pail of water from a well into the stables. He greeted his mother with a big kiss but ignored Luke in favor of his black Friesian stallion. Kynon treated the horse as an old friend. Luke saw his opportunity.

"Kynon, would you like to ride my horse again?"

"Yes, sir."

Luke assisted Kynon to mount the horse but kept a firm grip on the reins. "Your mother tells me you were out and about on the night of Sir Daffyd's abduction."

"Yes."

"Did you see anything that might help my inquiries?"

"No, sir."

Luke threatened to lift the boy from the horse. "My horse does not carry liars. I hope nobody saw you that night. If the murderer saw you, you might be his next victim."

Kynon began to cry. "Please, sir, if I tell you what I know, promise not to tell mother. She thinks I am lying."

Kynon explained, "After Mother and I returned from Mr. Cadwallader, I sneaked out in my father's special boots and headed up the highway in the direction of the Pass in the hope of following Tecwyn and the shepherd. It was a wet, sleety night. I walked quickly to alleviate the cold and soon came in sight of the shepherd. I assumed Tecwyn was just ahead of him, but there was no moon.

"As I neared the ridge, I saw that the shepherd had left the highway and walked along the top of the ridge.

"I was very tired and cold. I moved inside a small cave on the edge of the road. I must have dozed off, but I was alerted by the sound of two shots. "Almost immediately, a horseman galloped down the road. He stopped on the verge level with my cave to store his musket and replace his carbine in its holster. He pulled off his mask.

"It was—"

As Kynon leaned over to whisper the name, he seized the reins and pulled away, trotting briskly out of Cadwallader's Farm onto the road. Luke let fly a series of military oaths that brought Bronwyn running from the house where she had delivered her cakes. "What did you say to my boy?"

"The lad needs to be taught a lesson. He pretended to tell me whom he saw in return for a ride. When I released my grip in anticipation of his evidence, he took advantage and galloped off without giving me a name."

"Colonel, he is a good lad, but he does enjoy a lark. He will tell you when he returns your horse. I must go back inside. Mr. Cadwallader requires some more of my healing potion, which I can mix from the herbs in his garden."

Luke ambled down the drive toward the road and walked slowly in the direction in which Kynon had ridden. Twenty minutes later, the boy and horse reappeared on the horizon. They were cantering happily back to Luke. On reaching him, Kynon dismounted, "I needed to get well away from where we were. Mother cannot hear me now. The man I saw in the vicinity the Pass carried weapons that could have delivered two shots in a short time."

He whispered the identity of man to Luke who was both amazed and relieved. "Thank you, my boy. If you are right, then much of the malaise affecting Rhyd is explained."

"Don't tell Mother!"

"I won't tell anybody, until I have proof to support what you have told me."

Luke rode slowly back to Llanandras. He could hardly believe what Kynon had told him, but it fitted in with other evidence that was emerging.

40

LUKE RECEIVED A MESSAGE. EMLYN Vaughan wished to see him urgently.

Vaughan lay abed in his own house, cared for by Bronwyn Hedd and other village women versed in herbal medicine who took it in turns to minister to a dying man. Vaughan had never married and employed no female servants.

Six of Luke's dragoons patrolled the outside of the house, and two others stayed within, one at the door of the bedroom and the other seated beside Emlyn's bed.

Luke was taking no chances. He was sure the would-be murderer would try again.

As soon as he arrived, Bronwyn told him, "Emlyn is not responding to our treatment. The fire and the smoke have damaged him severely."

"Will he survive?"

"No. He has great difficulty in breathing. This is your last opportunity to talk to him."

Luke entered the bedchamber and immediately recognized the dire straits of the patient. Emlyn smiled and signaled for Luke to come close to the bedside.

He murmured, "I know who tried to kill me."

Emlyn then began to cough and wheeze alarmingly. Eventually, he whispered, "On the night Daffyd was abducted, I received a visitor who claimed that all his horses were disabled, and he wished to borrow one of those that I lease to the brotherhood. He had been an active member years earlier. He told me he had to reach the Pass urgently. I told him that all but one of the brotherhood horses had already been taken that night. He was highly agitated if not distraught. He was seething with rage. I offered him a drink to calm him down, but he ignored my overtures and galloped off on the only horse available as if Satan himself was on his tail. The next morning, I found the horse tied to my railing in a very distressed condition. To treat a horse so was completely out of character for this person."

"Who is this person?"

Luke bent over the dying man who mumbled a name followed by an expulsion of air. Emlyn Vaughan was dead.

Luke asked Bronwyn, "Did Emlyn tell you who attacked him?"

"No, he was more concerned about Sir Daffyd. He claimed that Daffyd's would-be killer was someone very close to him."

"Bronwyn, prepare him for burial but do not let it be known that he has died! I will spread the news that Emlyn is about to tell me the identity of Daffyd's would-be assassin. Hopefully, that will incite him to try again."

Bronwyn dressed the body, and it was taken in secret in an army cart to the barracks at Llanandras.

Emlyn's bed was filled with items to create the impression that he was still there, and Luke's men were concealed within the house, one hidden in a large cupboard that dominated the bedchamber.

Next day, Sir Daffyd summoned Luke. He entered Daffyd's library to find Cranog, Edwyn, and Merlyn already present.

Sir Daffyd spoke, "I have invited you here to witness a momentous event. We have two lawyers present so I am convinced that what I do will stand up in court, although it is based on a lie, a fact that must remain in this room. I had hoped my dear friend Huw would be present, but Edwyn says he has taken to his bed with an unknown illness. After I finish here, I will visit him and explain what we have accomplished."

"What do you propose?" asked Merlyn.

"I have decided on my heir."

"And who is that?" queried the long-suffering Cranog.

"I will name you, Edwyn, as my heir."

Edwyn paled. "But that cannot be. I am the son of Huw and Jane Cadwallader. I am not one of your bastards, sir."

"Calm yourself, Edwyn! You are indeed the son of your father. That is where the lie rests. I cannot do what I am doing and leave my estates to a stranger. It has to be to a blood relative. Therefore, for the purposes of this procedure, you are to acquiesce in being one of my bastard sons."

"No, this is appalling," shouted Edwyn. "I will not have my mother's reputation sullied in this way. I reject your proposition."

Gwent was equally astonished. "Sir, why choose an outsider when there are at least half a dozen lads in the community who are your genuine offspring?"

"None of them have the capabilities possessed by Edwyn. The whole purpose of this exercise is to protect the Morgan dynasty into the future."

Cranog was distressed. "Father, I am happy to relinquish my position, but not if it upsets Edwyn. This is most insensitive."

Luke commented, "Sir Daffyd, you can accomplish this end without upsetting anybody and based on a much sounder legal basis. Confirm your niece as your legitimate heir. Edwyn is courting Rhoslyn. Their child would eventually inherit your estates."

Gwent was surprised. "I did not know Rhoslyn and Edwyn were lovers."

"Neither did I," announced an astounded and stern Daffyd.

"And it cannot be. They are brother and sister."

A deathly silence took over the room.

A shattered and then infuriated Edwyn screamed, "How can that be?"

Daffyd gave a clinical response. "Your nominal mother Jane was infertile, but she was very anxious to have a child. Your father sired you on the body of a loving friend. My sister-in-law had a similar problem, and my brother produced a daughter using the same woman. Edwyn and Rhoslyn have the same mother."

"And who would that be?" screamed a hysterical Edwyn.

"Bronwyn Hedd," answered Daffyd who, dismayed by the turn of events, left the room as if in a trance.

There was a deathly silence.

Merlyn broke the impasse by suggesting to Cranog, Edwyn, and Luke that they all needed a stiff drink.

As they each downed several drafts of Irish whiskey, Luke fumed. "What a daft proposal. I thought Daffyd had more common sense than that."

"Colonel, we Welsh gentry are governed by our hereditary. To Daffyd, the survival of Morgans into the future is all he cares about. He never contemplated the hurt his scheme would cause the Cadwalladers," explained Merlyn.

Edwyn, who had remained silent, excused himself. He would tell Rhoslyn the catastrophic news immediately. Cranog left with him.

Merlyn and Luke continued to drink.

Luke eventually asked, "Did Daffyd mention his plan to anybody before today?"

"Months ago, he intended to inform Huw, but I don't know if he did."

Luke jumped to his feet. "Good God! Follow me!"

The two men ran into the hall, and Luke asked the nearest servant, "Have you seen Sir Daffyd in the last few minutes?"

The woman answered, "Yes, sir, he just left and said he was going to visit his old friend Mr. Cadwallader."

"I hope we are in time," shouted Luke as the two men ran to the stables and mounted the first available horses.

They galloped at breakneck speed to the Cadwallader farm.

They entered the house, and a servant revealed that Sir Daffyd had been alone with Huw for some time.

They burst into the bedchamber. Daffyd was slumped across the bed, bleeding profusely from multiple stab wounds.

Huw was sitting up in bed, holding a bloodied dagger.

He oozed hatred as he questioned his victim.

"How could you do it? You were my best friend from childhood. I trusted Jane with my life, and the two of you betrayed me."

Luke was relieved to see that Daffyd was not dead.

With difficulty, he responded to his attacker, "You silly old fool. I never slept with Jane. Edwyn is not my son. It is a lie, so that he can inherit the Morgan fortune. He is the most capable man in Rhyd. I could never have children by Jane. Neither could you. Did you never wonder why Jane moved to Scotland during the period of her alleged labor and did not return for twelve months? She claimed the child was sickly, and they could not travel home for some time. From the moment Jane left with her pretend pregnancy, our mutual friend Bronwyn consoled you. You are Edwyn's father, and Bronwyn is his mother."

Huw looked traumatized. "You told me on the night of your abduction only that you were to make Edwyn your heir. I know the law. That could only mean that Edwyn was one of your bastards. In heredity, blood rules."

"I am sorry, old friend. If you remember that night, it was a very brief conversation, and I was interrupted before I explained the situation in full."

"What have I done?" cried a distraught Huw.

He then fainted.

Almost simultaneously, Daffyd lost consciousness.

Two weeks later, Luke formally interviewed Huw Cadwallader.

"Tell me about the night of Daffyd's abduction!"

"Just before he rode to the Pass, Daffyd dropped in to inform me of his plans for that night and his decision to make Edwyn his heir. Before I could comment or question him, he left. I was in a rage. How could a friend seduce my wife to whom I was devoted? How could she betray me with my closest companion? The thought that Edwyn was not my son was overwhelming. All I could think about was revenge and preventing the spread of this devastating knowledge. As soon as Bronwyn left, I ran across the fields to Vaughan and asked for a brotherhood horse. Mine were quite striking beasts that would be easily recognized. I rode post haste to the Pass and awaited the arrival of Daffyd's party, which had been delayed at the Red Kite.

"I shot first with my musket and then almost simultaneously fired again with my carbine loaded with soft bullets."

"How did you feel when Daffyd returned from the dead?"

"Angrier than before. If Daffyd went ahead and named Edwyn as his heir, I would be a humiliated, and an indelible stain would be attached to the character of my late wife. The rest of Rhyd would be laughing behind my back. It was a thoughtless plan. I am proud that Edwyn rejected it."

"Well, now you know that your wife was innocent, and that Edwyn is your son. Nevertheless, stripped of all excuses and emotions, you murdered two men, Tecwyn Hedd and Emlyn Vaughan, and attempted to kill Sir Daffyd. You must pay the penalty."

Edwyn entered the room and immediately interrupted the conversation.

"Surely Father has already paid for his alleged crimes. Daffyd will not prosecute the attempts on him, and technically, Emlyn died from the effects of fire and smoke inhalation. There is no reliable evidence that Father was responsible. Finally, it could be argued that a man who was mentally disturbed conducted all of these criminal acts. Don't bring your strict English interpretations of the law to the valleys of Wales!

"At the moment, the local magistrate is still Cranog, who with his father's blessing will dismiss any charges brought against Huw."

"But, Edwyn, as an officer of the law, you cannot ignore Huw's murder of Tecwyn Hedd!"

"Tecwyn Hedd was a vicious guttersnipe whom the community is well rid of. He sexually abused his female relatives and as good as murdered his brother to further these animalistic plans. I will not allow my father's years of service to the state and this community be rendered worthless by your concept of justice," replied a determined Edwyn.

"If this is Welsh justice, I will have no truck of it. You have two days to come to your senses. I return at noon the day after next to arrest Huw for murder. I will bring with me a troop of dragoons and will inform the community in advance.

"The law of the land must be upheld, especially where it concerns the misdeeds of those devoted to its maintenance. You know what has to be done."

Luke, brought up in a tradition of military honor, believed he had provided a window in which Huw would take his own life.

Evan was surprised at his colonel's approach. "Luke, why are you being so vindictive toward this man who in his own mind had a matter of honor to settle?

"You have said very favorable things about Ned Jenkins whose behavior led to the death of many more people than Huw's misplaced actions. In your own past, you have ignored the technicalities of the law and exercised your power over life and death according to your own judgment. "Why do you ignore the crimes of Gwent and Kimball, and concentrate on this one distraught and confused man?"

Luke brushed aside his deputy's argument as that of another Welshman who did not appreciate the justice of the English law.

Luke waited two days to hear the news that Huw had committed suicide. It never came.

At the appointed hour, Luke and his men arrived at the Cadwallader Farm to be met surprisingly by Lady Rhoslyn Morgan, who announced she was acting for the Cadwalladers.

"Edwyn's father has gone beyond your reach."

Luke removed his hat and offered his condolences.

Rhoslyn, pale and tense, replied, "No, Colonel, he is not dead. He is somewhere in the Bristol Channel en route to the Americas."

Luke was appalled.

He did not understand the Welsh.

What astonished Luke even more was the rest of Lady Rhoslyn's news. Huw had not migrated alone. Edwyn, his recently discovered birth mother Bronwyn Hedd, and her youngest son Kynon had accompanied him.

Next day, as his men prepared to leave Llanandras for good, Luke summed up their achievements. "We played our part in the isolation and defeat of the insurrection against the Protector. We have solved all the murders and attempted murders. All that remains is for me to recommend to the government those capable of administering this area in the name of Oliver Cromwell. All of the possibilities have stains on their character. I will have to think carefully on this matter."

EPILOGUE

TWO MONTHS LATER, LUKE HEARD that the Cadwallader party had not reached the Americas. Their ship had run aground off the Irish coast with the loss of all hands. Sir Daffyd died from infected wounds that had refused to heal. Cranog inherited the Morgan estates, and a pregnant Lady Glynnis was proving yet again an effective lady of the Manor. The news of approaching fatherhood changed Cranog's mind and personality. He would be bard and lord of the manor and following Luke's recommendation was reappointed a magistrate.

Rhoslyn on discovering that Edwyn was her half-brother was utterly devastated. With promptings from her stepmother Lady Alis, she converted to Catholicism and with the help of Lord Kimball entered a French convent.

Sir Conway Jenkins also died within a few months of Luke's departure, allegedly from a broken heart at the loss of his two eldest sons and much of his property. James, his heir, ceded what was left of the Jenkins lands to his sister Elizabeth and migrated to a Puritan colony in the Americas.

Merlyn Gwent regained much of his family's traditional land. Some was confiscated from Price, and large areas were obtained for a nominal cost from the Cadwalladers.

When he married Elizabeth Jenkins, despite a significant age difference, and incorporated her lands with his, he became the area's largest landowner.

With Papists and Baptists content with the government and most of the gentry reconciled to the need for law and order, Luke reported that Wales was safe for the Protectorate.

It was, at least for the immediate future.